Tate Hallaway was born in the magical town of LaCrosse, Wisconsin. Tate has been a fan of vampire fiction since she first read Poppy Z. Brite in high school. Her first short fiction accept-ance was to a vampire 'zine called *Nocturnal Ecstasy Vampire Coven*. Tate lives in Saint Paul, Minnesota with three black cats. Tate's first novel was TALL, DARK AND DEAD.

Praise for Tate Hallaway's novels:

'Hallaway presents a terrific and enjoyable read. The charac-ters are lively, and the story stays strong and balanced throughout . . . readers can only hope that there will be a sequel' *Romantic Times*

'Tate Hallaway kept me on the edge of my seat with *Tall, Dark and Dead*. Every time I thought I knew where the story was going, she threw something new into the mix. A thoroughly enjoyable read!' Julie Kenner, *USA Today* bestselling author of *Carpe Demon*

Dead Sexy

Tate Hallaway

HEADLINE PUBLISHING GROUP
An Hachette Livre UK Company
338 Euston Road
London NW1 3BH

headline
review

First published in 2007 by HEADLINE REVIEW
An imprint of HEADLINE PUBLISHING GROUP

First published in paperback in 2007 by HEADLINE REVIEW
An imprint of HEADLINE PUBLISHING GROUP

1

Cataloguing in Publication Data is
available from the British Library

ISBN 978 0 7553 3657 9

Typeset in Amasis by Palimpsest Book Production Limited,
Grangemouth, Stirlingshire

Printed and bound in Great Britain by
Mackays of Chatham plc, Chatham, Kent

Headline's policy is to use papers that are natural, renewable and
recyclable products and made from wood grown in sustainable
forests. The logging and manufacturing processes are expected
to conform to the environmental regulations of the country of origin.

For Shawn, as always

Acknowledgements

Thanks as always to my brilliant and insightful editor, Anne Sowards, and to my supportive and hardworking agent, Martha Millard. Many thanks also to my editor at Headline, Piers Blofeld. My writers group, the Wyrdsmiths, must be thanked for keeping me on track; also a shout-out to Ms. Ember for making the sex 'less creepy' and to Naomi Kritzer for thoughts on polyamory. Last minute readers Sean M. Murphy and Shawn Rounds have my eternal gratitude.

1

Aries

Key Words:
Impulsive and Dynamic

Who knew there were so many dead things in Madison, Wisconsin?

As I peeked over the top of the tarot card display, I saw a zombie standing at the register holding a copy of *The Complete Idiot's Guide to Voodoo*.

I struggled to not smack my forehead against the bookcase in frustration. Given how my day started, a zombie customer was just the icing on an already screwed-up day. I'd spent the predawn hours dealing with the fact that I had one too many men in my life, and neither of them was alive. Sebastian, my current vampire lover, dropped me off at my apartment around five a.m. I had to get into work early today, and, of all stupid things, I'd managed to forget my store keys at home. This would have been only minor on the hassle scale, except that I happened to notice Parrish – my vampire ex-lover, who Sebastian wasn't supposed to know was still alive, much less in town, even much more less living in my basement –

skulking around the hedges of my backyard, obviously wanting to talk.

Sebastian, of course, had wanted to come in, help me unload my bike from his trunk, steal several more kisses, and all sorts of deliciously gentlemanlike things that were completely the opposite of what I needed if I was going to find out what the hell Parrish wanted so badly that he would risk exposing his presence to Sebastian. I ended up handing Sebastian some lame lie about wanting time to decompress before work, which I could instantly tell he didn't buy, but he was too well mannered to argue. After all the contorting I did in order to talk to Parrish, I found out all he wanted was to cop a snuggle himself before going off to bed. Worse, when I fended Parrish off with just a hug, he smelled like cheap sex and booze, and I swore the scent still clung to me despite a very hot shower. The whole thing had put me in a foul mood. I'd already mis-shelved several books and managed to knock over and break one very expensive blown-glass chalice.

Zombies just added to the suckiness of the day.

To the untrained eye, I'm sure the zombie looked like your average University of Wisconsin hockey jock riding a wicked morning after. Glassy-eyed and slack-jawed, his German-farmboy blond hair hung in wilted clumps across his broad forehead. His jersey seemed threadbare and slept in, and his jeans had unidentifiable sludge ground into the knees and where the cuffs brushed the floor. All fairly unremarkable, really, unless you noticed the blackened toenails on bare feet and the slight grayness of his skin.

But I could smell the grave dust from two aisles away. This

poor boy had partied a little too hearty one night and woken up dead. Well, mostly dead, drugged, *and* possessed.

As somebody's slave.

Which begged the question – what was an active voodoo sorcerer doing in Madison, Wisconsin?

Granted, Madison is an exceptional place to live, especially if you are out of step with the ordinary. Despite the fact that cornfields and cow pastures are less than twenty minutes away from the center of town, the politics lean toward the frighteningly left. Madison is home to the Great Midwestern Marijuana Festival and birthplace of the satirical newspaper *The Onion*, for Goddess's sake.

Thanks to all the students at UW, few people ever look at me funny when I walk down the street in full Goth mode. Piercings and tattoos are commonplace along State Street. You'd be more likely to get gawked at if you strolled along in a business suit, but, then again, given that the capitol building is just up the road, maybe not.

The thing was, Madison is so accepting – so, well, liberal – that black magic really doesn't jive with the shade-grown, fair-trade, bicycle-delivered coffee-drinking crowd. Slavery is really not okay, you dig? And zombies are slaves to their voodoo masters, no question about it.

Plus I had to wonder what good was a jock zombie? Did he still go to classes? Had his grade point average slipped? Or did his professors just write him off as a slacker boy gone bad? The zombie's blunt fingers dragged slowly along the titles on the bookshelf. When I noticed the spittle hanging from his lower lip, I felt a pang of pity.

I shook my head. I couldn't afford to start thinking like this. If I took in every ghost, golem, or ghoul that wandered into Mercury Crossing, Madison's premier occult bookstore and herb emporium, I'd be one seriously busy little Witch. Ever since I'd cast the spell that made the Vatican Witch hunters think Sebastian and I were dead, my life had been inundated with the denizens of the spirit world. It was like they recognized me as some kind of kindred spirit – a fellow not-quite-dead thing. That thought gave me a shiver.

The zombie started moaning.

I replaced the Aquarian deck in its plastic holder and made my way behind the counter to the register. The smell of freshly turned grave increased the closer I got to the zombie. My eyes watered, but I made an effort to smile. 'Can I help you?'

'This,' he hissed, flopping the book onto the counter clumsily.

I didn't even pretend to look at the price, I just stowed the book under the counter and came back up with a bag of sea salt. The zombie looked confused, but then they always did.

'I think you'll find this more to your *taste*,' I said, hoping he'd buy the clue and open his mouth enough so I could splash a few grains on his tongue. Salt was the going cure for zombies. It was that or red meat, which was really not very practical to store in any kind of quantity behind the register. Besides, I'm a vegetarian.

'Book,' he insisted. The Neanderthal ridge of his brow knitted into a frown.

I put the salt down on the counter. 'Are you sure?'

The zombie nodded slowly, as if I was the one with the addled brain. 'Book.'

I thought about arguing with him. In his eyes, however, I saw an intensity that made me think he wouldn't be swayed. Even so, I was about to try again, when he held up a wad of mud-streaked dollar bills. Did I even want to know where those came from?

He dumped the money on the counter. A spider scurried out from between the curled and soggy bills to shelter itself somewhere under my register. I thought I saw a family of sow bugs scuttle along the edge of the countertop and head for the safety of a dark shadow.

Ew. Even the creepy-crawly people didn't want to hang out with this zombie. The magic holding him must be seriously ugly.

Retrieving the book from under the counter, I rang it up. 'The customer is always right.'

Two minutes later, I realized I'd been played. The damn zombie had given me counterfeit money. I didn't notice right away because of all the dirt, but the whole thing just looked wrong. There was no holographic picture or metallic strip, and the left-hand seal was blue instead of green. The more I looked at it, more discrepancies popped up. The top read 'silver certificate' instead of Federal Reserve Bank. What seemed strange to me was that there was something about the zombie's dollar that made it seem real, despite all the oddities – like it had its own internal consistency. Which was a strange way to forge money, I thought, though I was certainly no expert.

Covering the bill in grave sludge, on the other hand, was very clever. I hardly wanted to touch the stuff, much less examine it too closely.

I was still comparing the zombie fakes to real bills when I heard the jingle bells on the door chime.

Glancing up, I saw a cop.

He wasn't wearing a uniform, no shiny badge hung off a Sam Browne belt, but I could tell. He wore a trench coat, a button-down shirt, black tie, slacks, dress shoes. Nothing flashy – no earring, no necklace, not even a wedding ring. Though, for some reason, I had the impression gold would look good against his warm, brown skin. Inky black hair was clipped short over his ears. He looked clean, respectable – normal. That was the big giveaway. Nobody dressed that mundane walked into an occult bookstore.

So with a squint, I checked out his aura. He held it close to himself like a gambler not wanting to show his hand. The color was pure gold.

Whoa. This cop was psychic.

Even my best friend, Izzy, who was a fairly strong, if latent psychic, only had flashes of gold in her aura. I'd never met anyone with an aura so pure, so magical. If he hadn't had the purposeful stride, the firm set in the jaw, and the intense so-blue-they-were-almost-gray eyes that caught mine and wouldn't let go, I might have reassessed my opinion that he was a cop.

'Good timing,' I told him. I mean, wow – it had been less than ten minutes since the zombie scammed me. If he hurried, he might still be able to catch the guy.

6

'Garnet Lacey?'

'Dude,' I said, impressed. He knew my name, and full-blown peek-in-your-mind-and-know-what-you're-thinking stuff was a one-in-a-million talent.

Normally cops weren't my favorite people – mostly because my interaction with them typically involved apologizing for hosting a rambunctious party or jaywalking. However, being a telepathic cop was really using your powers for good. I mean, he could be out in Vegas making a mint hustling poker, but instead here he was tracking down zombie counterfeiters. 'Wicked cool,' I said.

His jaw clenched, and he frowned at the tarot display I'd spent all morning rearranging. I felt a flush of embarrassment. Ugh, I probably made him feel like an exhibit on display at a zoo, acting so impressed with his powers like that.

He cleared his throat and squinted at me Clint Eastwood style. 'Are you Garnet Lacey?'

I shot him a quizzical sidelong glance. Wasn't he already reading my mind? Maybe he wasn't used to having his powers so easily accepted. He should know that of all places to show off, an occult bookstore was an easy A. To spare him further discomfort, however, I got down to business. I held up the bill to show him. 'Can you believe the nerve? This doesn't even remotely look real.'

He peered distractedly at the dollar in question. I seemed to have derailed him in some way. So much for the attention span of Madison's finest.

'I'm investigating a murder,' he said, pulling out one of those flip wallets you see in movies about cops and flashing me an

ID. Except instead of a detective's gold badge like I expected, it had a photo on one side and a seal on the other with the acronym FBI in big, blue letters. 'Special Agent Gabriel Dominguez,' he said by way of introduction.

Right. Counterfeiting is a federal crime. Then something clicked. 'Wait,' I said. 'Did you say murder?'

'Yes.'

Oh. The zombie. I shook my head, 'Yeah, poor kid.'

I put the bill down on the mud-streaked counter. I absently rubbed at the smears of dirt on the glass wondering if I should tell Special Agent Dominguez that the dead guy he was looking for had just left.

I gave Dominguez another looking over. Being psychic didn't guarantee he'd had run-ins with the occult underworld. His eyes hadn't lingered overlong at the silver 'L' in Theban script that hung in the space between my breasts, and he hadn't startled the way some sensitives did when they felt the dark presence of the Goddess Lilith behind my eyes.

In fact, sadly, Dominguez looked pretty square. I mean, sure, it was a kind of hottie 'Twern't nuthin', ma'am,' Lone Ranger kind of square, but he still seemed like the sort who might choke if I started casually mentioning reanimated corpses.

I double-checked his aura. This time I noticed flashes of midnight blue, which gave him a very calm, very Zen spirit. He'd definitely be the man to watch your back in a fight. I bet the guys at Quantico or wherever found him very steadfast and trustworthy. No spooky Fox Mulder. This guy was a Scully, through and through.

Hell, he might not even know how psychic he was. He might just think he had extremely keen powers of observation or imagine himself intuitive about human nature. Then again, if he was reading my mind right now, he knew. I looked up at him and thought really hard: *zombie went that way.*

He frowned at me. I had the sense from the way his lips pressed together that he was getting exasperated. It wasn't the look of someone who was merely annoyed that I had just shouted into their head; he had that why-can't-we-communicate-in-English look I've seen when I try to explain the difference between horary and humanistic astrology to someone who simply wanted to know what sign they were.

I began to suspect that my dear Agent Dominguez was blocked. Some traumatic event in his life had caused him to completely ignore his abilities. I could mentally shout all I wanted. He'd never listen me.

So, I tested him. I imagined myself leaning across the counter and giving him a long, passionate kiss on the lips. Then, I ran imaginary fingers through his short-cropped black hair, feeling the sharp stubble on the back of his neck.

He scratched behind his ear. 'Um, several "guys", actually. More than one,' he said as if correcting me, meeting my eyes, but only just barely. 'I'm investigating the murder of six dead priests.'

I was so pleased to have gotten a reaction from him that it took me a second to parse what he'd just said. Then, it didn't make any sense. 'Zombie priests? No way was that kid a priest. Seminary student, maybe in a stretch – if they have a hockey program, but no way was he old enough to be a priest.'

9

Special Agent Dominguez looked at me like I had gone completely insane. There was a crack in his hard-core cop persona, when a tiny smile played at the edge of his lips. 'Did you just say "zombie"?'

I hadn't meant to. I knew this would happen. Either people choked or they laughed at me when I mentioned the color of their auras or noted that they might be feeling a bit clumsy because Mercury had just gone retrograde.

I guessed I should be grateful that Dominguez seemed to have put me into the 'she's amusing' category. At least that attitude could work toward 'weird, but compelling' or 'cute, if a bit odd'. The people who choked or snorted various beverages out their noses usually couldn't even be convinced of my entertainment value. Often they felt obliged to try to 'correct' my worldview by imposing their own. I didn't have a lot of patience for that. Besides, sharing my body with the Goddess Lilith on a regular basis made me feel pretty superior about the validity of my claims. I *knew* magic was real. How many other people had had their faith so profoundly proven to them? When I called, a Goddess answered.

Still, being the resident weirdo isn't always the first impression I want to make with people like Agent Dominguez. I don't know. Maybe it's the whole hidden-shoulder-holster appeal, but just once I'd love to have a cop look at me and say, 'Which way did you say the zombie went, ma'am?' Instead of giving me that did-you-get-a-load-of-her smirk.

And, dang it, Dominguez was kind of cute for a mundane. I shouldn't be looking (not to mention mentally kissing), since I have a boyfriend. But, well, I'm a sucker for a man with broad shoulders and a slender waist, and all I can say is that this cop was not the sitting-around-the-doughnut-shop kind of guy.

Plus, he was a psychic, even if he didn't know it. He was one of us. He shouldn't have still been grinning at me like that.

'What?' I asked a little belligerently, since I could feel a blush heating up under his stare. 'Like you've never heard of zombies?'

'You're kidding, right? You're kind of taking all this stuff' – he waved at the crystal balls and magic wands in the display case – 'a bit too seriously, aren't you?'

'Yeah. Ha. Ha.' I didn't want to get into all the reasons I did with the special agent, so I reached under the counter for the special cleanser I'd cooked up for my post–dead things encounters. It was part moon-charged rose essence, part holy water, with a dash or two of clove oil. I'd put the concoction in a spritzer bottle on which I'd marked 'necromancy zapper' with a black Sharpie. It was good stuff. It not only cleaned up any kind of spill (outside of blood) and magically purified the place, but it also smelled like pumpkin pie. I sprayed it liberally all over the muddy counter.

I wasn't really aiming for him, but I wasn't terribly disappointed when I splashed the special agent's sleeve and made him jump back.

'Hey, watch it,' he said. Then, using those psychic powers of his, the special agent deduced that it was a good time to get back on subject. 'Actually, I'm looking for a gal, not a guy. Have you seen this woman?'

I was expecting to get my first glimpse at this voodoo sorcerer who'd been cooking up all these zombies I'd seen lately, so I leaned in curiously as the agent pulled a photo out of his wallet. He flipped it over, and I found my knuckles tightening around the one-hundred-percent-recycled paper towel I held in both hands. I gaped in horror.

It was me.

The photo was some kind of digital reprint from my driver's license, and it was a couple of years old, but it was *me*.

I wasn't surprised Dominguez hadn't recognized me; I barely recognized myself. The photograph he laid down on a dry spot on the counter showed a blond Norwegian woman in an Indian-print dress. She looked innocent and sweet.

I did not. In fact, I'd been so grouchy after the Sebastian/Parrish fiasco this morning that I'd decided to play up the whole walking-dead look. I'd powdered my face a shade paler than normal, gone bloodred on the lipstick, and gelled my dyed-black pixie haircut into spikes. So much eyeliner and mascara surrounded my eyes that they looked sunken and bruised. When I'd left Sebastian's house this morning, I borrowed his best movie-vampire gear – a white poet shirt, black leather pants (mine, from a previous sleepover), and a velvet great coat.

More distinctly, the woman in the photo had blue eyes so pale they had almost been washed out by the reflection of the camera's flash. Mine were purple – a deep, rich, unusual shade, like the inner tongue of a bearded iris. The new color was a magical scar left over from the horrible Halloween night a year ago when I had called down the Goddess Lilith and ended up fleeing Minneapolis after I dumped the bodies of six Vatican assassins into the lake inside Lakewood Cemetery.

Six priests.

Oh.

Oh, shit.

2

Taurus

Key Words:
Practical and Sensual

My lip quivered with the desire to say, 'I can explain, officer.'

Only, I couldn't.

If Special Agent Dominguez smirked when I mentioned zombies, I highly doubted that he'd believe me if I told him that a Goddess had appropriated my body that night.

A Goddess whom, I might add, was currently causing my stomach muscles to clench. She wanted out, and She wanted to destroy the threat. The more frightened I was, the more likely She was to slip her leash.

I put a hand on my belly to steady myself, but all I wanted to do was shout, 'It was self-defense. Honest!'

I remembered that night well. I'd come late to the Samhain ritual and opened the door to discover that the Vatican's Ordor of Eustace had murdered my coven. The order was a secret, possibly unsanctioned organization, whose mission was to continue the work of the Inquisition, in a way. They firmly believed the quote from Exodus, which states, 'Thou shalt not suffer a Witch to live.'

And there were six of them, one of me. They had bloody knives and silver bullets; I had a plate of chocolate chip cookies. I used the only weapons I had at my disposal: surprise and magic.

Self-defense.

Right?

Anyway, it shouldn't matter, should it? After all, it wasn't me that did the killing, it was Lilith. I called; She came. I went away. Then I woke up with blood on my hands.

Hmmm, okay. That part was going to be tough to explain.

My mouth worked as I struggled for a way to articulate that even though I'd summoned Lilith, I had no idea She'd possess my body and use it to take out the Vatican agents. I hadn't asked Her to *kill* anyone. I'd simply begged for protection. She was the one who'd decided that required a more permanent solution.

My knees trembled, and I put a hand on the counter to steady myself. From the look the special agent shot me, I realized I'd waited far too long to answer his question. Even if the guy weren't psychic, he'd have to know I was hiding something.

'Yeah,' I said, sticking to half-truths, since that was all I could trust myself with. 'She works here.'

'Do you know when she might be in?'

I shook my head. That was also partly true, since I was feeling a sudden compulsion to run for the hills. I was glad I still had my bug-out bag and cat carrier ready in the hall closet in my apartment. They might come in handy.

In fact, I wondered what the special agent would do if I just bolted for the door right now. I glanced over his shoulder at the street outside, trying to calculate the distance I'd have to cover before he tackled me . . . or drew his gun.

Of course, this great escape of mine hinged on the idea I could move with any kind of speed or accuracy in the black leather kitten heels I wore. Kicking them off wasn't really an option, since the heels were attached to knee-high boots. I suspected my dear special agent would have a bit of a heads-up that I was making a break for it if I had to find a place to sit down so I could scrunch off my footwear.

Dominguez must have picked up on my sudden sense of panic, but he misunderstood it. He gave me a sympathetic glance. 'I know this is quite a shock. But Garnet's involvement might not be criminal. If she's a friend of yours, you should tell her I just want to talk to her about what she might have seen.'

'So Garnet's not a suspect?' I tried not to sound as anxious or interested as I was.

Those steely blue eyes caught mine. 'Not yet.'

Even as those words scared me to death, they made me laugh. I mean, the guy sounded like he read his line off a cue card on *Law & Order*. I could almost hear the music swelling. Bum-bum!

'You're a Leo, right?' I have no idea how those words came out of my mouth or how the solicitous smile appeared on my lips. Maybe it was some kind of defense mechanism, a kind of judo flirt. 'You're totally a Leo. I can tell.'

'Taurus,' he said, with that kind of whiplash look people get in their eyes when I suddenly change the subject based on some astrological quirk I've noticed. 'Why?'

The tone of his last question sounded more like the rest of

it might have been, 'why are you asking me this right now?' but it was too late. My mouth was open and words were falling out. 'That explains the edging of blue in your aura. Zen Sensual.'

His eyebrows rose at that. 'Zen what? What the hell are you talking about?'

I get that a lot. 'Taurus is ruled by Venus, the Goddess of love and beauty,' I explained. 'Your Sun energy – that's what people are talking about when they ask your sign, your Sun sign. Anyway, um, Taurus is very steadfast, loyal, but also secretly very . . . sexy.'

'Uh-huh,' he said with a tone that screamed, 'cuckoo', but there was a twinkle in his eyes. Something I'd said caused me to pass into that 'insane, but sort of cute' phase, I could tell.

'You should let me do your chart,' I said. Then, thank the Goddess, I stopped talking.

Dominguez stared at me. I had no idea what he was thinking, but his gaze flicked over me one inch at a time. I held on to my smile, but it was starting to fray at the edges. In another minute or so, I'd probably pass out, throw up, or confess all my crimes starting with the time when I was six and I accidentally walked out of the Piggly Wiggly with a gumdrop in my coat pocket. Finally, he gave me a twitch of a grin. 'Yeah, sure. Why not? Sounds like a hoot.'

'Great!' I said with entirely too much enthusiasm. I scrambled around for a piece of scrap paper and a pen. 'So, tell me where you were born.'

'Barcelona.'

'Spain, really?' Yeah, I thought with a smile, I could see a little Antonio Banderas in him. I wanted to ask him how he came about such startlingly blue eyes, but it seemed a little rude to ask questions about his ethnic origins.

'I don't remember it. My parents only lived there the first few months of my life. Is that all you need?'

'I need date of birth: month, day, and year.'

'May 2, 1970.'

I looked up at that. He was younger than I'd thought. Maybe it was the strain of being psychic and not really knowing it, especially in the kind of job where you see the things he undoubtedly saw and where nice people like me lied to you on a regular basis, but I'd have put him at forty. He had fairly pronounced lines near his mouth and eyes, like he spent a lot of time squinting in the sun or laughing. It looked good on him, actually. Like he had some mileage on him, like he'd lived a bit of life.

When I realized I'd been staring, I added, 'Do you happen to know the time you were born? I need it to be pretty specific, hour and minute. It's sometimes on birth certificates. Or your mother might remember.'

'Ten thirty-four p.m. My father checked his watch.' At my look of surprise, he explained. 'He likes to tell me how involved he was. I guess he helped the doctor catch me or something.'

I nodded, scribbling all the information down. 'I can have the chart for you in a couple of days.'

'Good, because I'd like to stop by some time when you know Garnet will be in.'

'Garnet? Uh.' I asked, having forgotten momentarily the ruse I'd been playing. Then I felt the blood drain from my face. Luckily, my makeup covered my reaction somewhat. Desperate for a distraction, I grabbed the counterfeit dollar from the counter. 'What about this? Do you think someone's up to something?'

Dominguez took the bill I all but thrust at him. He gave it another cursory glance, then pulled out an evidence bag from his pocket and stuffed it in. 'I'll send it to the lab.'

'Cool.' We stared at each other. I felt completely transparent under his gaze, only not in a good way. 'So do you keep a supply of those baggies on hand?'

'Yes,' he said without elaboration. 'You couldn't check the schedule for me and let me know when Garnet will be in, could you?' When he broke our silence, I nearly jumped. 'I know you don't want to get your friend in trouble, but I only want to talk to her, you understand?'

That's what they always said in the movies right before they set up the ambush. 'Uh, sure. But what makes you think Garnet knows anything about these murders?'

Dominguez gave me the once-over, his eyes clearly deciding whether or not to trust me. 'A rental car belonging to the victims' – I cringed a little bit when he used that word – 'was found near where neighbors claimed a Wiccan coven gathered regularly. People remembered it because the house burned to the ground on Halloween. It made the papers. Eleven bodies were recovered and positively identified. There was a presumption of a twelfth member, but, of course, coven membership is highly secretive.'

Duh. Especially when you have Vatican assassins out to get you. 'But if coven membership is such a secret, how do you know she was part of that one?'

'We don't for sure. That's part of what I want to ask her.'

Except you got my name, so someone in the magical community in Minneapolis must have cracked under pressure. Or maybe, if I wanted to be generous, it was someone who thought she or he was doing me a favor. 'Yeah,' I muttered.

'Could you check that schedule for me?' Dominguez asked again. 'I really believe she has information that could be critical to solving this case.'

'Shouldn't Inter . . . ?' I stopped myself just in time. I'd been about to ask why the FBI was investigating this, since I'd have thought Interpol would be in charge of a case involving foreign nationals, but then I couldn't remember if he'd told me that the dead priests were from the Vatican or not. 'Shouldn't I . . . yeah, I should go get that schedule right now.'

I blinked at him stupidly for a moment. Then I practically tripped over myself hurrying to the storeroom.

When the door shut behind me, I let the back of my head rest on the cool wood. I closed my eyes and tried to take in a deep breath to calm my pounding heart. I sucked at being a criminal mastermind. I would *so* suspect me if I were this guy – psychic or not.

I stared longingly at the back door. My bicycle was parked in the alley outside. It would be easy to open the door, hop on, and ride away. But then what? If Dominguez had found me here at the store, he probably also knew where I lived. Although maybe not. I wasn't listed in the phone book, and my landlord was just some guy, not a corporation. Still, running would make me look very, very guilty.

Grabbing the schedule from where it was taped to the wall,

right below the Serenity Prayer, I took in another steadying breath. Breathe, Garnet, I told myself, go to your special place like they told you in that meditation class. Except I never did settle on a particular image, since I kept falling asleep during the sessions. Besides, if anything, my astral coping mechanism tended to involve shoving ugly thoughts and memories into a large closet with the words 'Do Not Disturb' scrawled in blood on the door.

So I did a deep-breathing exercise, ran my fingers through my hair, smoothed my leather pants, squared my shoulders, and . . . almost fainted when I saw my coworker, William, chatting with Dominguez when I opened the door.

William worked at the bookstore part time while attending the university. After three years at school, he still hadn't declared a major. That kind of summed up William, generally. I'd have thought after he discovered vampires were real, he'd finally embrace a particular brand of spirituality. But no. William was currently into shamanism. He'd let his mouse-brown hair grow long enough to put into a ponytail and was wearing a 'Free Leonard Peltier' T-shirt. Little round John Lennon glasses, which I suspected were also merely an affectation, perched on the end of his nose. Normally seeing William made me smile, but my heart froze.

William's hand lifted in a wave. In a second he was going to blow my cover. I made a slashing motion across my throat. William's eyes went wide. I had no idea what he thought my gesture meant, but he nodded solemnly.

My heels dragged. The distance between the storeroom and the register felt far too short. Had William already identified me? What had they said to each other? Was I about to leave the store in handcuffs?

Both men watched my progress. Sweat prickled under my arms. As I got closer I noticed that William was holding the photo of me. He shook his head. Handing it back to the special agent, he said, 'No, I've never seen her before.'

'Really? I thought she worked here.' Dominguez looked to me.

'No,' William said with a sly smile. 'Trust me, I'd remember a hottie like that.'

Nice. I wasn't sure if I should be relieved or insulted.

'So, you don't know Garnet Lacey?'

'Garnet Lacey?' William looked at me, then back at the FBI agent. I tried to give William a stare that suggested this might be the thing I didn't want him to talk about, but he was too busy snatching the photo back from Dominguez. 'That's a picture of Garnet? No way!'

'I've got the schedule.' Hoping to distract Dominguez, I waved the paper under his nose. Of course, my name was all over the thing, given that I was the manager.

'Garnet is supposed to be working right now,' Dominguez said after a quick scan of the list.

'She called in sick,' I said. 'I'm Marlena. I get called in to fill in odd hours here and there. That's me,' I said, pointing to Marlena Ito's contact information on the bottom of the sheet.

'Ito?' Dominguez gave me an appraising look.

'Excuse me? Did I ask you where you got your blue eyes?' I huffed indignantly.

'Marlena,' William said. 'Check out this picture of Garnet! Did you even know she was a blonde?'

'She's changed her hair?' Dominguez asked, reaching in his pants pocket for the ubiquitous cop notepad.

'I'd say,' William said with a snort. 'I can't get over this. Can I keep this?'

'No,' Dominguez said, grabbing the photo back.

'She's a redhead now,' I supplied.

'So, you're really FBI?' William asked. Dominguez was busy taking notes on his pad, but he nodded slightly. 'What's the deal with Area 51? Have we made contact with the aliens? Give it to me straight.'

Dominguez hardly missed a beat. 'That's the military.'

'Right, I knew that,' William nodded. 'Who killed Kennedy?'

'Not my department.'

'But you're homicide, right?'

'Nice shirt,' Dominguez said with a sneer.

'Oh, thanks,' William said, apparently completely oblivious to Dominguez's tone and the fact that Peltier was in jail for his alleged role in the deaths of FBI agents.

Dominguez gave me a long-suffering look. He fished in his pocket for a business card and handed it to me. 'Please tell Garnet to call me, won't you?'

'Sure,' I said, absently tucking the embossed card into my wallet.

'Typically evasive,' William muttered, as we watched Dominguez head out the door. 'Freaking FBI.'

I nodded, not really hearing him. Dominguez paused to look back at us, and I gave him a smile and a wave. Then he disappeared into the crowd as he headed down State Street.

My knees buckled. I fell to the floor hyperventilating.

'Oh my god, Garnet!' William said, scrambling around the counter to kneel next to me.

He gaped at me in horror, and, as I was having trouble controlling my breath, I did the same in return.

'You haven't fainted. You're hyperventilating,' he said with a deer-in-the-headlights-oh-crap-I'm-in-charge-during-a-medical-emergency quiver.

I wanted to help calm William down, but I couldn't. My brain had gone tilt. The only coherent thought in my head had to do with spending the rest of my life in a federal prison with a room-mate named Bull.

'You need a paper bag,' William announced. He turned away from me for a moment and began scrounging around behind the counter. I heard him mutter something about handles versus plastic. Then he jumped upright. 'Don't go anywhere,' he commanded, 'and don't die.'

I put my head down between my knees, though all it did was bring the floor closer. We needed to mop back here. Thanks to an unseasonably early snowfall, the hardwood was gross. Luckily the little bits of mud and slush couldn't penetrate my leather pants, though the thought of ending up face down in it kept me struggling for breath. Focusing on the need to tidy up helped for a moment. Suddenly I remembered that there was frost on the ground the night I used a pitchfork from the garden shed at the covenstead to poke holes in the tarp-wrapped bodies of the Vatican agents before Parrish and I loaded them into the back of his van.

25

Goddess, why did I ever think we were going to get away with it?

An urge to throw up almost overwhelmed my desire to breathe, especially once William returned with a brown paper lunch sack that smelled like yesterday's tofu curry salad. He pressed it to my face. I tried to wave it away, but he held it around my mouth with a surprising amount of determination. His face was close to mine, and I could see moisture glistening in his eyes as he pleaded, 'Please, Garnet. Don't you dare pass out on me, I never know if I'm supposed to call the hospital or not.'

I laughed, but it came out as a cough. The rhythm of the bag had steadied me. I managed to croak, 'No hospital.'

'So I should cancel the ambulance?' When he saw my eyes widen and heard my breath hitch, William raised a hand. 'Bad time for a joke. Very bad time. See, I suck at this.'

I was wracked by another laugh/cough, but I patted William's knee. 'I'm okay.'

William cautiously removed the bag. A finger lightly touched a corner of my eye. 'Your makeup is smudged.'

I nodded, staring at the dirt-encrusted floor. I heard William settle his back against the counter.

'This is about Minneapolis, isn't it? And what Lilith did, right?'

I blinked up at William. Sometimes I forgot that I'd trusted him with one of the darkest secrets of my soul.

'You've got to tell them the truth, *Marlena*. Don't you ever watch TV? You don't lie to the cops, they always figure you out.'

'William,' I said. 'Who's going to believe that a Goddess killed those Vatican agents? Especially when I tell them She did it while inhabiting my body.'

'A jury of your peers?'

'Where am I going to find twelve Witches possessed by Goddesses?'

When the bells over the door jingled, I held my breath. Could Special Agent Dominguez be back already with reinforcements?

William apparently had the same thought because he froze midreply and looked ready to squeeze himself into the cubby next to the cleaning supplies. We sat there motionless, staring meaningfully at each other like Butch and Sundance at their last stand in Bolivia.

'Hello? Garnet? Anyone?'

My shoulders relaxed their tension. It was Sebastian. 'I'm here, hiding under the register with William.'

'Right, of course,' Sebastian said, sounding particularly British, which was funny, since he was Austrian. 'Perfectly reasonable.'

Brushing off my pants, I stood up. Sebastian looked dead sexy, as usual.

Sebastian wasn't a traditional vampire. He'd been made by an alchemical formula, so he had none of the usual troubles with sunshine. Weather affected him, but only just barely. There was a slight windburn blush along the sharp line of his cheekbones. Yet despite the forty-degree temperature and wet wind outside, Sebastian merely wore a thin, broken-in leather jacket and jeans. The jacket was unzipped to the navel and showed not only a crisp, white T-shirt, but also the hint of what lay beneath, which I happened to know was a smooth, hard plane of well-developed pectorals that

27

tapered down to a slender waist, and well, more. A very nice more.

Noticing me, he smiled. Sebastian had one of those light-up-his-eyes, generous, infectious smiles – the kind that I always found myself grinning back to, even when, like now, I felt as though my universe was crashing down around my feet. Just seeing him looking at me like that steadied me a bit. I almost felt safe again.

'So, uh, are you ready to go, then?'

'Go?' I asked.

'Lunch?' Sebastian prompted. 'Remember?'

I stared stupidly at Sebastian, still feeling shell-shocked and a bit woozy. I glanced at the clock on the wall. It was early, only ten a.m.

Sebastian followed my gaze. With an apologetic grin, he shrugged. 'I felt a "disturbance in the Force".'

In other words, Lilith had alerted Sebastian that I might be in trouble. She was annoying that way. Lilith didn't live inside *just* me any more. Sebastian had partial custody thanks to the ridiculous amount of blood-and-magic bonding we did during the spell I cast to contain Lilith, fool the Vatican agents into thinking we were dead, and save Sebastian's life. Did I mention it had been a seriously ass-kickin' spell? One of the unintended consequences was that Sebastian and I were now linked forever on a deep level. We felt each other's distress. We experienced each other's pain.

And sex was beyond fantastic.

'The Force is real?' William's voice came out as a strange muffled echo from his hiding spot under the counter. 'And vampires can feel it?'

'Oh, hello, William,' Sebastian peered over the counter at William's long legs sticking out from the cramped cubby. 'You really *are* under there.'

'I'm hiding from the cops,' he announced.

Sebastian looked to me for an explanation, but stopped when he saw my expression. 'I hate to use the cliché, darling, but you look like you've seen a ghost.'

I nodded. 'Six of them, actually.'

'Six?' William paused midspritz; he'd crawled out from his hiding space with a bottle in hand and automatically started cleaning up the mud on the counter. William was a nervous cleaner. 'Lilith took out six Vatican agents at once? Wow. She must have made you into some kind of super ninja killer, Garnet. Fly on the wall and all that, man.'

Both Sebastian and I gaped at him with open mouths. Me, because I couldn't believe William had managed to describe the worst night of my life in some kind of B movie context, and Sebastian because . . .

'Is he serious? Is he implying you killed six Vatican agents?' Sebastian asked. Sebastian didn't know about my past, about what Lilith had done. Oh, he had firsthand experience with the Order of Eustace and their mission to rid the world of all the practitioners of true magic – he had a couple of bodies of his own buried in his rose garden – but he hadn't, until two seconds ago, known I did too.

William glanced between Sebastian and I with a sheepish look. To me, he said, 'You never told him?' To him, 'You seriously didn't know?' Back to me, 'Oh, shit, Garnet. I guess I figured . . .'

Yeah, you'd think I'd have gotten around to telling my boyfriend about the single most life-changing event in my life, except the thing was, I'd been so busy making sure that the agents didn't send Sebastian to his final grave that it just kind of slipped my mind, and, of course, then it became sort of awkward to slide into casual conversation.

More to the point, the whole event was my ugly secret. I barely let myself think about it.

'Not me,' I insisted feebly. 'I didn't kill anyone. Lilith did.'

'Of course,' Sebastian said somewhat dismissively, as if the distinction wasn't terribly important. 'When?'

Which was an interesting question when you thought about it. My lover didn't look at my slender five-foot-something frame and say, 'how,' or even, 'why.' Well, he could guess why, and he knew about Lilith.

'Last Halloween. They attacked my coven.'

Sebastian blinked. I couldn't quite read what he was thinking in his expression, but he seemed to be taking a moment to read-just his image of me, because then, in a measured tone, he said, 'I see. Now their ghosts are haunting you?'

'Not ghosts. FBI,' William supplied.

I tried to give William the 'stop talking now' glare, but he'd turned to alphabetize a couple of books that had gotten misplaced by a customer.

Sebastian ran his fingers through his hair, which was not a good sign. We'd been dating five months now, and I knew that gesture. It meant I was giving him a headache. I'd seen this expression a lot.

'FBI,' Sebastian repeated. He caught my gaze. Unearthly light reflected a starburst pattern in his chestnut-brown eyes. 'Garnet, that's not good. If the law has come knocking, they've found a body.'

I nodded. The worst part about all this is that I'd been warned months ago by my coconspirator and ex-lover, Daniel Parrish, that the FBI would be tracking me down eventually. He'd showed up in town . . . well, to declare his undying love for me, but also to inform me that a freak drought had dried up the lake where we'd dumped the bodies. At the time, I'd had bigger things on my mind, most notably the sudden appearance of a Vatican agent in town. When things settled down and no cops showed up right away, I forgot about it. Okay, I didn't *want* to think about it, and that was just as good as forgetting as far as I was concerned.

'A body is a very, very bad thing,' Sebastian was saying almost to himself. 'Never leave a body where they can find it. Never.'

William make a choking sound.

It wasn't like Sebastian to talk so casually about disposing of corpses – especially in front of William, but he was a vampire after all. It didn't surprise me he had a little experience in this matter.

'Look,' I said. 'We did the best we could, given the circumstances. I mean, it *was* fairly clever of us to remember to put rocks in with the bodies so they wouldn't float to the surface.'

Now William stared at me in horror. He took a few steps backward and pretended to rearrange the titles in the Feminism and Magical Theory section. His act would have been much more convincing had he put down the bottle of cleanser first. As it was, he continued to clutch it in one hand, while pulling books out with the other.

Sebastian stopped shaking his head and pinioned me with that intense gaze again. *'We?'*

'Dude,' William said, apparently recovering from his initial shock. 'That was the royal "we". As in Lilith.'

Sebastian raised a skeptical eyebrow and turned to me for confirmation.

Actually, it was me and Parrish, but I was just as happy not to correct William. The last thing I wanted was for Sebastian to be reminded of Parrish. Sebastian hated him for various and sundry reasons, not the least of which being that he was my ex, and another vampire, and, well, more than a little bit of a bad boy with a tendency toward public displays of sex, violence, and blood sport. In fact, the last time Sebastian saw Parrish he'd tried to kill him, and nearly succeeded. That was the biggest reason why I continued to let Sebastian believe he'd run Parrish out of town.

Sebastian pulled his hair back again, only this time he glared pointedly at William. William, for his part, continued to organize books, oblivious to the vampire's venomous look. To me, Sebastian said, 'About lunch, are you ready to go?'

Clearly, Sebastian wanted to get away and continue this discussion privately. 'Sure.'

State Street is the main tourist destination of Madison. The stores catered both to UW students and to visitors, so they tended to be a strange combination of utilitarian and luxury items. The most successful stores had a bizarre intermarriage of both, like the boutiques selling Indian-print dresses for students *and* expensive beaded evening gowns for tourists. It was nearly Halloween, and a lot of the display windows reflected the season – apparently mummy mannequins also had a penchant for cheap, imported clothes.

As we passed one shop, a warm blast of air carried with it the smell of gourmet-flavored popcorn. My mouth watered at the scent of chili pepper and cheese.

Pigeons bobbed in meandering circles underneath nearly leafless maple trees. They erupted in flapping, cooing flight as we passed.

Sebastian and I continued a few blocks down State Street to Cecil's Deli. The building was set back from the street a short distance, making it even more a hole-in-the-wall than all the other narrow shops on the pedestrian mall.

The warm air inside smelled of pastrami and rye bread. Tables and booths crowded the tiny space, and most of them were filled with college students and their ubiquitous textbooks lying open beside them. Sebastian and I slid into an empty booth with smooth plastic seats and a vaguely sticky, red-and-white-checkered vinyl tablecloth.

A waitress unceremoniously handed us each a laminated menu and set down water in industrial-strength glasses so scuffed they had become opaque. The water tasted slightly metallic, but it was ice cold and delicious. I gulped mine down to the chipped ice.

My eyes flitted over the dense, hand-printed menu, but my mind was elsewhere. 'What am I going to do?'

'I still can't believe Lilith was so sloppy as to leave an identifiable body.'

I grimaced at my mostly empty water glass. 'Lilith did the

killing and left,' I explained, after a glance around to see if anyone was listening. Most of the college kids had their ears plugged with iPods. As an extra precaution, I leaned in close and kept my voice low. 'I was in charge of the afterward. It was my first homicide, okay? Disposing of bodies is hardly my area of expertise.'

Sebastian chuckled darkly. 'I suppose not. Still, it's almost a full year later, to the day. That's pretty good for a novice.'

I suppose I shouldn't have felt slighted by being called an amateur murderer, but I did. 'Hey! Those bodies would still be undiscovered if not for the drought.'

'I'm sure they would have,' Sebastian said in a tone I could have mistaken as condescending, except for the gentle hand that reached across the table to smooth my clenched fist. The warmth of his callused skin always surprised me. Sebastian had been made by magic, not blood, and his flesh didn't carry the chill of the grave.

The image of stone-cold corpses made me think about those Vatican assassins all wrapped in gardening tarp. Ugh, what a horrible mess. Death. Why was so much of my life about death?

What I really wanted at that moment was to lean across the table and give Sebastian a long, slow, life-affirming kiss. Touching him would make me feel more grounded, at center. I opened my mouth to ask him to come sit beside me so I could lean into his strength just a little.

Of course, that was the moment the waitress showed up. She was youngish, student age, athletic in a boxy sort of way, with pink streaks in her shaggy short blond hair and a triangle of the same color in her ear. If she overheard any of our conversation about bodies, she didn't give any indication as she deftly took down Sebastian's order for a Reuben and mine for a breakfast plate with eggs over easy. I watched her shuffle away, wondering at the jerkiness of her gait . . .

I sniffed at the air. 'Do you smell grave dust?'

Sebastian shook his head. 'Patchouli. Horrible stuff.'

'Yeah, that could be it.' My eyes followed our waitress as she made her slow, steady progress through a sea of dodging wait-staff.

Sebastian took a sip of his water. His eyes watched me with a curious expression, as if he were thinking very hard about something.

'What?' I snapped. I hadn't meant to, but being scrutinized when I was in the frame of a murder didn't sit well at the moment.

His voice was low and casual, as if we were discussing the price of tea in China. 'You said something about rocks?'

I nodded, not really wanting to remember the exact details of dealing with the dead Vatican agents. The truth was Parrish did most of the actual handling of the corpses. I'd felt far too sick, too grief stricken, and far too wrung out, having been so recently possessed by a Goddess whose moniker was Mother of Demons.

Sebastian cleared his throat. 'How on earth did you have the presence of mind to do that?'

I nearly laughed. I had been completely *out* of my mind that night, not in it.

'Ah,' he said lightly. 'I thought so.'

'Thought so, what?'

'Parrish helped you, didn't he?'

'You sound jealous,' I teased.

Sebastian's reply was to study the checked pattern of the tablecloth.

Before I could speak, the waitress returned to deposit a coffee mug in front of me, and a glass and a can of soda for Sebastian. On the table she placed silverware swaddled in white paper napkins. Sebastian and I stared coolly at each other over her ministrations.

When she left, I whispered, 'You *are* jealous.'

He shrugged, rearranging the glass and plate slightly. 'You know what they say, "true friends help you bury the bodies."'

'*They* say that?'

He peeked up at me through those thick, almost girlish lashes. 'Well, at least some people do.'

I snorted a short laugh. 'Sounds like somebody's been hanging around the wrong people.'

As soon as the words were out of my mouth, I wished for an undo button. It might seem like an innocent remark to a casual observer, but the people Sebastian hung out with when he wasn't with me had been the crux of a number of arguments between us lately.

It wasn't that I disapproved of his friends, because the ones that I'd met I liked tremendously. Being originally from Austria and, I imagined, due in part to his obviously foreign accent, Sebastian tended to attract international and (to me, at least) exotic companions. Students studying abroad and expatriated professors used Sebastian's farm as an overflow youth hostel. I liked that. It meant there was always someone interesting around.

His friends weren't the problem.

It was the ghouls.

Ghouls are volunteer blood donors for vampires. Most of them are vamp groupies, addicted to the sting and the rush of the bite. It's a sexual thing, the bite. Thanks to the highly aphrodisiac quality of the act, the majority of vampires don't have to kill to feed. They just have to cultivate a string of willing victims, groupies, chew toys . . . competition.

I sipped my coffee to hide my wince. I knew what was coming.

Sebastian let out a sigh. 'Oh, Christ, that again.'

'I didn't mean anything by that, honestly.' I said, but I doubted he'd believe me. It was my fault he wouldn't. After all, there had been plenty of times in the past months when I intended every jealous little poke.

'How else do you expect me to sate the hunger?' Sebastian asked.

I picked up my napkin roll and broke the brown paper seal, avoiding answering. What *did* I expect him to do, starve? I'd made it fairly clear early in our relationship that I wasn't especially comfortable with the idea of dating someone who considered me a food source. So he only bit me during sex play, never taking more than a nibble, and only for fun. I was sporting one of his love bites on my inner thigh this morning actually, but it was hardly more than a scratch, a tease.

Even though Sebastian was an unusual sort of vampire, he still needed blood to survive. I denied him mine. A vampire has to hunt, I supposed.

Still, I didn't have to like knowing he had others.

'Garnet,' he said, his baritone voice soft, like a caress. 'You know those women aren't important to me.'

'I really don't want to talk about this.' That was no lie. I never knew quite how to feel when a man started telling me that the other women in his life weren't important. The feminist in me always had a strange desire to rally to these other women's defense. Besides, it always seemed like the kind of line he could be telling them when they asked after me. I shook my head, not quite willing to paint Sebastian in such a cold and calculating light. 'Look, in the great scheme of things your ghouls just aren't that important to me right now.'

He looked unconvinced.

It was my turn to let out an exasperated sigh. I reached a hand into the pocket of my pants and rubbed the cloth satchel full of herbs I kept there. It was an anti-jealousy charm I'd made shortly after I discovered I was emotionally linked to Sebastian through Lilith's blood bond. Inside was High John the Conqueror root for strength and rosemary for remembering the good times Sebastian and I have. I closed my eyes momentarily and tried to visualize dissipating the green haze of jealousy that surrounded me.

It didn't work.

For this relationship, I was practicing tolerance. Trying, anyway. The whole ghoul issue had broken up Parrish and me, and I didn't want a repeat performance. Besides, possessiveness was pure negativity, bad vibes. I didn't need that baggage.

I had enough going on.

Speaking of which. 'What am I going to do about Special Agent Dominguez?' I asked.

Food arrived. This time, when the waitress reached around me to put a large oval plate overflowing with eggs and hash browns on the table I swore I caught the scent of grave. I tried to look in her eyes for signs of life, but she kept them politely averted. As she placed the sandwich in front of Sebastian, I squinted at her aura.

All she had was the faint deep purple glimmer of a newly made zombie.

Sebastian took a huge bite of the Reuben. 'Ah, I love sauerkraut.'

I poked at the yolk of my eggs with a triangle of butter-soaked toast. Two zombies in one day. I shook my head. Not my problem, I thought, watching the waitress shuffle around the room with a large pot of coffee. I have bigger things to worry about. 'Seriously, Sebastian. What am I supposed to do about the FBI?'

'I suppose killing him is out of the question.'

Sebastian wasn't entirely joking, despite his thin smile, so I felt the need to say, 'Yes. If we made an FBI agent disappear, they'd definitely send reinforcements.'

'Oh well,' he said lightly. He took another thoughtful bite of his sandwich. 'It was just a thought.'

I was familiar enough with Sebastian's tone to know he was just playing rogue, but I'd also been with him when he'd effortlessly dispatched the Vatican assassins. He was certainly capable of being a killer. 'You wouldn't really kill someone that lightly, would you?'

He shook his head around a mouthful of Reuben. 'No, for a lot of reasons. But as you're discovering, when people die it attracts a lot of attention. Vampires don't need that kind of publicity. We wouldn't last long.'

I didn't suppose they would. Not only would they have the kinds of troubles I was having with law enforcement and whatnot, but there was always someone left behind, someone grieving.

Like me. Only I never stopped to grieve for the coven. I never found the time. I'd been on the run, not just physically, but also mentally, since the day I left. Now, with Halloween fast approaching, so many things reminded me of them. Just the other day, I saw that the hat shop here on State Street had a sale on pointy Witch hats. My coven always wore those at social gatherings around Samhain as a joke. We would have put them on for the 'cakes and ale' part of the ritual that night, only the Vatican interrupted us before we could.

I poked at the yolks of my eggs with a fork. Of course, the flip side of all this was that somewhere, someone else was thinking about the Vatican agents the same way.

Should I even care? I asked myself. I mean, these people were the real murderers, storming into our ritual and killing us based on some ancient, badly translated lines in the Bible.

I looked around at the faces of the strangers eating brunch. They were all people with friends and family. Did the value of human life change based on the strength of someone's religious convictions? Wasn't a person a person, no matter how small, as Dr Seuss once said? Did I have the right to strike them down to avenge my friends? To defend myself?

'Should I have done something else?' I asked, taking a bite of egg finally. 'Should I have called the police instead of burying the bodies?'

Sebastian considered as he crunched a pickle. 'What would you have said, "hello, I've just killed six people, care to arrest me?"'

'Well, it was self-defense, wasn't it?'

'Of course it was.' He reassured me with a sincere tone and concerned eyes. 'Besides, there's nothing wrong with taking justice into your own hands. You have to take up arms against evil when you see it. You can't count on the law to do it for you. History has amply proven that.'

The bread I'd been chewing stuck in the back of my throat. Is that what I'd done? Had I meted out vigilante justice?

I felt sick to my stomach. Images I'd kept buried from that night started resurfacing randomly. I'd come to with my hands clenched around one of the Vatican agent's throat. The tendons between my thumb and forefinger ached with the effort of crushing his trachea.

My eggs threatened to come up. I held them back with some effort.

Sebastian's voice cut through my panic. 'Are you okay?'

'I just feel sick about this whole thing,' I said, holding my napkin up to my mouth with a trembling hand.

His hand gripped my shoulder just tight enough to steady me. 'Don't worry about anything,' he said. 'I'll take care of you. Luckily, I have a ridiculous amount of money,' Sebastian reminded me with a little self-effacing laugh. 'I can hire a cadre of the best lawyers for your defense, and buy you a villa to hide in until this blows over. How do you feel about the south of France?'

'I don't have a passport,' I said distractedly. Somehow, while

I was still reliving that night in detail, Sebastian had rushed ahead to the trial. It was sweet of him to offer to buy me a good defense, but I hadn't even really come to terms with the fact I needed one.

'Oh well,' he said, removing his hand from my shoulder. He apparently needed the use of his appendage in order to consider the situation, because he scratched his chin thoughtfully for a few moment before saying, 'With enough money, I'm sure we can find a way around that.'

'Yeah,' I muttered. I took a bite of the hash browns experimentally. Some part of my brain registered them as crisp and salty, but I could barely choke them down. I pushed the plate away. 'I'm going home,' I said, standing up. 'Or maybe back to work. I don't know. I can't stay here. I can't sit still.'

Sebastian seemed to understand. Like a perfect gentlemen, he'd gotten to his feet the instant I had. 'Can I take you? Or would you like to come around to my place? I could put on the kettle and stoke up the fire.'

Tempting though that was, I shook my head. 'I'm too anxious. I've got to walk.'

He nodded and reached for his jacket.

'Alone,' I added, feeling kind of bad about it. Thing was, Sebastian wasn't the vampire I wanted right now. Parrish had been there. We'd lifted the bodies into his van together. This was *our* problem to solve.

'Of course,' Sebastian said chivalrously, though I sensed in his voice a hint of sadness at being dismissed.

I reached out and gave his arm a squeeze. 'I'll be all right,' I said. 'I promise.'

He pulled me into a kiss and gripped my waist protectively. When he released me, he gave me a smile. 'You'd better be.'

After stopping back into the store to tell William I was taking an extended break, I hopped on my bike. I lived several blocks away from State Street on the second floor of a creaky old Victorian. Actually, I had access to the attic too, which more than made up for my drunken, disorderly downstairs neighbors. Getting a whole floor to devote to my witchcraft made stepping over the passed-out and half-naked bodies on my way to use the laundry facilities almost worthwhile. Besides, being so out of it made my neighbors much less likely to notice the fact that in a corner of my storeroom in the basement was a coffin.

I pedaled my mountain bike down the residential streets. Most of the early snow had melted. Only a few patches of white hid in ruts and dents of browning lawns. The temperature hung just above freezing, leaving slushy mud puddles in the gutters for me to swerve around. Everything looked tired. Most trees had lost their leaves. Those that hadn't were well past their autumnal glory; all that remained were ragged assortments of faded yellows and muted oranges. Gardens had become untidy. Squirrels had long ago looted the heads of sunflowers, leaving only broken stalks. Flowers were now sprouting seeds and dried-up husks.

The sky, on the other hand, was a brilliant shade of blue. The sun was so bright that I wished I'd thought to wear my shades.

My house had a tower, the only one of its kind on the block, and was painted a hideous shade of pink. The worst part was that the paint was new. My landlord had decided to 'freshen things up a bit' earlier this summer, and, in a fit of metrosexual fabulousness, apparently thought hot pink would make some kind of fashion statement. It did, though not, I imagine, the one he'd intended. It sort of screamed: *Look at me! I'm overdressed and ugly!* I suspected he'd been watching too much HGTV. I should probably consider myself lucky I didn't have crepe-paper flowers glued all over my bathroom wall.

When I reached my house, I carried my bike up the cement staircase and stashed it in the hall. A green-glass tulip leaf chandelier hung from a pressed tin medallion on the ceiling. It was dusty and worn, like so much of the place, but I'd been charmed by its faded glory from the first moment I'd stepped into the building. The open staircase curved gracefully around a leaded glass window on the landing, and despite the chipped wood and missing spindles, it always reminded me of a scene out of *Gone With the Wind*.

I looped the chin strap of my safety helmet over the seat of my bike. In the autumn, the hallway was always overly warm and smelled faintly of stale beer. The hardwood floor was often sticky, particularly near the overflowing recycling bins full of crushed cans and cheap brown glass.

I wrinkled my nose and headed for the basement door.

The stairs were steep. I had to fumble a few steps on the rough concrete floor until my hand found more than cobwebs. The light switch was one of those pull strings that you expect to turn on a bare bulb, but in this case switched on a frosted glass globe filled with the corpses of far too many insects. The basement was unfinished and unloved. Concrete walls were spotted with seeping, crumbling sections. Pipes hung low overhead, a jumble of new copper, old lead, bits of PVC, and tons of plumbing patch. The whole place smelled dank and moldy. I felt kind of bad for Parrish, living down here with the centipedes and half-used paint cans.

My storage space was actually a divided coal room. The owner had put up drywall and added doors with padlocks. I never kept mine locked – for obvious reasons. Parrish had declined the use of my much nicer attic space because he didn't want the hassle of having to wander through my bedroom every night. He claimed he preferred the privacy of getting to come and go as he pleased, but I think he was more afraid that Sebastian might stay over. If I was queen of denial, then Parrish was its emperor. Parrish confessed to me one night that he believed that as long as he never saw Sebastian and me together, he could just pretend we weren't an item.

But to protect him, I'd warded his door. He and I could pass through the spell easily, but anyone else who approached would have trouble even seeing the door – they'd mistake it for part of the wall. I felt a faint hum when I touched the knob. Lilith thrummed deep inside me, responding to the magic.

Even though I knew he was in torpor, I knocked before turning the knob. When he didn't respond, I pushed open the door. Despite knowing what to expect, I always freaked out a little at the sight of Parrish's coffin. Plain wood, it looked a bit like a freight box, except it was so obviously *that* shape.

The rest of Parrish's possessions filled the room. He had two steamer trunks, a leather suitcase, and a chest of drawers I'd found for him at a flea market a couple of months ago. On the top of that were his toiletries and a pile of manga, no doubt stolen from some bookstore.

In the top drawer he kept a pad of Post-it notes and a black pen. I pulled it out from on top of rows of neatly rolled socks and wrote, 'I'll be home by eight, come upstairs.' Then I signed it the way I always did when there was trouble: 'Meadow Spring'. Meadow Spring was my craftname back in Minneapolis. Parrish knew that the last time I was Meadow Spring was the night he helped me bury the bodies.

I knelt down and stuck the note on his coffin. My hand rested for a moment on the rough wood. I knew that if I lifted the lid, Parrish would look dead. His eyes would be open and glassy, and he'd have a creepy, vaguely peaceful smile on his face. The rest of him would be an embalmer's wet dream: soft, silken auburn hair lying around his perfectly pale face like a mane. There would be no bruised, sunken skin, no blemishes of any kind, despite the fact that the last time Parrish was required to take a breath was over two hundred years ago.

'Hey,' I whispered, though I knew he couldn't hear me. 'Guess what? It's crisis time and I need you again.'

As I left I swore I heard a groan, like Parrish rolling over in his grave.

On my way back to work, I popped into the coffee shop next door to the store to check in with my friend Izzy. Though I was anxious to get back before William ran the place into the ground, I wanted to make sure Izzy hadn't accidentally narced me out to Dominguez.

The lunch rush was on at Holy Grounds, and I had to wait

in line. Though mostly your standard exposed-brickwork urban-modern-artsy coffeehouse, Holy Grounds played up its location, which was directly adjacent to Mercury Crossing. A large, richly-painted mural in the back of the store showed a brown-skinned, plump, open-armed mother-Goddess symbolically birthing the five elements. The other, smaller canvasses hung around the room showed more pagan themes: a spinner transforming into a spider, a triple-faced Goddess, and a naked man with antlers. Under the oil paintings, warm dots of light came from lamps whose shades dripped with colorful beads. A nest of comfortable couches occupied the back wall.

Besides the usual crowd of highly caffeinated students arguing politics or movies in the corner, there was a contingent of Birkenstock, power-suit, vanilla-shot-soy-latte types and a Druid. I stood behind the Druid and admired the quality of the wool in his dark green cloak. Someone, possibly even himself, had embroidered Celtic knot work in golden thread all around the hem.

'Your usual?' Izzy asked me after the Druid had wandered over to join the crowd waiting under the PICK-UP sign.

I probably didn't need the caffeine, but I nodded. I looked at the person behind me in line; she was busily chatting on her cell phone. Even so, I leaned in close and said in what I hoped was a casual, relaxed voice. 'Hey, Izzy, did an FBI agent come in here today asking about me?'

Izzy arched one of her dark eyebrows at me and shook her head in disbelief. Her fingers ran nimbly across the buttons on the register. 'You're some kind of trouble magnet, aren't you, girl?'

47

Speaking of goddesses, Izzy always reminded me of that famous bust of Nefertiti. Except in place of the pharaoh's head-dress, Izzy had a fuzzy cap of hair, which had become significantly puffier in the last few months. She'd been talking about wanting to do something different with her hair, maybe trying cornrows or dreads.

'Let me guess,' Izzy continued as she took my five and made change. 'He was the good-looking Latino – regular coffee, black.'

Did I mention Izzy is a strong latent psychic? I nodded, counting the coins in my hand absently before tossing them into the tip jar. I really needed to get a less expensive addiction. 'You didn't say anything about me, did you?'

'Honey, I am happy to say you didn't figure into our conversation at all.'

Before I could reply with more than a laugh, the next person in line occupied Izzy's attention. I stood next to the Druid and waited for the honey latte I didn't really want. I tried to hang around to see if I could get more of a chance to chat with Izzy, but after several minutes of anxious dawdling I gave up. The crowd showed no signs of abating. So I grabbed a to-go cup for my drink and waved an apologetic good-bye to Izzy over the press of bodies.

Then I did what I always do in times of crisis. I fussed. When not helping customers, William and I neurotically cleaned the store top to bottom. I even voluntarily scrubbed and disinfected the tiny employee bathroom and finally got around to hanging up those ridiculous Witchy motivational posters that had come gratis from Bear Claw Press. 'The Goddess Loves You' made me smile, especially since the artist had included a montage of

48

photographs of Goddess statues from around the world, including several of Kali and other goddesses whose love was, let's say, suspect at best.

Lilith twitched across my belly.

'Oh, hush,' I told her with a fond smile.

I returned the cleaning supplies to their cabinet in the store-room and plunked myself down on the chair by the desk over-flowing with invoices, orders, and receipts. I rummaged through the paper randomly and put my feet up on the safe. I still had to figure out what I was going to do about the FBI agent. I supposed I could take Sebastian up on his offer – provided he really could get me out of the country without a passport. I had some vacation time coming. The south of France probably didn't suck this time of year.

I sighed. I already knew I didn't want to run. I'd seriously considered that option the last time I was in trouble when it would have been easier to make a break. These days I had a lot more roots planted. All of those could be yanked, anyway, if I landed in jail for life. At least if I stayed here, maybe Izzy and William would visit me in prison.

I had to deal with this here and now.

After all, how many times had I heard that 'murder had no statute of limitations'? If I disappeared for a few months now, who's to say they wouldn't be back for me later?

Last time I'd solved my problem with magic. Maybe there was a spell I could use on Agent Dominguez. But what? Given how psychic he was, he'd probably detect a direct memory assault.

When I made the Vatican agents think Sebastian and I were

dead, I'd changed the way they saw events unfold, as they were happening – kind of an illusion distorting the moment. To make Dominguez forget about me, the spell would have to cover events that happened in the past with witnesses I had no control over. I was a pretty powerful Witch, but there was no way I could cast a net of forgetfulness over the whole world. Besides, I was pretty sure that even if I could, I'd be foiled by a paper trail. All it would take to jog Dominguez's memory would be a memo with my name on it . . . or those case notes he kept in that notebook in his pocket.

What I needed was some magic that would make him open to hearing me out, something that would make him sympathetic to the extenuating circumstances. I should cook up something that could melt his heart and make him listen to me, make him want to help me.

Desperately.

You know what I needed? A good old-fashioned love spell.

3

Gemini

♊

Key Words:
Intelligent and Changeable

A love spell was a bad idea and I knew it.

I went back to sorting through the invoices. Then I let myself get distracted by the things that absolutely needed to be done for the day – I paid the rent for my absent boss, balanced the books, and phoned in orders for the popular items we were running low on, like smudge sticks and other incenses.

As I did my busywork, part of my mind kept coming back to the idea of the love spell. Love – or lust – could be a powerful motivator. People have been known to throw themselves on their swords for love. I knew at least one person who'd quit a great job and moved to another country for love. And I wouldn't be asking Dominguez to rush into a burning building for me, just listen. The love spell could be tiny, hardly anything, only a little nudge to make him find me irresistible enough to not want to see me wasting away in jail. What was the harm in that?

It's not like I'd be cheating on Sebastian, not really. I mean, I wouldn't have to *do* anything other than string Dominguez along long enough for him to help me clear my name. I could break the spell at any time he started taking things too seriously.

Plus, he had shown an interest. Dominguez had had a modest response to my flirting. It wouldn't be complete coercion. And anyway, so what if it was? This was a life-or-death situation.

By the time William and I'd closed up for the day and I'd walked the daily deposits to the bank, I had a list of ingredients in my pocket. Even though ideally I'd have preferred a waxing moon in a sign ruled by Venus, tonight would do. After all, time was of the essence. I wanted Dominguez absolutely smitten next time he saw me.

I could tell before I even got my key in the door that Barney, my cat, did not approve of my plan of action. As I came up the stairs I heard a series of sneezes culminating in a very unladylike snort.

When I opened the door, Barney was nowhere to be found. Normally anxious that I might somehow forget to fill her food bowl, she usually greets me as I come in with a warm chirp (she's part Maine Coon) and a bump on the leg to direct me toward the kitchen.

I tossed my backpack and my bike helmet on the couch, and hung up my coat on my tree. I headed straight for the tub. My plan was to ritually bathe with some handmade rose soap and then head up to the attic right away so I could have the spell in action before Parrish came back from his evening meal. I wasn't even going to pause to dress; I've found nakedness vastly improved love spells.

I had one of those old-fashioned, claw-foot tubs deep enough to accommodate a lot of bubbles. I turned the faucets to a water temperature one degree below scalding, lit a few candles, and flipped on a CD of Spanish a cappella lullabies to put me in the lovin' mood.

I was just about completely relaxed and in a near trance state when Barney hopped up into the sink. She reached out a fat paw – she actually had an extra claw, a dew claw, which made her large paws seem even bigger – and hooked the plastic shower curtain.

'Yes?' I asked her, as if I didn't know what she wanted to say.

After blinking her yellow eyes innocently, she shook her head so hard her ears flapped.

'I know,' I said, scrubbing the lightly scented soap under my arms. 'Binding spells are bad juju, but I've thought this through. I'll make sure to seal the spell with wax I can break.'

Barney let the shower curtain go with a tug. She bounded onto the toilet seat and turned her back to me. The fur across her shoulders rippled with disapproval.

Well, I didn't expect Barney to understand. She was allergic to magic – or at least pretended to be. She would act indignant no matter what spell I proposed, even if it was a 'mouse-a-plenty'.

I stepped out onto the rag rug. Toweling off quickly, I opened the door with the intention of gathering the burrs I needed for the spell from my tower room. Barney scooted past my legs and nearly tripped me on the way out. I shook my head at that cat. She never liked to let go of her point. I was sure she'd be knocking things off my dresser in the middle of the night just to remind me how wrong I was for not listening to her.

My tower room was where I grew my herbs. Since dating Sebastian, for whom herbalism was a specialty, my collection had expanded to include a number of odd plants. In fact, I could thank him for the three sandburs I plucked from a clay pot near the other roadside weeds I cultivated, like catchfly and Queen Anne's lace.

It really wouldn't be cheating on Sebastian to cause a little harmless attraction to blossom in Dominguez's heart, would it?

When Barney sneezed and batted a plastic Tupperware container off the top of the refrigerator, I nearly reconsidered. Then, I glanced at the perfectly round hole in my window. It, and the bullet imbedded in the plaster on the wall behind me and just over my shoulder, was a memento courtesy of the Order of Eustace.

Sometimes the situation demanded dire action, I reminded myself.

Besides, Sebastian would understand. I was sure of it.

Burrs in hand, I headed for my attic.

My ritual space used to be intentionally bare to remind me that I'd left behind my life of magic.

Now it overflowed.

Just beyond the white pentacle I painted on the rough-hewn wood flooring sat bookshelves/herb cabinets that Sebastian and I built. Okay, the truth was I designed them and Sebastian did all the heavy lifting and nail pounding, but, hey, I bought the pizza *and* the beer. Even so, I was really proud of them. They were four vaguely crescent-shaped bookshelves, which I had painstakingly aligned with a compass so that the openings between them corresponded to the cardinal points.

Magical doodads were piled on them. Jars of dried herbs, loose beads, oils, gemstones, string, ribbon, mirrors, fabric swatches, paints, feathers, sealing wax, and candles of every conceivable size, shape, and color.

Then there were the found objects: twisted oak branches, a glass full of rainwater, rocks, acorns, a bunch of bittersweet, a bowl of organic compost, and dried leaves and flowers. I had a pile of practical Witchy needs too – matches, salt, notepad, pens, all-purpose goo remover, and a fire extinguisher.

I was happy with the clutter, but as I looked around I still felt a little sad. All the things I'd collected were still so impersonal. I'd had to leave all my magical history behind – gifts given to me over the years, like the Bast statue from the Chicago museum's gift store that Jasmine bought for Barney hoping to cure her allergy – what a disaster that had been! I laughed at how foolish the two of us had been, trying to use magic to fix her magically induced sneezes!

My smile faded with the memory of Jasmine lying dead in the circle, her face twisted in pain. Her prayer beads – ones she'd crafted herself – had been broken. I'd saved them.

Walking over to the loose floorboard, I pulled out a black silk scarf. Since I was doing this spell so that Dominguez would have sympathy for what happened that night, I carefully laid the broken chain on the altar. It was silver. The beads were alternating groups of amethyst and mother of pearl. Where the crucifix would normally hang on a rosary, a silver Nile Goddess pendant hung. I smoothed the chains with tender brushes of my fingertips.

I left the other item hidden. It was a cross. It had belonged to one of the priests Lilith killed. I'd ripped it from him, the way I'd imagined he'd ripped Jasmine's. It occurred to me now that it was hard evidence linking me to the priest's deaths. I should get rid of it. Or, at least get it out of the house.

My fingers continued to stroke Jasmine's necklace. I'd deal with that later. I had a spell to cast.

I rummaged through my things until I found two fat, red votive candles, a scrap of scarlet silk, sealing wax of the same color, and stamp I got from a scrapbooking store with the impression of a heart in it. I set them all on my altar, which was still draped in red since the last full-moon ritual.

Facing east, I sat down on the floor. I could feel dust and bits of wood adhering to my damp skin. The air was warm and close and familiar. I took a moment to breathe in the old wood and frankincense scent of the attic. My shoulders relaxed for the first time since Special Agent Dominguez walked into the store this morning. I sat quietly, just decompressing, for a long moment. Through the skylight over my altar, I watched the day fade. It was still early, maybe five o'clock, but this was October in Wisconsin. I listened to the creaks of the house and the sound of pine branches scraping against the dormer window.

When I felt ready, I pulled out the bankers' box I kept under the altar table. I removed a stick of jasmine incense – funny that the spell called for the scent when I'd just been thinking of her. Lighting it, I stood up. Starting in the north, I walked the outline of the painted circle. As I did, I imagined a transparent bubble forming between the world and me, creating a magical space. Without much effort on my part, the guardians materialized. They were each aspects of Lilith. In the east appeared the faint image of a young warrior woman who was dappled on shoulders and thighs with the feathers of a snowy owl. Her long black hair was tossed by the wind and her hands rested lightly on a broadsword. A creature as dark as smoke took shape in the south. Only glowing specks of embers for eyes were visible. As I passed the western point, the watery image of a woman wavered into existence, like the reflection in a rippling pool. She was full bodied and naked, her hair cascaded in waves and she carried a chalice in her hands. Last, in the north, there stood an old woman with eyes sharp as flint and hair the color of polished steel. She held a silver coin in her gnarled hand and was the most solid image of them all.

I took a moment to regard the circle I'd cast. It just barely registered in the visual range, swirling incandescent greens and blues like a soap bubble. I reached a hand up over my head and felt an electric tingle. My magic had always been strong, but after merging with Lilith it was . . . well, honestly, it was frightening how powerful I could be.

Standing in front of my altar, I put the incense in its burner. Lilith rose to the surface; her presence prickled my skin like a light electrical current. It used to be that when I called Lilith, she possessed me completely. Now I had more control.

I knelt down to begin my spell. Taking the red cloth, I spread it out in front of me. I carefully picked out one of the sandburs. I imagined Dominguez in my mind, and said, 'This thine eye, I bind to me.' I placed the burr in the cloth, then I chose a second one. 'This thy hand, I bind to me.' With the last one, I swore I heard Lilith's voice echoing over my own as I said, 'This thy heart, I bind to me.'

I pushed the sticky seeds together until their barbs locked. I folded up the silk around them and made a kind of pouch in my fist. Using the flame from one of the candles, I lit the red bar of sealing wax. I carefully dripped it over where I pinched the cloth together by my thumb and index finger. Pressing the stamp in the cooling wax, I imagined locking the spell.

A loud sound like a door slamming shut startled me. I gasped and nearly dropped the charm. I looked around for the source of the noise. Seeing nothing, I shrugged. It was probably one of the storm windows dropping suddenly. It happened sometimes, especially when it was windy. The wind certainly seemed to have picked up; I could hear it groaning over the roof.

Standing up, I held the spell bag in both hands, over my head. Closing my eyes, I visualized drawing power from the guardians and from Lilith to activate the spell. I chanted the names of the Goddesses, 'Isis, Istarte, Innana, Hecate, Demeter . . .' A light, breathy voice joined me, followed by a crackly hiss. A smooth, sexy baritone added her voice, then a dusty old warble. At last, they all seemed to merge into one powerful voice, whose strength shook the windows and rattled the beams.

When the power was at its apex, I saw a bright red light, like a laser, shoot from the center of the spell bag and disappear into the night. I imagined it searing Dominguez like a French kiss on the eyes, hands, and heart.

Spell complete, I knelt to put a hand flat on the floor. I let the excess energies roll off me, grounding. The air pressure dropped, causing my ears to pop. I shook my head. Strange, that had never happened before.

Deliberately, I closed the circle and dismissed the guardians. When I finished walking it, I said, 'The circle is open, but unbroken.' Before I left the attic, I made sure all the candles were snuffed out and my materials put away. I grabbed a leather cord and fashioned a necklace to wear the charm around my neck.

As I headed down the stairs to take a shower to clean off my dusty butt, my peripheral vision caught sight of a glowing palm shape in the center of the pentacle on the floor. Both it and the pentacle seemed to pulse with an unearthly light. I blinked and the image was gone.

I heard someone let himself in while I was dressing after my shower. Given that the sun was down, I assumed it was Parrish. As usual, I felt tired after performing the spell work, so I'd slipped into my pink Hello Kitty pajama bottoms and my favorite navy-blue oversized sweatshirt. I tucked the charm necklace underneath, close to my heart.

'Hey, make some coffee, will you?' I shouted out to the living room. I yawned, stretching until my muscles popped.

The springs in the living-room couch squeaked as he hauled himself to his feet. Somewhere in the kitchen, Barney sneezed.

That caught me by surprise. Traditional vampires, of whom Parrish was one, didn't set off Barney's allergies. My theory was that a vampire's magic was expressed only at the moment of his transformation from dead to undead (and possibly during the bite). So when not actively biting or 'Becoming', Barney's sensitive nose merely registered them as a dead thing. Given how much she liked to present me with lifeless mice and other such lovelies, her affection for him made a kind of twisted sense. To her, Parrish was like something the cat dragged in.

When Barney sneezed again, I got a little nervous. Sebastian, you see, was full-time magic. 'Sebastian?' I called. 'Is that you?'

Over the clattering of tins in the cupboards, I heard, 'Of course, darling. Who were you expecting?'

That's when I heard the clomp of motorcycle boots on the stairs.

4

Cancer

Key Words:
Nurturing and Tenacious

I rushed into the living room hoping to divert Parrish before Sebastian noticed him. It was too late. Sebastian stood in the doorway of the kitchen holding my coffeepot in his hand like he wished it were a bludgeoning weapon while crushing a coffee filter in the other.

Parrish, for his part, acted completely nonplussed. He grinned when he saw me, showing off descended fangs. He'd come straight from breakfast.

When he'd died, Parrish had certainly left a beautiful corpse. His past-the-shoulders, silken mane of auburn hair gave him the air of a heavy-metal rock star – a fashion statement, I should note, that he courted quite intentionally. Dusty jeans, worn out in all the right places, hugged his long, lean legs. His T-shirt was so tight he might as well not have been wearing one. Over that, he wore a motorcycle jacket that made his six-foot-plus frame look like he might have once had a membership in Hells Angels, if Chippendales had a chapter.

Parrish was a bad, bad boy.

'Got your note, Meadow Spring,' Parrish said, holding up the sticky on his finger. 'If there's trouble, you know I'm at your service, lady.'

I smiled. Parrish might be bad, but he wanted desperately to be a gentleman.

From the kitchen doorway, Sebastian snorted derisively. 'Chivalry was dead before you were born, Daniel Parrish.'

Standing in the opposite corner of the living room, as if it were the other side of a boxing ring, stood Sebastian. Where Parrish was all shine and show, Sebastian exuded a quiet strength. He looked almost like a regular guy, dressed as he was in broken-in, faded blue jeans, and a black button-down shirt. His clothes didn't especially cling to him, but neither did they hide his trim, sculpted body. His black hair was bound neatly into a ponytail, and he had a calm, yet deadly expression on his face that would rival any ninja master's.

'Sebastian Von Traum,' Parrish said, pretending to notice him for the first time. 'Always a pleasure.'

'Likewise.' When Sebastian returned Parrish's cold smile, I could see that his fangs had dropped too.

Great, my vampire boys were ready to bite each other.

Unfortunately, I already knew who'd win if it came down to trading blows. Parrish looked tougher with his penchant for leather and steel and a long, sordid history in the criminal underworld, but Sebastian had eight hundred years on him. In vampire terms, Parrish was still minor league; Sebastian was in the majors.

Having been smacked down by Sebastian before only made

Parrish pricklier. It wasn't going to take much for him to be spoiling for a rematch.

I needed to say something. But what? Sebastian wasn't supposed to be here. The only reason I could figure why he'd decided to drop by was Lilith. I should have guessed that my spell work would make him all tingly. He always could tell when I drew on Her power.

And it wasn't like he didn't have a key to the place. Sebastian was my boyfriend, after all. He had a toothbrush in my bathroom and extra underwear in a corner of my sock drawer.

So how did I explain Parrish, who was supposed to be dead . . . or at the very least drummed out of town? It was pretty obvious thanks to Parrish waving the note around that I was still in contact with him. Not cool, since it was a jealous rage that caused Sebastian to try to kill Parrish the first time.

Meanwhile, Parrish and Sebastian were doing that creepy vampire thing where they stood preternaturally still, not breathing, and glared murderously at each other.

'The FBI came into the store this morning, Parrish,' I said, breaking the silence. 'Like you said they would.'

Parrish turned to look at me, his face instantly softening into concern. 'Are you all right?'

'Yeah,' I said. 'It was all pretty crazy, but, well, I'm not sure he knows I'm me.'

Parrish chuckled lightly. 'And exactly how does that work, love?'

'He was flashing around a picture of Meadow Spring. He didn't recognize me. Well, I mean, I wasn't exactly Mata Hari, so he might suspect, but . . . well, you know . . . the eyes.'

'Yes, they're very, very different,' Parrish agreed.

I heard the faucet in the kitchen come on and realized Sebastian had left the room. I mouthed, 'hang on,' to Parrish and went in to investigate. I found Sebastian pouring water into my coffeemaker. He'd replaced the filter and the pot, and found the coffee in the freezer.

'You okay?' I asked him from the doorway.

He kept his back to me as he poured beans into the grinder. 'Unfinished business, Garnet.'

That's what he'd accused me of when Parrish first reappeared in my life. He didn't believe me when I told him things were over between Parrish and me, and I certainly seemed to be proving him right.

'It's not that . . .' I started, but he cut me off by turning to pierce me with a hot glare.

'How long have you kept him a secret from me?'

Parrish had come stumbling back to my apartment two nights after Sebastian had left him for dead. I took him in. I tended his wounds. I even found a willing ghoul to offer some, shall we say, transfusions. Sebastian wouldn't understand any of it.

And, really, why should he? He was right. There was a lot of unfinished business, and most of it was wrapped up in with letting go of who I used to be in Minneapolis before Lilith, the Vatican agents, and all this.

My feelings for Parrish were complicated by what happened that Halloween night. I'd broken up with Parrish the night before. I'd had it with the ghouls, not knowing where he was or what he was doing most nights . . . and, to be perfectly honest, Parrish was difficult to love. He was more than a little self-centered and had really embraced a kind of rock-and-roll lifestyle I wasn't terribly comfortable with. Yet, he was the first person I thought of when I found myself standing in the middle of a circle of blood and death.

Not only did he come running when I needed him, but he asked no questions, expected nothing.

That kind of heroism was hard to come by in a man. Hell, that was hard to come by in anyone.

'That's what I thought,' Sebastian said when I didn't respond. 'He's been here the whole time, hasn't he?'

The worst part of this conversation was that Sebastian had yet to raise his voice. He didn't even sound angry, only far too calm.

I would have preferred yelling, honestly.

Sebastian took in a long, steady breath. 'You should go back in there. I'm sure you two have things to work out.'

I didn't understand. What did that mean? 'What about you?'

'I'll be in when the coffee's done. Does he take cream?'

'I have no idea. He can't usually drink.'

Sebastian's mouth twitched into a smug smile. 'Right.'

I hesitated in the doorway. Sebastian, meanwhile, had turned his attention back to the coffee. I knew he was hurt, and this cold calmness frightened me. I desperately wanted to know how much damage I'd caused. 'Sebastian,' I said, putting a hand lightly on his shoulder. 'This isn't what you think. Parrish and I aren't lovers.'

'I never thought that.' His voice remained even and measured, and he never turned to look at me.

'I only asked him to come because he knew the old me, you know?' I let my hand slip off.

'Of course.'

'I didn't mean to hurt you,' I said.

'He's waiting for you, Garnet.'

I didn't know what to make of Sebastian's calm insistence, so even though I knew I probably shouldn't, I went back into the living room.

Parrish pretended to admire a statue of Kali that sat on a brick-and-board bookshelf near the door. When he saw me come in, he quickly replaced it. 'I wish you would have told me you were planning on having a guest,' Parrish said teasingly.

'So you could sharpen your fangs? I don't think so.'

'Seriously, Garnet, I thought the idea was to keep lover boy in the dark.'

Oh, could you be any louder with that little comment, Parrish? I walked over and stomped my bare foot onto his boots, probably hurting myself much more than him in the process. 'Knock it off,' I whispered.

A wolfish grin that spread across Parrish's face. 'He's jealous.'

He's hurt, I thought but didn't dare say. Parrish had no qualms about throwing something like that into Sebastian's face. 'Look, I think we should talk later.'

'As you wish.' Parrish sketched a courtly bow and leaned over to give me a peck on the forehead.

Before he could move away, I caught his lapel and pulled him closer. 'Come back before you turn in,' I whispered in his ear.

He nodded and left.

I closed the door behind him. When I turned around, Sebastian stood in the doorway. The dark look in his eyes told me he'd witnessed our final exchange.

'He's leaving.' Sebastian said through lips so tight they made the question into a statement.

'Uh, yeah. It's for the best, don't you think?'

Sebastian nodded slowly. 'I see.'

I didn't. I waited for him to elaborate. The way the muscles of his jaw worked, I knew something was going to be forthcoming soon.

'You never are going to really let me in, are you?' Sebastian asked. His tone was still cold and measured. I didn't like it one bit.

'Into what?'

'You can't even talk to him with me in the room, yet you expect me to believe you're not having some kind of secret love affair.'

'We're not!' I blurted so forcefully that I'm sure I seemed guilty. I hated how defensive I sounded, especially since Sebastian was still so cool and collected.

'So, you're denying you're still in love with Parrish?'

I shouldn't have hesitated, but I did. Thing is, I was never sure I ever, 100 percent loved Parrish. When I considered how selflessly he came rushing to my aid, sometimes I felt I ought to have loved him a lot more than I did. Weirdly, I wanted to love Parrish, because there was so damn much about him that I liked, but how did I explain all this to Sebastian when I could barely articulate it to myself? Anyway, it hardly mattered. That ten-second delay had sunk me, and I knew it. So I changed tactics. 'He's not my boyfriend, you are.'

'For the moment that's true.'

That was certainly an ominous statement made more so since I was still the only one to have raised my voice. 'I know I should have told you the moment Parrish came looking for my help, but, Great Goddess, Sebastian. You tried to kill him. I thought maybe you'd do it again if you knew he was in town.'

'You seriously thought I wouldn't know about all the other vampires operating in a city the size of Madison?'

'Did you?'

'I knew he was still around. He's got a bit of a reputation.'

You could say that again. Lately, in order to pay the bills, Parrish had taken up the dubious profession of biter for hire. Apparently – and I *so* didn't want to know any more about this – there was a large contingent of Goth types who so desperately craved the experience of a real vampire bite that they were willing to pay Parrish ungodly amounts of cash for it. The good news was Parrish was well compensated; the bad was that he was a vampire equivalent of a gigolo.

Parrish kept telling me this particular line of work was temporary. He found it distasteful, pun intended no doubt, and he still considered himself a professional thief. Parrish had made his living as a highwayman when such things as stage-coaches and king's highways still existed. Now, he robbed banks, but in order to do that successfully, he always told me, the key was not to do it very often. Thus, 'blood whoring', as he called it, to fill the gaps.

It seemed sleazy and dangerous to me, but when I asked

Parrish about it he always shrugged it off, saying that he might as well get paid for doing something he had to do anyway.

'None of that really matters,' Sebastian said. 'I'm not actually terribly surprised you took him in. I'm not even all that bothered by the fact that you still care for him. What I'm upset about is that you lied to me about it. You kept him a secret for months.'

I didn't know what to say to that. I felt miserable.

Sebastian nodded at my silence. 'And I might even have been okay with that, but I come in from the kitchen to find out that you fully intend to continue with the evasion and secret keeping. I'd hoped that somehow, despite how awkward it might have been, you could have included me in your little tête-à-tête about your current situation with the FBI. You don't seem to trust me with it.'

'What do you mean?'

'How could we have been going out all this time and you never managed to mention your murderous run-in with the Vatican Witch hunters?'

'It never came up,' I said, though somehow when the words escaped my mouth the statement managed to sound more like a question. 'I wanted to tell you.' Actually, that was a lie. I preferred not to think about what happened last Halloween. The memory was still too painful. 'I was waiting for the right time.'

Sebastian watched me intently with the kind of concentration usually reserved for someone speaking English with a thick, alien accent. 'Yet William knew.'

'Uh. Yeah. I ended up telling him and Izzy when the Vatican was after us.'

'Izzy too.'

'Well, Sebastian, we were kind of busy with our own problems, remember? Besides, you'd gotten staked to the wall.' I pointed to where the stub of a longbow arrow stuck out of my solid oak window frame. I'd since varnished it to match and hung a spider plant from it. 'And, then there was the Feather fiasco where we weren't exactly talking.' He'd ended up lunching on William's then girlfriend, freaking everyone out, including me. 'And, then we were fighting for our lives, and . . . Well, when it was all over, I was just as happy not to bring it up again, you know?'

'No, I don't know. I'm having a real problem with this, Garnet. I don't understand how you failed to share what I can only imagine must have been a defining moment for you.'

I broke. 'I didn't fail to share anything; I didn't want you to know,' I yelled. 'What's so fucking wrong about not wanting my boyfriend to think of me as a cold-blooded killer?'

'Your argument would be more convincing if everyone else in town didn't seem to know.'

'They're my friends, not my lover. That's different.'

'Yes,' he said quietly. 'I think that's the problem.'

I frowned at him. I felt all mixed-up. 'Sebastian, you're more than a friend. That's why I didn't want to tell you. I want you to like me.'

'Like who? The real you, or the "you" you present me with? That's what you're asking me to do. Love your lies.'

'Lies? That's a little harsh, isn't it?'

'Is it? If I hadn't come over, what would you have told me you did tonight when I asked? Would you have mentioned

Parrish or would you have made something up?'

He knew the answer and so did I.

'So,' he continued, despite my shut-up-about-it glare. 'This "right time" to tell me about the Vatican assassins came and went, didn't it? You told me something else. Some lie.'

'Get over yourself, Sebastian,' I snapped. 'This is not about keeping things from you. This is about a past I don't really like to talk about, okay?' Despite my best efforts, I heard my voice snag. I clenched my teeth. I didn't want to cry right now, I wanted to make my point. 'Not telling isn't the same as lying.'

'I suppose you're right,' he said, conceding the point calmly, damn him. 'But not telling and lying both keep me at arm's length, don't they? That's what I'm hurt about. It makes me wonder what you think of me. Do you imagine me some kind of delicate flower that will wilt at the suggestion of bloodshed? You do remember I'm a vampire? I have a little experience with what might lead someone to kill.'

Yes, but did he? It was different, murder and feeding. I knew Sebastian would kill to defend himself; he'd done it when the Vatican attacked us. He hated Parrish enough to go after him, but he'd left him alive. Sebastian lived in a different world than Parrish – one filled with sunshine and jobs and ways to make a living that didn't involve breaking the law.

Sebastian must have read some of my thoughts in my expression. His face darkened. 'Oh, I see. Mr Stagecoach Robber is the only one who really understands what you're going through because of his criminal past, eh?'

'No, because he was *there*,' I blurted out before I considered the consequences.

Sebastian's jaw twitched, and the passion drained from his expression. 'I can hardly compete with a little shared murder, can I?'

'What the hell does that mean?'

Sebastian grabbed his jacket from where it lay strewn across the arm of my couch. He shrugged into it. Over his shoulder he added, 'It means, Garnet, that you and I are officially on a break. Your coffee is ready.'

Sebastian stalked past me toward the door. 'Oh, and when you see Parrish later be sure to tell him that if he's sleeping near here I will find his lair and destroy him.'

I grabbed his sleeve and pulled him around to face me. 'Don't you dare! You so much as touch a hair on his head we're far more than on a break, Sebastian Von Traum, we're over.'

Though he somehow kept his expression cool, his eyes flashed. 'I'll be honest with you, Garnet,' he said evenly. 'The truth is, despite what I just said, I could never do permanent damage to anyone you care about that much, because I care about *you* that much.'

Well, that certainly derailed my argument. I decided I hated fighting with someone who'd clearly had several hundred years to perfect the art of the parting zinger. My only response was, 'Yeah, well. Good.'

'Yes, but I've proved your point, haven't I?' Sebastian said. 'Your beloved Parrish wouldn't hesitate. I'm clearly not vamp enough for you.'

I could hear the mixture of self-loathing and unadulterated jealousy in Sebastian's voice. 'That's not true!'

72

'Unfortunately, Garnet, I now know you're a good liar.'

He didn't let me counter that. He disappeared down the stairs to the front door. My mouth hung open as I stared at the cracked plaster and dingy wainscoting of the empty steps.

Barney bonked the back of my calf as if urging me to follow after him.

I shut the door. 'There's no point right now,' I told her. 'I really screwed this one up. He'll come back when he's ready to talk.'

My brave words didn't even convince Barney. She bonked me once more, softer, then padded off. Loud munching came from the kitchen.

Which reminded me that I had a pint of Ghiradelli chocolate ice cream in the freezer.

I crawled under an afghan on the couch, and I ate ice cream until I felt bloated. Since I didn't own a TV, I emptied my mind by reading all the latest gossip about various celebrities in *In Touch* magazine. Barney curled up into a warm, snoring ball on my feet.

As I scanned the fashion photos of 'Who Wore It Best', I had one of those despondent moments when I decided I didn't understand men at all. The stereotype would have me believe that most guys preferred a girlfriend who didn't burden them with unnecessary baggage. Sebastian should be happy I wasn't much of a talker when it came to my past. Who wanted all that crap dumped on them, anyway? It's not like he could do anything about it now.

Yeah, okay, maybe I should have told him before today, if

only because it was bound to come up sooner or later. I just preferred to leave my past buried. Even before the FBI showed up looking to make me into a murderer, I wasn't exactly in a hurry to let people in on the gory details of my crime of passion – especially not my boyfriend.

I swirled the chocolate melt around the bottom of the bowl. Every noise made me twitch. I knew it was too much to hope that Sebastian would have an instant change of heart, but I couldn't help myself. At some point, I glanced at the clock over the bookshelves. It was well past midnight. I should go to bed, but the thought of lying in the darkness surrounded by all the I-should-haves and why-didn't-Is made me nauseous.

When the phone rang, I leaped up to answer it so fast that Barney landed very hard and very uncatlike on the floor. I got the receiver in my hand before the second ring.

'Yes?'

But the voice on the other end wasn't Sebastian, or even Parrish; it was Izzy. 'Oh good, you're awake. I need a favor.'

Izzy had once helped me pull Sebastian off the wall where he'd been pinioned with a longbow arrow. Despite the hour, I didn't even hesitate. 'Of course.'

'Do you still have sea salt under the counter at your store? I need a zombie zapper.'

'Yeah, but Izzy, I'm fifteen minutes away by bike.' That wasn't even counting in the time I'd need to find socks and shoes and get bundled up for the weather.

'I'm still at the coffee shop. I just need your security code.' She was whispering now, and I thought I could hear low moaning in the background.

Cripes, it was like *Night of the Living Dead* over there.

'Yeah, of course.' Even though Izzy was my best friend, my gut clenched a little as I relayed the numbers to her. Then I felt guilty for even feeling the least bit hesitation. Izzy was clearly in trouble.

'Thanks.' I could hear buttons being punched and the beep of the lock releasing.

'Izzy, what's going on?'

The line went dead.

It hadn't quite sounded like she'd snapped off her cell. The sudden silence felt much more ominous somehow. I hit Izzy's cell number on speed dial and got her voice mail.

I hunted up a pair of running shoes and then headed to my bedroom for a change of clothes. Barney hopped up onto the bed with a questioning, 'Brrt?'

'Izzy is probably okay,' I told her as I wiggled out of the pajama bottoms and into a pair of jeans. 'But I thought I'd just ride down to the store and make sure.'

Sitting her butt down on my grandmother's quilt, Barney watched me dress. Her steady, unblinking yellow stare was the closest thing to agreement she showed. Barney was worried too.

After pulling on the thickest, warmest wool socks I had I gave Barney's ear an affectionate tug. 'I'll be back before you know it.'

I had my jacket on and my bike in my arms when Parrish came in the front door.

'You're out late,' he said, just as I said, 'You're in early.'

I answered first. 'I thought I'd ride by the store. I think . . .' Normally I'd censor the part about the zombies, but this was Parrish I was talking to. 'Hordes of the undead are attacking my best friend.'

Interested, Parrish leaned on the railing. It creaked under his weight. 'Which kind?'

'Zombies.'

'God, them again.'

I set my bike down. I stood just under where Parrish's elbow rested on the staircase railing. The pleasant smell of leather and sandalwood drifted between us. 'So it's not just my imagination. There are a lot of them all of a sudden.'

'Yeah,' Parrish shrugged. 'Word is, it's Katrina.'

'Like, as in the hurricane?' When Parrish nodded I still didn't quite believe what he was implying. 'Seriously?'

He shrugged. 'Listen, I came by to talk. If you want, I could go with you to check on your friend.' He looked at my mountain bike, and then said, 'We could take mine.'

His was a motorcycle and much faster. Very tempting, but I said, 'I should probably go on my own. I don't think it's such a good idea, riding off alone with you anywhere right now.'

I waited for the lewd rejoinder about how irresistible he was or some such, but instead he shifted upright and moved out of my path to the door. 'I'll wait for you.'

I hefted my bike, but Parrish said nothing. He crossed his arms in front of his chest and leaned against the wall, which hummed lightly with the sound of the neighbor's Grateful Dead tunes. He bowed his head and closed his eyes. At that moment, I knew he wouldn't push it. He'd ask no questions or make

76

any demands. He'd sit here and wait for as long as it took.

'Izzy could be in real trouble,' I said. 'Your bike is much faster.'

Of course a motorcycle, especially one as loud as a Harley, is no place to have a conversation. We rode in silence with me clinging to his back, my face pressed into his leather jacket to try to stave off the cold and biting wind. It was one of those fuzzy gray October nights where the heavy cloud cover reflected the yellow lights of the city. There was moisture in the air, as though it might snow. The streetlamps were surrounded by a halo of haze.

Since State Street was a pedestrian mall, we had to park the bike and walk up the street. Both shops were closed and dark. Peering into the window of Holy Grounds, I couldn't see any obvious signs of struggle. I let myself into the store using my key. Izzy had reprogrammed the security lock, and when I noticed that I felt instantly relieved. She hadn't left in a hurry or under duress.

'She's okay,' I told Parrish, as I relocked the store. 'She probably forgot to recharge her battery again.'

'Do you want to swing by her place just to make sure?'

I did. I knew Izzy could take care of herself and the locked door was deeply reassuring, but it never hurt to be sure.

Ten minutes later we cruised past Izzy's house. It was an Arts and Crafts bungalow on Mason Street between Hoyt Park and Forest Hill Cemetery. I expected the place to be shuttered and dark for the night, but there was a light on in the kitchen. I thought I could make out two figures sitting at the table.

Parrish pulled up to the curb, but I shook my head. Everything seemed all right, and, besides, I'd forgotten my gloves, and my hands were raw with cold. I wanted to go home.

'You'll feel better if you talk to her,' Parrish said.

'It's almost one a.m.,' I said, feeling another twinge of Minnesota Nice. I mean, Izzy and I were the call-after-midnight kind of friends, but show up at the door? Somehow it seemed ruder.

He cut the engine. 'Go on.'

I pulled myself away from the relative warmth of the bike. Icy frost clung to the long expanse of grass in front of Izzy's house. A sheen of white covered the sidewalk, sparkling like glitter under the streetlamp. The front of the house was dark. The doorbell on the exterior of the three-season porch was broken, so instead I walked along the paved driveway toward the side door. I'd taken no more than a half dozen steps when a motion-sensitive light snapped on and illuminated a crow.

The bird stood in the center of the frosty drive, one beady black eye trained on me. Taking a bold hop toward me, it bobbed once like a deep bow, and proceeded to yell at me. Or caw. Whatever. It felt personal.

Then apparently finished, it took off in a flutter of oily wings.

As someone who takes this sort of thing seriously, I watched the crow disappear into a tangle of oak branches.

I looked at Izzy's house. Clearly, the crow was some kind of sign, but what did it mean? Was Izzy in trouble?

I took another step toward the door. The crow cawed once, loudly.

So, I wasn't supposed to go to the door. I sidled up to a window. Through it, I could plainly see Izzy. She was sitting at her kitchen table eating a bowl of Froot Loops. I raised my hand to rap at the window, and I felt something grab at my hair. Wings hit my ear. The damn crow was dive-bombing me.

'You're making me think Izzy is in real trouble,' I hissed at the crow. It perched on one arm of one of those old metal clotheslines in the neighbor's backyard. The crow puffed up its chest feathers and shook its head.

'No? She's not in trouble?' Creepily, it bobbed its head in affirmative. I reminded myself I was a Witch and tried to roll with the fact that I was clearly having a conversation with a bird. 'Why won't you let me talk to her?'

Maybe the question was too complicated, because it cocked its head at me.

After taking one last look at Izzy, I told the crow, 'Okay, but when I get home, I'm going to call her.'

I turned on my heels and headed back to where Parrish waited on his bike. The crow flew overhead, its cries of 'Ah, ah, ah' echoing in the night.

Parrish gave me a long look. From where he sat, he'd seen everything. 'Crows at night. That's so wrong,' he said. 'This place is creepy.'

Somehow that seemed more ominous coming from a vampire.

'Yeah,' I said, clambering on the back of his motorcycle. I slipped my arms under his jacket and hugged him tightly.

Wordlessly, he started the engine, and we drove toward home.

As we turned up the street, I watched perfectly spaced rows of white granite headstones roll past.

I thought I saw something moving between the trees, but decided it was just a deer . . . or more likely my nerves imagining things.

Back at home I invited Parrish upstairs. The apartment stank of burned coffee. The pot Sebastian had made now had a black ring of sludge stuck to the bottom. I set it in the sink to soak while Parrish settled himself down at my kitchen table.

Parrish crossed his arms on the scarred wood of the oak table and watched me. On my way to the refrigerator to offer Parrish something to drink, I accidentally kicked Barney's food bowl and scattered some kibbles.

'Shit,' I said louder than I intended. I bent down to pick them up, feeling ready to cry.

Suddenly, there were hands on my shoulder guiding me upright. 'Leave it,' Parrish said. 'It can wait.'

'But,' I said, gesturing to the mess on the floor. 'I know how to fix this.'

Wordlessly, Parrish pulled me into a bear hug. I allowed my head to sag against his chest. I needed to be held much more than I realized. Letting him support me, even for a moment, made it all better somehow. Even as I was comforted, I couldn't help but notice how the autumn chill unnaturally permeated his skin. His arms were powerful and capable, but I strongly felt the absence of his heartbeat. It was like being surrounded by a statue of a man.

I broke contact. Parrish hugs were dangerous. They just

implied clothes coming off and guilty mornings after. Parrish was temptation walking. If I ever wanted to patch things up with Sebastian, which I did, now would be such a bad time to relax my vigilance in this department, despite how good it felt to be held. 'I'm okay,' I lied.

He gave me a sad little smile that said he'd let me get away with saying so for now. His hands held my shoulders. 'I'm sure you are. But you don't have to be so strong with me.'

That almost broke my resolve. I held the quiver of my lip in check by act of supreme will. Parrish had seen me at my worst. He'd seen my hysteria, my grief, all the ugliness of that night and he still loved me. I took in a deep breath, intending to steer the conversation back to safer ground.

Instead, he pierced me with those storm-gray eyes and said, 'We'll get through this.'

As much as I appreciated him throwing his lot in with me, I had to say, 'It's me the FBI is after.'

'My dear lady, I am an accomplice after the fact, or at the very least a coconspirator or an abettor.' When I frowned at him in confusion, he said. 'Garnet, we drove them to Lakewood Cemetery in my van. Forensic evidence is going to point to me as clearly as it will to you.'

'What forensic evidence? You're a vampire.'

'Just so, but I have hair and skin and fingernails. I leave footprints. My clothes shed fibers. The tires on my car make tracks. I can be witnessed by passersby. I am not so entirely formed of magic that I can defy natural laws.'

Yet, somehow, I thought he could. 'Do you really think they're looking for you too?'

He let his hands fall off my shoulders and cracked his neck in that way guys do when they're thinking about something uncomfortable. 'Most certainly, though my connection to the agents' death is slightly more tenuous. Anyone who knew us as a couple would likely be aware of the fact that you broke things off with me the night before the murders. Officially, we were no longer romantically linked. Of course, most of the people who knew us well, namely your coven, are dead. So it wouldn't take much to connect the dots given that I've followed you here.'

I shook my head. I'd only partly heard all Parrish had said, my brain having stopped working after 'murders', I repeated aloud, feeling my knees tremble slightly.

Parrish steered me over to a chair and sat me down. He knelt beside me and cupped my face with his still-cold hands. His eyes sought out mine. 'I shouldn't have used that word. Forgive me.'

'It's what it was, though, wasn't it?'

Parrish flashed me a quirky grin. 'There's murder in self-defense, and then there's killing people and sucking their blood. I'm hardly a firm moral compass on this issue, my love.'

'What am I going to do?'

'First of all,' he said. 'You're not going to panic. We don't yet know precisely what led this lawman to our door. It is within the realm of possibility that he has no hard evidence at all, but is merely attempting to flush us out.'

I nodded. Dominguez had said something about me not yet being a suspect.

'Second, you're going to remember that you did nothing

wrong. You're guilty only of defending yourself. If you must confess to anything at all, it will be to responding as any reasonable person would – in self-defense.'

'But . . .'

Parrish put a finger gently on my lips to stop my protest. 'Stay out of the second-guessing game, Garnet. What's done is done. Doubts will damn you. You must believe in your innocence.'

He made it all sound so reasonable; I felt half convinced. I nodded absently, not really believing.

His hands gripped the sides of my face and compelled me to look into his eyes. 'You *are* innocent, Garnet. Completely. Lilith did the killing, not you. I'm not asking you to believe something that isn't true. This was not your doing.'

It wasn't, was it? I was the vessel Lilith had used, that's all.

'Yeah,' I said, this time with more conviction. 'I didn't ask Her to kill anyone.'

He gave me a looking over, as if checking my resolve. He nodded in approval and let his hands drop. 'That's my girl. You're going to be fine. You have nothing to worry about.'

Except I did. There was all that forensic evidence he mentioned earlier. 'What about you?' I asked. 'What are you going to do?'

Parrish shrugged and stood up. Leaning against my refrigerator, he said, 'Normally when the constables show up, I go to ground.'

I nodded. Then I suddenly wondered if he was being more than very British at that moment, 'Wait. Do you mean literally?'

He flashed me another mischievous smile. 'You can't hang a dead man twice.'

'You can't hang a vampire at all,' I noted. 'Aren't public executions usually daylight activities?'

'I was being metaphorical,' Parrish said with an exasperated eye roll. Pulling out a chair, he sat. 'Anyway, the point is still the same. Being dead has its advantages. Justice is considered served if the criminal is already a corpse.'

'Yeah,' I said distractedly. I'd used a similar idea to distract the Vatican Witch hunters who'd come after Sebastian and me several months ago. I cast a spell to convince them they'd successfully killed us. I could consider something like that with Dominguez, I supposed, but since he wasn't actively trying to kill me, I wasn't sure it would work. It was one thing to redirect energy already in motion, another to cast an illusion involving an unexpected outcome.

Besides, unlike the Vatican organization, which operated in the shadows, the FBI would probably expect Dominguez to return with things like a death certificate or an obituary. Those things were much harder to fake.

While we both sat silently considering my options, Barney hopped up on the table and presented herself for some love. Parrish obliged by scratching her neck ruff. She leaned into it, purring. Barney had always had a soft spot for Parrish.

'You're a Witch, Garnet. Couldn't you put a hex on him?'

Barney's teeth snapped at Parrish's fingers. He pulled back, surprised. I shooed her off the table. 'That's kind of my plan. Barney doesn't approve.'

Parrish held his fingers close to his chest, as though

protecting them, and he eyed the cat warily as she stalked off. 'Clearly.'

I didn't want to think about FBI agents anymore. I got up and wandered over to the fridge. I rummaged around half-heartedly and settled on a super-green smoothie. What I really wanted was some caffeine, but the thought of coffee made my eyes water. 'I really screwed things up with Sebastian,' I said, closing the refrigerator door.

Parrish let out a sigh of breath and nodded. 'He'll come around.'

Sitting down, I pulled the plastic ring off my drink. I felt strange not offering something to Parrish, but unless his fangs were descended he couldn't eat or drink.

'I don't know. We said some things . . .'

'Sebastian's been around a long time, my darling,' Parrish said kindly. 'Doubtless he understands the concept of a heated exchange of words. I'm sure this isn't the first time someone he loved said something they later regretted, or vice versa.'

'He doesn't fight hot,' I said. 'He's very measured. Very cold.'

'Hmm.' Parrish gave me a pitying look. 'That's unfortunate.'

I nodded, taking a swallow of the smoothie.

'It was about me, wasn't it?' Parrish asked a little too glee-fully. 'Your argument.'

He knew it was, but I didn't want to give him the satisfaction. 'Not everything is about you.'

'Sure it is,' he teased. 'How much does he want to kill me?'

'A lot,' I admitted.

'I'll be careful. After all, he has me at a distinct disadvantage.'

Sunlight killed Parrish. Sebastian could easily drag Parrish's coffin into the open and expose him. Even though I wasn't entirely convinced Sebastian would really do it, the thought of how easy it would be scared me. 'You should move into my attic.'

Parrish laughed. 'Do you want to finish with him for good? Because you should know I *will* take you up on this. I'd move back into your bed if you'd let me.'

I thought about that a second too long. So, even though I shook my head, Parrish flashed me a wolfish grin as I said, 'That would be a bad idea.'

'Let me know when you change your mind.'

I chuckled. It was so like him to say 'when' and not 'if'. Parrish was nothing if not sexually arrogant. I hated myself for how attractive that made him.

'There's that smile I love,' Parrish said, touching the corner of my mouth with a thumb. 'I still love you, you know.'

I knew, but I couldn't deal with this now, here in this kitchen that smelled of Sebastian's coffee and reminded me of the hurt in his voice and all the stupid things I'd said and done. 'Parrish,' I started, though I wasn't sure where I was going so my voice just trailed off into a sigh.

He let my halfhearted protest hang in the air between us. Then his fingers plucked playfully at the short hairs above my ears. 'I'll never get used to this no matter how many times I see you.'

I tended to be thrown by pictures of the old me. I hardly recognized myself as a blue-eyed blonde. That person no longer felt like me. The spiky hair, on the other hand, suited me. I'd convinced myself that maybe I'd had a perky Goth hiding deep inside me all along. 'I don't know, Parrish. I was very Marsha Brady before, don't you think?'

Parrish gave me a blank look.

Then, I remembered that despite being two hundred years old, he had almost none of the shared TV culture. *The Brady Bunch* had had a squarely afternoon time slot, and while he might be able to catch them on Nickelodeon reruns, why would he bother? Parrish spent his nights on the hunt, not catching up on cheesy TV shows.

'Pollyanna?' I tried.

'Ah! I read that one, but I don't remember Pollyanna's hair.'

'Never mind.' I gave up. Sometimes trying to communicate over the age barrier stumped me. Sebastian and I had the occasional moment like these, but, being on the daytime schedule like the rest of the world, he was much more plugged-in. Plus, Sebastian had an affinity for gadgets, which made him seem very modern. He'd even bought his classic car off eBay. Sebastian claimed his fondness for electronic stuff came from the scientific inquiry of an alchemist, but I secretly believed it was because he had the heart of a geek boy.

Crap. I missed him.

I stood up. 'I really need to get some sleep,' I told Parrish. 'Work tomorrow.'

'Of course,' he said.

We walked to the front door together. Before he headed down the stairs, he turned to me. 'You'll let me know if you need help with the police, eh?'

'You're always the one I think of when the cops are after me, Parrish.'

Parrish smiled just enough to show off the tips of his sharp canines. He tousled my hair and gave my cheek a quick peck. 'Brilliant.'

I returned his smile warmly. But after he slipped down the stairs and out of sight, I retreated to my bedroom. I tore apart my closet until I found one of Sebastian's old sweatshirts. Snuggling into it, I breathed in his scent and cried myself to sleep.

I woke up in the morning to a driving rain and a pounding headache. It was so dark outside that I checked the glowing red numbers on my alarm clock twice hoping for a reprieve. Thunder boomed in the distance. I grudgingly pulled myself out of the warm folds of my comforter.

My eyes ached. My head hurt. Brushing my teeth helped, as did the scalding shower. Discovering the coffeepot soaking in the sink did not. I tried to be cheerful as I scrubbed it out, and I flipped on the radio only to discover it was still tuned to Sebastian's favorite country and western station. I quickly turned the knob on Patsy Cline before she broke my heart all over again. The college station was playing something weepy by Tonic, so I switched it off.

As I poured a bowl of flax flakes for myself and some kibbles for Barney, I decided to get coffee at the café.

An hour later, I stood at the bus stop. Rain dripped off my umbrella. I'd dressed for the weather: simple wide-cuff black jeans, an oversized wool sweater, and combat boots. If it wasn't for the scarlet bat on the back of my ankle-length coat, I'd have looked positively normal.

The interior of the bus smelled of wet, grouchy people. I wedged into a hard plastic seat next to a businessman balancing his laptop on his knees. The strong odor of his cologne mingled with the stink of warm bodies. Steam obscured the passing scenery so badly that I overshot my stop by three blocks.

I stomped through the puddles as I made my way back up State Street, cursing all the overhanging awnings that sent down unexpected splatters of water. By the time I reached the coffee shop, I felt like a drowned rat. I probably looked like one too.

But the coffeejock behind the bar took my order with a smile. I guessed the trivia question right and got twenty-five cents off my latte, and according to my watch I had a whole half hour to kill before I had to start the process of opening up shop. I put my feet up on a nearby chair and scanned the latest issue of *The Onion* for something funny. Despite myself, I got caught up in one of their crazy pothead columns. I was chuckling to myself when the door chimes caught my attention.

The rain did beautiful things to Dominguez. Curls plastered themselves to his head in a way that made me want to be the bearer of a warm towel and a hot cup of cocoa. Our eyes met. He smiled.

My hand strayed to the spot under my sweater where the spell charm hung around my neck. I smelled the faint scent of roses as he pulled up a chair to sit by me. 'We meet again, Ms Marlena Ito.'

I laughed. 'Indeed.'

'Any progress on my astrological chart?'

I'd forgotten I'd promised to cast his chart. 'No. I had a family crisis last night.'

I tried to sound light, but he must have caught something in my tone. He leaned closer, and those crystal blue eyes sought out mine. 'Nothing too serious, I hope.'

'My boyfriend broke up with me.'

I swear I saw a twinkle in his eye. The corners of his mouth twitched like he was desperately trying to hold back a smile. 'That's terrible,' he said unconvincingly.

I couldn't help but grin at him. His enthusiasm was so cute.

The table was narrow enough that his knees brushed against mine. Instead of making all the usual apologies, we just smiled stupidly at each other. I ran a finger along the edge of my coffee cup trying to remember why I'd been so freaked out when I first saw him. Sure, he had a few rough edges, but the more I looked at them the more I decided they were really hard angles, the kind I liked on a man.

'You're at loose ends today?' he asked.

'I wish,' I said. 'Work.'

'For a sub, you work a lot.'

Go with the truth, Garnet. 'I need the money.'

He nodded as though he completely understood. I suspected he might. He didn't have the demeanor of someone who'd had life handed to him on a silver spoon. He seemed like the sort who took odd jobs, maybe several of them at once, to pay for college.

Not like Sebastian, who died before universities were

invented, or Parrish, who lived the kind of rough-and-tumble life where reading was only important as a survival skill. Dominguez was normal. It was strangely appealing on this dark and rainy morning.

'Take me to lunch.' As soon as the words were out of my mouth, I regretted them. Sebastian and I always had a lunch date. I couldn't believe I was replacing him so quickly. Then I reminded myself that this wasn't a real date. I was trying to keep Dominguez in my romantic thrall. His broad, sexy smile made me fairly certain the spell was working.

'Sounds like a plan,' he said. 'What time do you get off?'

I had to bite my lip to keep from saying something wildly inappropriate. 'Noon.'

'Great. I heard about this excellent pizza shop I want to try.'

At least it wasn't the deli. 'I look forward to it.'

As he got up to find a place in line, I watched the way his pants hugged his backside. It was far too easy to imagine his body hardened by FBI training underneath those wet, clinging clothes. I found myself actually serious about being excited to see him again. It wasn't going to be any kind of hardship to spend time with this man.

The pre-Halloween/Samhain rush was on at the store. In between customers, William and I spent the morning decorating the front window with seasonally appropriate books and plastic jack-o'-lanterns. I hung up a cardboard cartoon Witch, and set out a cauldron filled with an aromatherapy steam machine. It was a nice effect. No doubt we'd soon be getting the call from the local Madison paper for an interview with a real Witch for their Halloween human-interest story in the next few days.

So many people came and went that before I knew it, the morning was over and I was looking into the startlingly blue eyes of Gabriel Dominguez again.

His smile gave him dimples. I liked how it made him look younger and more approachable.

William nearly choked when I told him we were off to lunch. 'Are you sure? I mean, we've been so busy.'

'Garnet out sick again?' Dominguez asked.

'It's a head thing,' William said, giving me a disapproving purse of his lips. 'I think it's serious.'

'Are you ready?' To distract Dominguez, I tucked my arm into his elbow. My fingers curled around the solid form of his forearm and something passed between us. Our eyes met. His were wide, searching. He'd felt it too.

'Uh, yeah.' He blinked. Dominguez looked down at me like he wanted to say more, his lips parted as if he might kiss me.

I leaned closer, inviting him to do just that.

William cleared his throat.

Dominguez broke eye contact, and suddenly the heat between us vanished, only to be replaced by a warm flush at my cheeks.

Whoa. This spell was a little strong. It was affecting me too.

I needed to keep a clear head if I was going to convince Dominguez to go easy on me. I smiled at that thought. He was already easy on my eyes, and it didn't take much to imagine how easy it would be to run my fingers through those thick, dark curls.

Suddenly, my fingers were there, feeling the curl of short hairs at the back of his neck and the corded muscles of his shoulders.

'Jesus, Garnet. What would Sebastian say?' William said with a shake of his head.

Dominguez's gaze, which had been focused on my lower lip, narrowed suddenly and sharpened. 'Garnet?' He broke from our embrace to flick his eyes over me, and then he added in a tone full of self-congratulation, 'I knew it.'

5

Leo

Key Words:
Theatrical and Romantic

The look I shot William should have killed him, but instead he stared back at me with eyes wide and full of regret.

'I mean . . .' William's gaze darted around as though frantically looking for a way to take it back. Finally, he stared hard at Dominguez, puffed out his narrow chest, and said, 'I swear to God I didn't say that.'

Meanwhile, my hand strayed to the amulet hidden under my sweater. Pulling it out into the open air, I pinched the fabric between my fingers. The barbs of the burrs poked my fingers sharply through the silk. The smell of jasmine and roses filled my nose.

Dominguez's eyes followed my movements intently, like a predator tracking prey.

William came out from behind the register. A customer with a handful of incense sticks watched with a mixture of annoyance and rapt attention. 'Don't arrest her,' William said. 'You can't. She didn't do it.'

I shot William the for-Goddess's-sake-stop-talking look.

'Sounds like you know a lot of details,' Dominguez said to William, even though he continued to face me. 'I'll be talking to you later.'

William turned white as a sheet. The customer leaned on the counter to listen more closely.

'It's okay,' I told William. Then, when that didn't shake him out of his stupor, I jerked my chin in the direction of the eavesdropper. 'Customer.'

William hesitated. I could tell he didn't want to leave me undefended.

'No, really,' I insisted. 'It's okay. I'll be back after lunch.'

'You're awfully confident,' Dominguez said.

Remembering Parrish's advice from last night, I used my most innocent voice to say, 'I've got nothing to hide.'

Even if I didn't convince Dominguez or myself, William slowly moved back behind the counter.

Releasing the spell bag, I reached for Dominguez's hand. I felt a rush as our skin connected. His palms were warm and smooth. 'Do you still want to go out? We could talk.'

He stared at our intertwined hands like they were writhing aliens. Then he looked into my eyes. 'Uh.'

Pausing from counting the packages of incense, William's eyes darted between Dominguez and the charm around my neck. 'Magic?' he mouthed.

I gave William a curt nod in response. To Dominguez, I said, 'How about pizza? You said you knew a good place?' I gave his hand a gentle squeeze.

'Uh.'

'Come on, Dominguez.' I pulled him gently in the direction of the door.

'Yeah. Uh, sure. Yeah,' he muttered as he got his bearings. With his free hand, he fished car keys from his pocket.

I grabbed my umbrella from where it was propped near the door, tucking it and my coat under my arm. Opening the door spattered my face with cold wind and rain. I desperately wanted to put my coat on, but I was afraid to break skin-to-skin contact with Dominguez. Instead I struggled awkwardly one-handed with the umbrella as we stepped out into the downpour.

We paused under the store's awning. Dominguez seemed to be trying to remember where he parked, so I gave him a moment to think it through, though I never let go of his hand. The storm was still so intense that even though it was noon, the sky was dark as night. The neon sign cast flickering sickly green shadows on the wet stained concrete at our feet.

'This way,' he finally declared, though he sounded less than convinced. I made a mental note to tone down the effect of this spell. I wanted Dominguez smitten, not addled.

The rain muffled the sounds of our footsteps. State Street was eerily empty of its usual traffic. The only person we passed was a middle-aged homeless man huddled in a doorway with newspaper over his head who watched our progress with tired eyes. I ducked my head to avoid a gust of wind. Raindrops battered the umbrella, sounding like a drum.

Before I knew it, we were standing in front of Dominguez's car. Practical, black, boring, and just a little too tidy, I could have marked it as a government-issue vehicle a mile away. The new-car smell clung tenaciously to the interior, despite the fact

97

that it had clearly seen a few occupants and more than its share of miles. I had to move aside a thick file folder before I could sit. Dominguez took it from me and held it close to his chest possessively. When he slammed the door and glared at me, I remembered I'd had to let go of his hand.

'Lying to a federal investigator is a crime, Ms Lacey.'

How about lying underneath one? I almost said, but luckily I stopped myself in time. I tucked the spell charm back into my shirt; it was clearly interfering with my ability to concentrate.

'It wasn't really my intention to lie to you,' I said. 'At first, I thought you knew who I was, and then when I discovered you didn't, I kind of took advantage of it. Cops make me nervous.' My sheepish smile died when I saw Dominguez's expression.

'Why lie at all? Are you trying to protect yourself or someone else?'

Oh, he was good. I felt completely cornered. So, instead of answering, I asked: 'Is it my fault you're a blocked psychic?'

Dominguez started to say something, then did a kind of double take. 'What?'

'You knew who I was when you first asked,' I said, crossing my arms in front of my chest. 'Deny it.'

'I had my suspicions,' Dominguez offered tentatively.

Before he could go on, I cut him off. 'You knew. You've been psychic your whole life.'

He studied the steering wheel, resting his thumbs on the leather grip. 'Not my whole life. Only since I turned twenty-eight.'

His surprise confession killed the hot retort I had ready. 'Twenty-eight?' I repeated. Though he didn't look up at me to confirm it, I took his silence as consent. 'Saturn Return,' I said as though that explained everything. To me, it did.

A Saturn Return is when that planet moves into the same position in the sky as it was on the day you were born. Because Saturn is associated with maturity, fate, and discipline, a lot of people's lives go to hell in a handbasket. It's a time of high stress. People tend to make major life-defining choices during their Saturn Return: buying a house, getting married, having kids, getting a divorce, moving across country, taking a new job, joining the French foreign legion . . .

And some of them, apparently, become psychic.

When I put it that way, it sounded a bit ridiculous, but I could see it. Saturn's role in astrology was as a kind of a personality crucible. Saturn was the voice of the parent who says shit like, 'If it doesn't kill you, it'll make you stronger.' You know, that dreaded 'character building'.

Whatever Saturn Return pressures hit Dominguez must have broken down some defenses. The walls came down, and out poured his psychic abilities.

Turning thirty sucks on general principles. But, man, finding out you're also a psychic must have really blew. 'Saturn Returns are life changers, all right,' I muttered sympathetically. 'I guess you really got hit, eh?'

'That's what Madame Zostro told me.' I had no idea who this madame was, but I could guess she was one of those store-front fortunetellers who always advertised that walk-ins were welcome. I was beginning to understand why Dominguez was willing to let me do his astrological chart. He was looking for some answers.

He nodded as though to himself. 'While all that might be true, you still lied to me about who you were, even after I identified myself as an FBI agent.' He glanced up at me mischievously. 'Even after *you* thought I was psychic.'

I was getting pretty tired of being accused of being a liar, even if, in this case, it was true. 'If you know all that, you understand my motivations.'

'I don't, really.' Dominguez put his hands on the steering wheel in the two-and-ten position, but didn't move to start the car. 'Now that he broke up with you, why are you still protecting him?'

'Who? Sebastian?'

'Parrish,' Dominguez said. 'Daniel Parrish?'

'Parrish isn't my boyfriend. Not anymore.'

He squinted at me and scratched behind his ear. 'Isn't that what I just said?'

'Parrish and I broke up a long time ago. Way before last night.'

Dominguez nodded, but his eyes looked at me as if he didn't believe a word I said. I felt like I was having this argument with Sebastian all over again too.

'Seriously,' I insisted.

Lightning flashed, lighting the street for a split second. Lilith tightened the muscles of my stomach. It bothered me deeply that Dominguez had connected Parrish and me.

Dominguez continued, 'Maybe it's just a coincidence that Parrish happened to move to the very town you relocated to.

Maybe your defensive behavior has nothing to do with him. All I know is you seem guilty of something.' His tone was cold and his eyes colder. I had to figure out a way to initiate a little physical contact, which clearly intensified the power of the spell. 'Do you want to tell me of what?'

The wind tossed a wave of rain across the hood. Our breath had begun to fog the windows. I twirled the umbrella between my knees. 'No?'

'What happened last Halloween, Garnet? What made you leave town?'

The concern in his eyes made me turn away. I watched rivulets of water make their crooked way down the windowpane, like tears.

The desire to confess overwhelmed me. All the death, all the secrets pressed like a stone on my chest, constricting it. I swallowed hard.

'You can tell me,' Dominguez said, putting a hand lightly on my thigh. 'I'll understand.'

'My coven . . .' Images from that night came back to me.

Naked bodies lying on the floor, dead, inside what was meant to be a protective circle. Nightingale's glassy gaze capturing mine, and that horrible, creeping realization of the meaning of the dark stain of a bullet hole marring her beautiful pale face. The smell of freshly baked chocolate chip cookies mingling with the coppery scent of blood. Then the click of guns, the sense of being caught in the crosshairs with nowhere to run. Blackness. Waking up to even more death, alone.

I didn't realize I'd started crying until Dominguez handed me a tissue. 'Do you know who killed them? Are you still in danger?'

101

I almost laughed. Where was the FBI six months ago, when the Vatican came here looking for Sebastian? I was alone then too.

A tremor rippled across my stomach.

No, not alone, Lilith was there. She was still here.

I dabbed my nose and tried to pull my thoughts together. I decided to stick to as much of the truth as I could. 'There's a group – a religious order – that take the whole "thou shalt not suffer a Witch to live" thing seriously. The Order of Eustace they called themselves, but really they're a modern Inquisition. Their members all have a tattoo of that chapter and verse – Exodus 22:18 – somewhere on their bodies.

'My coven always lived in fear of discovery,' I said. 'We were strict about using craft names. Even so, I guess the order found them.'

Dominguez had nodded encouragingly all the while I'd been talking. He didn't seem all that shocked to hear about a secret order of assassins running around. I got the impression that maybe the FBI knew something about the Witch hunters, but he'd wanted to hear my take on them. Before I could ask him about that, he said, 'And now those priests are dead.'

'Well, good riddance,' I spat before I could stop myself. 'I didn't know those guys, okay? My friends are dead too.'

Dominguez pulled a file folder from somewhere behind his seat. And tossed a pile of papers in my lap. 'You want to know them? Here they are.'

I looked down at the faces I hadn't seen since that night. They all looked so young . . . so grumpy. To be fair, the images had clearly been blown up from passport mug shots, so most of them had that vaguely disgruntled look of someone required to jump through a bureaucratic hoop.

On their own volition my fingers moved through the papers. There was just enough of the passport that I could read their country of origin. One had been a scruffy-looking Brazilian who gave the camera a slightly cocky, self-satisfied smile more suited to a soccer player than a priest. There was a black South African; a gruff, beefy Italian American; an Armenian from Jerusalem; a Texan with a goofy, frat-boy grin; and a solemn Irishman with lanky blond hair and anxious eyes.

And I'd killed them.

In fact, it had been this one, the one with those haunting, hunted eyes that my hands had been on when the presence of Lilith slithered from my mind and my muscles. I didn't instantly loosen my grip. I crushed his throat until I was certain he was dead. Then I banged his head against the floor, despite arms trembling from overexertion.

I remember feeling the cool whisper of Lilith's pleasure, and the sense of Her coiling deep inside my abdomen, settling in for contented sleep. I also remember how, with cold detachment, I surveyed the carnage. I'm certain that is why Lilith chose to stay with me – part of Her recognized me as kin.

But I wasn't a killer by choice. I'd done what I'd had to, hadn't I? 'Too bad the order was in the business of killing innocent people.'

Dominguez gave a little chuckle. 'You're sounding like a suspect now.'

I was taken aback by his comment. Now? Wasn't I one before? Could he read my guilt in my face? Could he see the dark

Goddess in my eyes? Maybe everyone could. My violet eyes were a kind of mark of Cain, after all. 'Do I really look like a killer to you?'

Dominguez shifted in his seat, as though to get a better look at me. The muscle in his jaw twitched. 'People don't look like killers, Ms Lacey. They just are.'

There was a sadness in his voice, and I found myself reaching out to pat his hand in sympathy. How much would it suck to be a psychic cop? 'You've seen a lot, haven't you?'

His eyes dropped to where I touched him. I could see his mouth working like he knew that the proper thing would be to ask me not to touch him, but he wasn't quite ready to do that. 'This isn't about me,' he said quietly.

No, it was about *me*. It was about what Lilith and I had done. The rain tapped insistently at the roof, and I could feel our breath mingling in the nearness of the car. We were close enough that I could catch the scent of rich, dark coffee that clung to him, and that dangerous otherness that was likely gun oil. 'Do you believe in magic, Dominguez?'

Dominguez smiled darkly. He moved to brush my hand away, and his fingers touched the back of my hand. My breath caught.

Our gazes locked instantly, intensely. I felt drawn to move closer to him, almost like there was a physical hand on my back pushing. I needed to stay focused on the task at hand. Speak, Garnet. Tell him that you need help, and only his big, strong, capable self will do. My mouth opened.

And he kissed me.

His lips were surprisingly soft and sensual. I don't know why, maybe it was the whole cop demeanor, but I expected coarse and pushy. Not that there wasn't heat, but it was a fire under control. Sexy in its potential.

I wondered what it would take for him to loosen up, to let the passion out. I ran my fingers through his hair and wrapped them around the muscles of his shoulders, pulling him into a more demanding kiss.

Dominguez broke our kiss, but his face stayed within the intimate zone. Fingers stroked softly at the hair that covered my ear. His eyes watched mine with a tantalizing openness, vulnerability. He kissed the tip of my nose gently, making me laugh at the sheer sweetness of the gesture. Then his lips brushed my cheeks, sending a corresponding flutter down my spine.

My hands caressed coat mostly, though what I wanted was a better feel of the slope of muscular shoulders and arms. Perhaps psychically sensing my desire, Dominguez shrugged enough out of his coat that I could slip it over his arms. Hooking my fingers around the knot of his tie, I began working it loose.

Dominguez's breath tickled my ear as he made an appreciative noise. He nibbled at my earlobe; his tongue darting out just enough to allow my imagination to screen a preview of other places he might lick with such skill. 'Oh, very nice,' I said encouragingly.

His tie slid off into my hand, and I tossed it blindly into the backseat.

Apparently, my Chippendales-like move inspired him, because he leaned back enough for me to get a good view, and started slowly, seductively unbuttoning his shirt. Each button undone revealed more chestnut-brown skin. I could see touches of dark, wiry hair scattered across the hint of well-defined pectorals. I must have looked appreciative because he smiled that secret you-think-I'm-sexy smile.

When he got to the last button and I could see shadows that implied a taut, washboard stomach, he stopped and gave me an expectant look.

I slid my hands under his shirt and felt the hard, smooth heat of his shoulders, even as I had a 'yummy' thought juxtaposed with a this-man-is-getting-naked-in-the-car,-in-the-middle-of-the-afternoon panic. Though the windows were fogged, anyone could walk by and see us like this. I imagined a policeman knocking on our window, and Dominguez calmly explaining he was an FBI agent interrogating a suspect, except, of course, he was the naked one. A laugh escaped at the thought.

Dominguez eyebrows shot up like he wasn't sure he liked the sound of that, although when my hands got to his chest his nipples told a different story. I suspected other things had also hardened, and I couldn't keep another laugh down.

His cheeks flushed crimson, and, perhaps to hide his growing embarrassment/arousal, he pulled me into a searing kiss. I yanked his shirt down, and he let himself be taken out of it.

Dominguez surprised me by sliding his hands up my waist to rest just shy of my breasts. It felt like kind of a dare, an I'll-go-further,-if-you-go-further sort of thing.

Oooh, this was getting fun.

Before I could make my next move, Dominguez worked a hand under my sweater. Even through the bra, Dominguez's fingers found my nipples. Spikes of pleasure shot directly to my groin. All conscious thought vanished, and I started to sweat. The bulky wool sweater had to go. In my frantic attempt to disrobe, my elbow got caught in the neck hole and tangled around a bra strap, and for a moment all I saw was warm, black weave and the silk pouch of the love spell. That was all I needed. The second I stopped to consider what we were doing – and why we were doing it – the passion, which had so quickly ramped up, died.

I awkwardly backed into my clothes, using my elbows to push away Dominguez's hands. 'Um,' I said, once my head popped back through the collar. 'We can't.'

I expected some kind of argument, a lot of heartfelt cajoling, or at the very least a look of intense disappointment. Instead, he smiled. 'I understand,' he said, despite the obvious straining against his jeans, which was probably extremely painful right about now. 'I love you,' Dominguez said. 'Will you marry me?'

And then he hugged me. His nose nuzzled my hair and neck, and his arms crushed my waist with passion.

I suppose, given that I'd just been the one to slam on the brakes, I should have ignored the broad naked body pressed against me. But my hands roamed along the contours of his back. My fingers massaged strong shoulder blades and torso. Fingernails raked across skin, causing his back to arch so deliciously.

And somewhere through the pheromone fog his words finally hit. 'Marry you?'

'I doubt Mama will approve of you,' he said, lifting his head from where it rested against my shoulder to look me in the eye. 'But we'll have to convince them our love is true.'

Except it's not, I thought. It's all a product of my overactive spell. 'I'm sure what you're feeling is intense, because Goddess knows I'm having the same problem, but it's not really love. Or even really lust. Not true, anyway.'

'It's true. I know it's kind of sudden, but I'm serious. I love you. I intend to marry you, Ms Garnet Lacey.'

What the hell did I say to that? I mean, okay, I was used to the occasional lover in the past who declared his undying affection for me particularly after great sex, but Dominguez and I hadn't even really got to the good bits, and, well, marriage? Seriously? When I broke away from his earnest, desperate gaze, my eyes strayed to the charm between my breasts.

'You don't mean that,' I said, untangling myself from him. I regretted leaving the warmth of his embrace not only because I suddenly felt cruel but also because he had no shirt and it was cold. Goose pimples rose on his skin. Everywhere.

'No, I do,' Dominguez insisted. 'I want you to be my wife, properly. A big church wedding.'

'I'm a Witch.'

'Oh, okay, well, we can work something out. Maybe we can compromise and get a Unitarian minister to perform the ceremony. They're nearly pagan.'

The Unitarians actually had a pagan organization called CUUPS, Covenant of Unitarian Universalist Pagans, but this really wasn't the time to discuss all that. 'I don't want to marry you, Dominguez. I don't even know you.'

'I need you. I can't live without you.' He put his hands gently on my shoulders, and nudged me into a soft, loving kiss.

The kiss was very nice, especially the way his fingers stroked the back of my neck, and it threatened to stir things up for me again. This was getting ridiculous. I grabbed the charm back in both hands and pulled at the seal until it broke. A short burst of gale-force wind whistled around the car, making the shocks creak and the car bounce.

Dominguez's hands shot from my body as if he'd been burned. 'Santa Maria,' I heard him say under his breath. He stared in horror at his hands, which he held out in front of himself like a doctor awaiting gloves. Then he crossed himself, noticed he had almost no clothes on, and folded his arms in front of his chest. Now, his eyes searched mine.

'What the hell happened?' He glanced around his car seat with a frown until he located his shirt. The sleeve had gotten draped into a coffee cup full of stale coffee. He looked at me accusingly as he wrung it out.

'Love spell. A little too potent.'

'A spell? You expect me to believe that?' he asked.

I showed him the broken charm. 'How else do you explain what just happened?'

We both glanced at his naked torso. I blushed. He jerked on his shirt. 'Hormones?' He growled. 'Being on the rebound?'

I quirked a single eyebrow at him; I'd love to know more about *that* story, but I decided to stay on target. 'Do you usually show so little self-restraint, special agent? Or do you ask all the girls to marry you?'

A frown creased his forehead as he buttoned his shirt. 'No.'

Lightning struck somewhere nearby, rattling the windows with the simultaneous thunder. We both jumped a little. After we'd recovered, I showed him the spell bag again. 'Magic.'

'You put the hex on me?' He had to reach past me to grab his tie off the rear dash. I came face-to-face with his rumpled shirt and, for the briefest second, smelled his skin. The scent brought to mind a naked image I had to jerk back from. In my haste to put space between us, I nearly whacked my head on the window. Noticing my reaction, his face crumpled in an angry-at-the-awkwardness-of-this frown.

'Uh, well. It's not a hex. It was just supposed to be a little nudge, you know? Okay. I need to work on the formula, clearly.'

He shook his head in disbelief. 'Okay. That's obstructing justice. You're under arrest.'

'I'm what?'

'Under arrest.' He produced handcuffs from somewhere. One snapped on my wrist expertly.

I stared at the cuff. After what we'd just nearly done, I gave him the I-hope-this-is-some-kind-of-fetish-and-not-the-real-deal look.

Dominguez stared back quite seriously, like he meant I was under arrest, for real.

He had to be insane. 'You're going to arrest me for casting a spell?'

His face flushed again. 'Uh.'

'I know I just spent minutes convincing you magic is real, but do you really think that's going to fly at the home office? Booga-booga,' I said, waving my hands at him like an old-fashioned sorcerer. 'I had to arrest her, boys, she cast a spell on me.'

I'd kind of hoped he'd realize how foolish that sounded, but the way his expression hardened told me my plan had back-fired. His eyes narrowed angrily. 'You also lied to me about who you were.' The second ring latched with a cold, metallic snap. 'That's also obstruction.'

My hands were locked together in front of me. I held them up, still stunned, still expecting Dominguez to produce the key and smile and say, 'Ha, ha, got you there. I'm such a funny guy, messing with your head like that.'

But he didn't.

Instead, Dominguez started the engine. The wipers must have been left on because they slashed across the windshield. Even on high, all they did was move the water around.

I looked down at the chain holding my wrists together. I'd never been arrested before in my life. I tugged and felt the cuffs cut into my wrist. I tugged harder. I couldn't break free. I was really bound. A wave of claustrophobia washed over me. I bit my lip. 'This is serious.' When he didn't reply, I asked, 'What's going to happen?'

'We'll go to headquarters. I'll charge you with obstruction of justice. Unless you decide you want to confess to something else in the meantime.' He gave me a quick glance, and I shook my head. 'We'll book you – take the mug shot, fingerprints . . . all the usual stuff. At some point a judge will decide bail.'

'At some point? I have work tomorrow. Who's going to cover for me at the store? What about Barney? Who'll feed her? I can't go to jail. I have stuff to do, responsibilities. I need to call Sebastian, let someone know where I am.'

'If you can't do the time . . .' Dominguez turned on the defrost to try to clear up the steam we'd created. He reached for his seat belt, but stopped. He leaned over to buckle me in, and it was all suddenly too restrictive, too close.

I felt Lilith rumble across my abdomen. Her fire spread outward from my still dully throbbing loins. Lilith's heat warmed

111

me, steadied me. Dominguez eyes caught mine. I don't know what he saw there, but he looked for a long moment.

'Are you all right?' he asked.

I couldn't suppress a chuckle. All right? How could he even ask that? I was going to jail. I was going to lose my job. Barney was going to starve to death. The click of the buckle echoed in my ear, like a clang of a cell door.

Almost as an afterthought, he said, 'I should read you your rights.'

Lilith laughed. I let Her.

I saw Dominguez's eyes widen. Then the last thing I felt was Her rending the chain of the handcuffs asunder, with a crack like the sound of all Hell breaking loose.

6

Virgo

Key Words:
Practical and Exacting

Rain pounded down around me. Its thundering beat melded with the rumbling of the freight train that shook the bridge over my head. The air smelled of rotting leaves and steel. Curled into a fetal position, my body was wedged into a thin, flat space at the top of a sharply angled concrete slope. Below, beyond a chain-link fence, I could see the lights of passing cars and hear the hiss of the tires as they passed into the relatively dry space under the bridge.

My wrists ached. Something smelled awful, like scorched skin. I suspected Lilith melted the rings of the cuffs, because I was no longer wearing them.

Unfolding myself, I continued to take a physical inventory. Broken fingernails. I was laying in something slimy. Mud?

Oh, right: blood.

Gobs of it congealed all over the shoulder of my sweater, spattered on my pants, clung to creases inside my palms.

This time I had no one to blame but myself. I'd *let* Her come.

Dominguez was dead because *I* killed him.

The coppery smell suddenly overwhelmed me. I turned my head to the side and threw up into a hollow made by one of the support beams.

My world spun out of control. A dark curtain dropped, and I saw concrete. Then nothing, not even pain.

I woke again to darkness. This time it was accompanied by the pleasant smell of damp hay. The storm rumbled in the distance and rain softly clinked against a metal gutter just outside the window, but I was tucked under a thick feather comforter.

'Mom?' I knew the moment after I spoke that I wasn't in Finlayson, but the scent of farm was so strong there was only one other place I could be. 'Sebastian?'

'You're safe here, Garnet.' The nearness of his voice startled me. In the darkness, it took me a moment to register the quilt-covered shape on the overstuffed chair as Sebastian. 'You've lost a lot of blood. You were shot.'

Shot? The instant I shifted in bed, I felt the tight bandage immobilizing my shoulder. The pain I knew should accompany a gunshot wound, however, felt fuzzy and distant. In fact, the pain I *didn't* feel had a pleasant edge to it, like maybe, even though I'd just killed someone, it wasn't such a big deal after all.

'You dosed me with one of your crazy home-grown narcotics, didn't you?'

'There are advantages to being an herbalist.' The smile was obvious in his voice.

'Heh,' I said, sounding, even to my own ears, like a total

114

druggie. I let myself revel in my altered state of well-being and listened to the after-rain sounds outside the window. Crickets creaked. Wind rustled.

I could sleep.

Except.

Part of my addled brain struggled with something I sensed was important for me to understand. How did I end up shot? Of course, Dominguez must have done it, silly. He's a cop. He carries a gun.

Yeah, except . . .

Shhh. Go to sleep, Garnet.

I yawned. That seemed like a sensible plan. I reached up to rub my eyes, only to feel a tight pull across my chest and a sharp stab of pain. Pain in my shoulder, where I was shot.

After Lilith rose. Yeah, that was the important part. If Dominguez wounded me after Lilith took over, he was at least alive long enough to pull the trigger. That might not mean anything, except that usually I woke up and had a body to deal with. I'd woken up alone. No body. Dominguez could be alive.

Hope fluttered in my stomach. Maybe the majority of the blood I'd been lying in had been my own. Dominguez might not be dead, after all. Maybe, just maybe, he'd been able to deflect Lilith's wrath. Perhaps when he shot me Lilith's power had ebbed enough for him to make some kind of escape.

If – and I prayed for that if with my whole heart – if Dominguez was still alive, he'd seen Lilith now. It might be possible to convince him of the truth. Even if my eyes didn't glow lava red when She possessed me, which they did, and which ought to be pretty convincing evidence that something magical was afoot, Dominguez wasn't just your average mundane. The guy *was* psychic. He would have felt the difference. Some part of him would have been aware of Lilith's presence. Something might just have registered in the back of his brain that said, 'This is not Garnet.' Maybe despite everything that happened, he'd still be open to hearing my side of the story.

It was probably too much to hope for, but with the love spell gone, it was all I had.

Okay.

I could sleep now.

Hmmm, warm and fuzzy.

I tried to roll over, only to be quite painfully reminded that was impossible. I let out my breath with a sigh, wishing I could hear the sound of Sebastian's even breathing beside me, but, of course, I couldn't. He made no sound at all. Not even shifting in his seat.

'I thought we were on a break,' I said into the darkness.

'Tell Lilith that.'

Right. Sebastian would have felt Her rising. That was probably how he'd known where to find me.

'Besides,' he said with a dark chuckle. 'I'm mad at you because I love you, not because I want you dead.'

I struggled to sit up a little straighter. A sharp pain stabbed deep, but I ignored it. The wind shook the window. 'You love me?'

'Uh . . .' Now I heard the creak of the leather seat. 'Hadn't I said that before?'

'No.'

116

'Oh.' Sebastian clicked on the lamp beside the bed.

I squinted painfully, waiting for my eyes to adjust, which they never quite did. Great. The drugs Sebastian had fed me must keep my eyes dilated. I could see well enough to take in the sorry sight that was Sebastian. He looked rough. Sebastian wasn't some kind of neat freak, but he always managed to look composed, even when grubbing around the undercarriage of a '58 Mustang. Now, he looked disheveled. He needed a shave, and his shoulder-length hair hung like a limp curtain in front of his eyes. Okay, actually, it was kind of a sexy look. Very rock-star-the-morning-after. Still, it wasn't his usual style.

Then, I noticed all the stuff. He'd totally been camping out by my bedside. There was an open bag of potato chips at his stocking feet along with an empty twenty-ounce plastic bottle of soda. An afghan was wrapped around his legs and torso. One of those dusty tomes Sebastian favored sat open on the end table at his elbow, an origami crane marking his place in the text. I started to wonder how long I'd been out and who, if anyone, had been feeding Barney.

'Well, I'd meant to,' he said, peering at me intently. 'Certainly before now. You're absolutely positive I never?'

'Never. Hey, did you feed my cat? Has anyone?'

'Your cat nearly goes into apoplectic shock when she sees me.' He chewed on his lip, exposing the sharp tip of a canine, and made thoughtful noises. 'Perhaps I planned to say "I love you" on your birthday?'

'That's months from now. Do you think Barney's okay?'

'She's a cat. She'll find a mouse or some bugs or something. Besides, she's not exactly rail thin,' Sebastian said dismissively.

Barney was a big gal – fourteen pounds of fur and jungle pouch.

'Anyway,' Sebastian continued. 'Is it really such a surprise? I do, you know. Love you, that is.'

I can't explain it, but there's something inherently charming about a flustered guy with a British accent. I tried to act immune. 'Sure,' I said mockingly. 'Now that I'm on my death bed.'

'Garnet,' he said, pulling his hair back from his face. His tone had turned serious. 'I've been in love with you for some time now. I may not have said so precisely, but you must have known it. Why do you think all this unfinished business you have with what's-his-name bothers me so much?'

I don't know why, but Sebastian's flip dismissal of Parrish bothered me. Even though it tugged at the bandages, I crossed my arms in front of my chest. 'You can't even say Parrish's name?'

'I don't like him much.'

'I figured that out.'

'Did you? Because I don't see you staying away from him. I wonder what happened that you ended up under some bridge like a vagabond, half dead. And with handcuff marks.'

I looked at my wrists, noticing the tightly wrapped gauze bandages around each. I looked like some kind of bad suicide attempt.

Okay, so the handcuff welts did seem a little like Parrish. Did I mention he was a bad, bad boy? Anyway, to be fair, I could kind of see how Sebastian made that assumption given that the first time they met Parrish was doing the whole S & M vampire master thing with a mostly naked babe in chains in front of an audience. And, let's just say, that wasn't much of a stretch for Parrish. The whole whips and chains thing came very naturally to him.

I suddenly realized I'd been smiling to myself, and Sebastian was waiting for my answer. Damn drugs. 'It wasn't Parrish.'

Sebastian shot me a look of pure skepticism.

'Seriously! Parrish sleeps all day, remember?'

Sebastian's expression didn't change.

'I was shot, Sebastian. Parrish didn't do that. He doesn't even own a gun. At least, I don't think he does. Well, actually, he probably has one being a bank robber occasionally, only you know he'd never use it on me.'

Sebastian continued to glare at me for a long moment. Had I said all of that out loud? The drugs were making me even more chatty than normal, if that was even humanly possible.

'It wasn't Parrish,' I said again, just in case I hadn't said so before.

Sebastian's frown deepened, and he turned to scowl at the wallpaper.

'It was Dominguez,' I said.

A twitch of an eyebrow broke Sebastian's scowl. 'Who?'

'The FBI agent.'

With a series of tics, Sebastian's frown morphed into confusion. 'I'm sorry? You're in love with who?'

I shook my head a little spastically thanks to the drugs. 'No, no, not in love. Lust. It was a spell.' I reached for the amulet to show him, only I couldn't find it. Or my sweater either. 'Hey, you took my clothes.'

'I had to clean and dress your wound; besides, that sweater

119

is ruined,' he explained hastily. 'Why on earth did you cast a spell of lusting on the FBI agent?'

I pulled the comforter more snugly under my arms. 'So he'd listen to me.'

'Listen to you . . . ?' He repeated, obviously trying to work through the crazy logic that got me there. He must have twigged my plan, because Sebastian's gaze flicked to the bandage covering my shoulder. 'I take it things didn't work out the way you'd hoped.'

'No,' I admitted grumpily.

He gave me the that's-a-shame pat on the knee.

When he didn't immediately remove his hand, I let out a breath I'd been holding. I put my hand over his and squeezed it tightly. I missed him so much. I didn't like when we fought, and this had really been our first nasty one. I hoped this was a sign that the fight was over.

'Dominguez accused me of being a liar too,' I added without meaning to, though it had been on my mind. Sheesh, what was in this stuff Sebastian slipped me – truth serum?

'Oh?'

There was a bit of ice in his tone, so I knew I needed to tread carefully. 'He seemed to think Parrish and I were an item also.' Okay, that wasn't terribly helpful.

Sebastian took his hand away. 'Can you blame him?'

'Yes! Why does everyone keep thinking Parrish and I are some kind of couple still? I broke up with him a year ago.'

'I can tell you why.'

'Go on then,' I said. 'Enlighten me.'

Sebastian sat back in his chair. His eyes drifted over to the rain-streaked window. He took in a slow, steady breath I knew he didn't need. He spoke in a flat voice, without looking at me. 'I feel it, Garnet. When you look at him . . . at Parrish. I feel all of it. I'm talking about . . . the emotion. Do you know how creepy and painful it is to look at that man the way *you* do?' A sad little smile played at the corner of his mouth. 'He's my strong protector, isn't he? The one I run to when there's trouble. My goddamned knight in shining armor. Fuck me, I feel really insane when the three of us are in the same room together. I alternately want to slug him and kiss him. How fucked up is that?'

It *was* weird. I'd feel more sorry for him if I didn't have a similar problem when I saw a woman on the street who looked . . . tasty – to Sebastian, to me; it got all very confused. 'What do you think it's like for me when you feed on a ghoul?'

His eyes snapped back to mine.

'I'm not going to let you derail this conversation with your petty jealousies.'

'Petty?' I sputtered. 'You're the one obsessed with my ex-boyfriend.'

Sebastian stood up as if to leave. Except he glared down at me, his jaw muscles jittering with what I could only imagine were restrained thoughts. 'You need to decide, Garnet. Are you going to live in the past with him or in the future with me?'

'With you,' I said. 'I've already made that choice. Why can't you accept that?'

'Because you still feel so much for him. You run to him in times of crises.' Then, quietly, almost as if he didn't quite dare say it out loud. 'Instead of to me.'

Sebastian wanted to be my knight in shining armor. I loved that impulse in a man. It was so alpha. 'You already are my hero,' I said, even though I knew it wouldn't help. 'This is an unusual situation – the whole FBI thing. It's not always going to be like this.'

'Yet it's very clear that you've turned to him before, and recently too. You seemed to have some kind of Bat-Signal,' he grumbled, crossing his arms in front of his chest defensively.

'What are you talking about?'

'Meadow Spring. What the hell *is* that, anyway? It sounds like the name of some cheap hotel.'

'That,' I said, through teeth clenched with a combination of irritation and embarrassment, 'was my craft name.'

A craft name is more than just an alternate moniker, it's meant to be a reflection of your true self, a way to consciously step out of the mundane world. Yeah, okay, Meadow Spring isn't nearly as cool as Coyote Moonspirit, but it meant something to me. When I'd chosen it, I'd just started down the environmentally conscious road; in fact, I was super green – fanatic about recycling, hybrid cars, low-impact living, and restoring native prairie. I wanted something that reflected my inner earth mother.

'Oh,' Sebastian said sheepishly. Then, with a hint of his earlier peevishness added, 'Another something I didn't know about you.'

'That's because I'm not Meadow Spring anymore. She died that night along with the rest of my coven.'

'No, you're wrong. She lives in Parrish,' Sebastian quickly corrected. 'That's why you can't let him go.'

My mouth opened, but no clever rejoinder spilled out.

We both waited for me to say something for several minutes. I thought Sebastian might be right, but I didn't know what to do with that information. After all, if letting Parrish go meant releasing the last bit of the surviving part of me that was Meadow Spring, wouldn't that be like losing my coven all over again?

Sebastian walked to the door, but stopped at the threshold. Without turning to face me, Sebastian said, 'I'll just be across the hall. I'll always be close at hand if you need me, Garnet. Always.'

With that, he closed the door behind him and I was alone.

Depressed, I flopped into a more prone position. I instantly regretted the sudden movement as pain lanced through my shoulder and back. Pain obliterated coherent thought for a good fifteen minutes. All I could do was lay still and focus on the cracks in the plaster ceiling until the ache subsided.

Then I wished Sebastian had left whatever herbal cocktail he'd cooked up laying around. I desperately wanted to alter my state of consciousness. There wasn't even an *In Touch* magazine or chocolate ice cream pint for miles. I had no way to distract myself from the mess of my relationship, but I was damned if I was going to cry anymore. Besides, I already had to dab the blanket with tears that had sprung to my eyes from my stupid move.

I decided to attempt to sleep.

Our argument and the pain had taken the fuzz off the drugs and I now felt wide awake.

I shut my eyes and listened to the sounds outside the window.

Crickets chirped. A cow lowed, long and mournfully.

Blinking my eyes open, I glanced at the window. A cow? Sebastian didn't have any animals, only herbs. He did, however, live right next to a cemetery.

After turning off the lamp Sebastian had switched on, I hauled my legs over the edge of the bed. Unsteadily, I pulled myself upright. My shoulder protested severely, but I still didn't hurt as much as I thought I should.

I froze when the moan came again. This time it sounded less like a cow and much more like a zombie to my paranoid ears. I kept telling myself it couldn't be. Sebastian lived miles away from the city. Why would there be a zombie here?

The cemetery across from Sebastian's farm was old. A stark highway lamp illuminated white gravestones speckled by moss and mold. The markers that hadn't fallen over listed crookedly at the head of sunken rectangular patches where simple pine coffins had long ago rotted away beneath them. Though the lawn was neatly trimmed, a number of markers were completely obscured by cedar bushes that had overgrown the simple offering they'd originally been.

There was no fence around the cemetery. It had probably been a family plot at some point in its history and was now a mostly forgotten piece of land wedged between cornfields. I scanned for any movement, but saw nothing.

Then a ghostly face materialized just on the other side of the glass, inches from my face.

I yelped and jumped back. Given my awkward position, being crouched between the bed and the window, it was more like I lurched off to the side, banging my shoulder in the process. In between gasps of pain, recognition dawned. 'Benjamin,' I said. 'You scared the living crap out of me.'

Benjamin let out a dry laugh, like rustling leaves.

Benjamin was Sebastian's house ghost. He haunted the place. Plus, thanks to an obsessive-compulsive disorder he'd probably had while alive, he also cleaned. My understanding was that Benjamin had killed the former lady of the house and then himself at some point before Sebastian bought the place. Benjamin didn't much like me (or women in general), but ever since I cast the spell that made the Witch hunters take me for dead, Benjamin started treating me like kin. Or, at least he no longer tried to kill me whenever I came over, and for my part I pretended to have meaningful conversations with him.

'Were you the one moaning out there?' I asked him.

Maybe if I had one of those ghost recording devices, I would have heard an answer on playback. Instead, I felt cold air brush past my arm. I decided that meant: 'yes.'

I carefully pulled myself back up onto the bed and watched in rapt fascination as things around the room began to tidy themselves. The afghan Sebastian had abandoned arranged itself in a precise fold over the back of the chair. On the end table, the book closed with a snap. The soda bottle made its way to the garbage can. Crumbs disappeared.

That last one kind of bothered me. Where had they gone, exactly? Did he eat them? I decided I didn't want to know.

A disembodied voice said: 'If you hurt him, I'll kill you.'

Benjamin had only ever spoken to me once before, and this experience was just as chilling. His voice was calm and clear, but just low enough to be almost inaudible. Plus, given that the book Sebastian had been reading was worming its way along the floor toward the bookshelf it came from, I'd have thought Benjamin was across the room. The voice sounded like it was just behind me, on the bed. I turned and saw an indentation on the mattress.

I stared at the spot on the bed where I thought Benjamin must be sitting. I wanted to be able to promise this murderous, protective ghost that Sebastian wouldn't be hurt by me, but it seemed equally unwise to lie. 'Right now,' I said in my most cajoling, explanatory voice, 'Sebastian is just a tiny bit obsessed with Parrish . . .'

I heard a hiss, and a picture frame on the end table crashed to the floor.

'Oh, so you don't want me to say his name? What is it with you guys?'

The hollow on the bed had smoothed out. It made me slightly more nervous not knowing where Benjamin was, but I found myself bubbling over with frustration.

'Okay, so Parrish means something to me.' Crash. A porcelain bowl threw itself on the floor and shattered. 'So what? We were friends. What's wrong with that? Yeah, I kept my relationship with Parrish—' Bang. Six books tumbled off the shelf. '—a secret. Look how Sebastian reacted!'

Just as I was about to start shouting, 'Parrish, Parrish, Parrish!' in my best schoolyard tease, the door banged open and Sebastian rushed in.

'Benjamin. Out. Now.'

A pile of magazines slammed to the floor, and then there was silence.

'I have no idea what you were saying to anger Benjamin, but taunting him,' Sebastian said to me, 'will only lead to beds levitating in the middle of the night or, worse, wallets and keys disappearing for good. Trust me, you want to play nice with the poltergeist.'

I pouted. I didn't need the lecture from Sebastian; I knew all that, the hard way. I mean this poltergeist was known to wield a knife on occasion.

Sebastian stood just outside of the door, his chest heaving slightly from the mad dash down the hall. I loved the pajamas he had on; they were my favorites. The cotton pants had brightly colored cartoon images of classic VW bugs all over it. A Limp Bizkit T-shirt clung fetchingly to his broad chest. If only he didn't look so angry, he'd be darn right hot.

'Sebastian,' I said, with what I hoped was a come-hither stare. 'Can't we just forget all of this stuff?' I sat down on the mattress and patted the spot beside me. 'Come to bed?'

I watched him consider it. The way his eyes lingered on me, I knew he wanted to. I thought for a second he was going to capitulate, but then he shook his head. 'No, Garnet. This is what we always do. We just "forget" about things and nothing gets resolved. I need . . . Crap, I need "closure" on this issue, Garnet.'

'Just sleep beside me,' I said. 'Hold me?'

He came to sit beside me. Sebastian encircled my shoulders lightly with his arm, and I winced a little from the pain of my bullet hole despite his gentle touch. His lips brushed my cheek. 'I do love you,' he said. 'But I can't sleep here. Every jostle and bump is going to aggravate that.' He lightly stroked the bandage. 'And you know I'm a restless sleeper.'

Actually, that was a lie. Like all vampires, Sebastian slept like the dead. In Sebastian's case he sleeps in the exact position he died in. Sebastian died violently in some kind of sword fight (he still had nasty scars on his back and on his abdomen), and his arms stretch out in odd, uncomfortable looking angles. And, stranger, his eyes are open.

But, in that position, he was a bit of a bed hog, and impossible to rouse or move. I conceded his point.

'I don't like it, but I understand.'

He kissed me lightly on the cheek, and stood up to go. He seemed to be on the verge of saying something, but apparently coming to some silent conclusion about me or the situation, he turned on his heel and left. I heard his bare feet slapping softly on the uncarpeted hallway, as he made his way to the guest room.

I didn't think I could sleep knowing that he was so close and yet so far away, but I did.

When I next opened my eyes, there was sun. The storm front must have been slow moving because the dark cover of clouds persisted a bit, but shafts of light broke through. They cast broken, spidery patterns on the nubby remains of the harvested cornfield. The air smelled fresh, scrubbed clean. I took in a deep breath and smelled coffee. A large thermos sat at my bedside. I looked around for one of Sebastian's usual notes, but didn't find any. Something about being deprived the exercise of deciphering Sebastian's florid script depressed me.

I found the mug Sebastian had set out for me. It was my usual cup. Of all of the nice pottery he had, I always preferred the cup he had hidden in the back of the cabinet that advertised the Fitzgerald Hotel in Vegas. I smiled as I remembered coaxing the story of how he'd gotten it out of him.

I gasped when I tried to reach with my left hand to twist off the top. The pain was intense. After taking a moment to breathe through it, I tried again. Only this time I kept my left arm as still as possible and using my right hand managed to get the top off.

I was just about to pour when I noticed my mug was already a quarter full of some mysterious amber liquid. I looked around for a place to dump it out. It dawned on me that this gunk was probably my 'medicine'. A sniff told me it was going to taste nasty. I thought about getting rid of the stuff on general principles, but as I was still reeling from the attempt to move my arm, I decided to risk drinking it. I poured the coffee on top of the mystery liquid. I took my first swallow without tasting it.

Hell, my first cup was all about the drugs anyway; I needed the caffeine.

I sipped and stared at all the stuff in Sebastian's bedroom that I'd come to think of as 'ours'. By my second cup, I decided I didn't want to be in this house anymore. The third cup fortified me enough to hunt up some clothes from my stash in his closet. I downed the fourth and fifth while dialing Izzy's cell.

'Where have you been?' she said before I could even say hello. 'William tells me you took off with that sexy FBI guy, and no one hears from you for days. What's been going on?'

'Days?' I was scrounging through Sebastian's kitchen for something to eat. I'd found a rock-hard bagel, some slightly withered grapes, and a jar of kosher pickles. Mmmm, breakfast. I was so hungry that the first crunch of pickle actually tasted good. I fished two more out of the brine. 'What day is it?'

'Sunday.'

Izzy's answer caused a near fatal snort of pickle juice. Sunday? I lost two days somewhere in there.

'Are you okay? What happened? Where are you?' Then, in a whisper, 'Have you been arrested?'

'I'm at Sebastian's,' I said, giving the bagel an experimental gnaw. When I nearly chipped a tooth, I gave up. Tossing it into the microwave, I hit thirty seconds. 'If you think you could come get me, I'll tell you everything. Hey,' I added, suddenly remembering. 'What happened with you and the zombies? I tried to stop by your place to see if you were okay, but I had a very weird run-in with a crow.'

'Really?' Izzy laughed. 'I can't wait to hear about it. Still, sounds like the usual Garnet-Witchy-fare. As for the zombies . . . Well, I'll explain everything that happened when I get there.'

'Sounds great.'

With a heavy clunk, I replaced the red plastic phone in its cradle on the wall, and marveled at the anachronistic cord that hung in tight ringlets between the receiver and the base. Sebastian had one other working rotary telephone in the house, which I swore he kept around just to amaze guests. I smiled, plucking at the wire just to watch it snap back into a coil.

The microwave beeped. The bagel steamed. The edges had turned into inedible rubber, but I could choke down the gummy middle, especially after liberal application of currant jelly. I drank even more coffee, feeling stiff and sore and sad.

Sebastian's kitchen was in full fall-harvest mode. Bundles of culinary herbs, like sage and oregano, hung from hooks over the doorway. Medicinal plants steeped in oils and alcohols housed in colored bottles arrayed haphazardly on the windowsills. A professional-grade dehydrator filled the kitchen with the scent of slow-drying mint and bee balm.

Glancing around at the bright linoleum countertops, I remembered the pleasant time we'd passed bottling, distilling, and canning all Sebastian's annual bounty. I'd learned I was slightly allergic to essential oils of rue that weekend. My hands had turned bright red with raised welts. Of course, Sebastian had some homemade hand lotion that had fixed me right up . . . and then we used the rest of the lotion in much more creative and exotic ways.

I put my dishes in the sink and glanced at the clock, wishing Izzy would break a few speed limits getting here. If I stayed too much longer, I'd cry.

It was still gray enough outside that I had the overhead light on. I jumped when Benjamin made it snap off and then flicker back to life. I guess he felt I was overstaying my welcome, as well.

I filled up my mug one more time and went outside, preferring to wait for Izzy at the end of the muddy drive rather than spend another moment with my memories.

Outside, everything was wet. The wind cut straight across the empty cornfields. A pair of mourning doves cooed to each other on the swaying overhead electrical wire. Sebastian's tidy front lawn was mostly brown, though a few stubborn patches held a trace of green. The flowerbeds were neatly cleared of debris and the perennials covered with a thick mound of straw.

The driveway was a beige sludge of sandstone gravel. As I made my way to the end of the drive where the mailbox stood, the cold wetness made my shoulder ache. I stared down the narrow asphalt stretch of county highway and tried to conjure Izzy's white truck.

I'd drunk the last dregs of my coffee and was starting to consider retreating inside to warm up when Izzy finally arrived with a honk and a wave.

I had a little trouble pulling myself up into the seat with my shoulder bandages, but I managed it. Izzy watched me with a deep frown.

'You're hurt,' she pronounced after I'd grunted and groaned the safety belt into position.

'I miss your little Toyota or Honda or whatever it was,' I said. At least the heat was on full blast. I could feel the moisture wicking away from my face.

'I needed the hauling room,' Izzy said, putting the truck in gear. When she bought it, Izzy's bungalow had been listed as having a lot of 'old-world charm'. She'd told me she quickly discovered that had been some kind of real estate code phrase for 'needs remodeling work.'

I nodded. 'Yeah, so, anyway, I was shot.'

The truck veered suddenly. Izzy jerked it back over to our side of the dotted yellow line. 'Like with a bullet? From a gun?'

Given that the last time anyone was shot in our circle of friends a longbow was involved, I supposed it wasn't an unreasonable question. Still, I laughed a little. 'Yeah. Just like that.'

I watched Izzy's face; she watched the road. She gripped the steering wheel with whitening knuckles. 'Please tell me this story doesn't end with a dead FBI agent.'

'I'm fairly certain it doesn't.'

'Lilith,' she said quietly, almost to herself.

Maybe it was my guilty conscience or perhaps there was something of an accusation in her tone, but I found myself suddenly on the defensive. 'He was going to arrest me for obstruction.'

'So you unleashed the Queen of Evil on his ass?'

Okay, so when she put it like that, it did kind of sound like using a wrecking ball to swat a fly.

'Sometimes,' Izzy said. 'I think you should seriously consider an anger management course.'

I think she meant it as a joke, but there was a serious overtone. I turned to watch the haystacks roll past. Each pothole we bounced over jarred my shoulder, and I tried to decide if she was right.

'This whole thing with the FBI? It scares me,' Izzy admitted, still pretending that the Sunday-morning traffic required her undivided attention. 'Somehow when you tell me vampires are real and there's a secret order of assassins who kill Witches for the pope, I can deal. The FBI. Damn, girl. That's real heavy shit, you know?'

I knew. Not only did the FBI spell trouble for me, but also for all my friends and relations. Pretty soon, if they hadn't already done so, agents would start hauling people in for questioning. The crap I'd brought down on my friends in the past hadn't really touched them in the same way because the Vatican agents were only after people who practiced true magic – in other words, just Sebastian and me. The bureau would be sniffing around everyone even vaguely associated with me to try to build the case. Dominguez had already threatened William.

'I'm sorry,' I said.

'It's okay,' she said, though I knew it wasn't.

We drove in silence for a while. We'd started down Mineral Point Road, which was technically still the highway, but it went near the center of town. A few houses had jack-o'-lanterns out already, even though Halloween wasn't for a few more days. When we passed a grocery store that had painted cartoon images of ghosts and mummies in the large windows, I thought to ask, 'Whatever happened to those zombies that were after you?'

'Salted them. Worked like a charm. They turned and headed back to their graves, I hope.'

When you fed salt to zombies they returned to wherever they'd died. 'You hope?'

Izzy shrugged, changing lanes. 'Most of these dudes looked like frat boys. The paper didn't say anything about a bunch of college-age kids dying, and you know they love to make a big deal about all that. "Frat Party Ends in Tragedy" – it's very front-page news. It made me wonder if they'd been buried at all.'

'For the ritual, do they have to be buried?' I asked. Izzy was much more of an expert on voodoo than I was; she had family in Louisiana.

Izzy tapped her index fingers on the steering wheel. 'I

suppose you can feed someone the zombie poisons at any time. Like slip it into spiked punch.'

'At a party,' I finished the thought for her, and we both nodded, considering it. An image of a bunch of zombies returning to lie dead in the front lawn of some house on frat row flashed through my mind. 'Like some fraternity version of Jonestown.'

Izzy nodded slightly, 'Yeah, like that. Makes sense. Suzette used to hang with those crazy party-boy types.'

I waited for a long moment, wondering if I was supposed to know what Izzy was talking about. 'Um, who?'

'From my work. The little perky blonde with the piercings.'

That must describe half the baristas from here to Poughkeepsie.

'With the Eeyore tat on her bicep.'

I nodded. I had a vague impression now. Not that I had any idea what we were talking about. 'What happened to Suzette exactly?'

'Just showed up one morning dead.' She nodded, turning onto my street. 'Things got rough when I told her I had to fire her.'

'For being dead?'

'Partly. The whole shuffling and moaning thing was getting on my nerves, but it was more that I couldn't stand being part of the scam.'

'What scam?'

Izzy shifted in her seat making the vinyl creak. Her long, gold-polished fingernails tapped on the wheel.

'The scam?' I prompted again.

She watched the road intently. 'Yeah, you know how these people keep going back to their jobs? What do you think is happening to their paychecks?'

'Being direct deposited as usual?'

Izzy shook her head. 'The coffee shop gets too much turn around to be set up for that. We hand out actual checks.'

'So, you think the voodoo sorcerer is ordering his zombies to cash out their checks for money?'

She nodded.

Murdering a bunch of college kids and turning them into zombies just to collect their meager minimum-wage salary seemed like a lot of effort for very little gain. Although, I supposed, if you got enough of them it could become pretty lucrative. Plus, then you'd have all these able bodies around to shovel the walk, do the dishes, take out the trash, and all the other jobs around the house no one wanted to do. Sounded kind of nice to the part of me that loathed housework. Nice, except for the whole killing and soul-slavery thing.

'Do you really suppose it's just for the money?' I asked

'Who knows?'

'But, why go to the trouble? Why make zombies at all? What are they usually used for?'

'Working in fields. Drudge work.'

'Flipping burgers doesn't seem all that different,' I observed.

'Slinging lattes, you mean,' Izzy said with a frown.

'Slinging lattes, selling books, it's all a matter of degree. Lots of people think jobs like ours are soul suckers.'

Izzy snorted a dark chuckle.

'What do you think?' I asked. 'Is this sorcerer doing us wage slaves a favor? Taking away our pain? Stealing our souls before our jobs crush them? Maybe this person is kind of doing the opposite of Marx, you know, instead of liberating the proletariat, he's providing an opiate for the masses.'

Izzy raised one finely sculpted eyebrow at time. 'Where'd you learn that? Did you even take Communism 101?'

'I dated a Marxist once.'

'One of your SNAGs, right?'

Madison was known for its overabundance of SNAGs, Sensitive New-Age Guys. Before Sebastian, I seemed to be some kind of magnet for that intellectually buff, but otherwise deeply beta sort of male. I nodded.

'Figures.' She snorted. 'But you know that's just crazy talk.'

I flashed Izzy a weak smile. 'Sounded better in my head.'

'So many things do.'

I stuck my tongue out at her.

She started to pull up to the curb when I noticed a shiny navy-blue minivan parked at the end of the block. There were a fair number of families down the street, but my neighbors tended to be the sort to buy used when they bought new. Besides, the van was particularly noticeable for its lack of political bumper stickers.

'Go around the block,' I said.

'You think the Feds have your apartment staked out?'

I pointed to the van as we passed it. The tinted windows reflected the white of Izzy's truck.

'I really can't deal with this,' Izzy said with a shake of her head. 'Give me a zombie army any day.'

My sentiments exactly.

Izzy slowed as she turned another corner. 'Are you sure you should risk it? Maybe you should hang at my place.'

I didn't really need anything at the apartment. I wanted to talk to Parrish – especially since Dominguez had confirmed that they were looking for him as well, but he wasn't available until sundown, which was hours from now. I worried about Barney, but she'd be okay for a little while longer. After all, she'd been known to rip into the Ritz crackers if she felt she hadn't been fed often enough.

I couldn't go back to the store. They'd certainly come looking for me there.

'I don't want to involve you in this,' I said to her.

'Honestly, I don't want to *be* involved, but you're my friend. I already am.'

Fifteen minutes later, we parked the truck in Izzy's garage. Sebastian's medicine had begun to wear off and my shoulder throbbed at the slightest movement. Getting out of the seat belt exhausted me. By the time Izzy got me lowered into the easy chair in her living room, I'd broken out in a cold sweat.

'I'm going to heat up some soup or something.'

I started to protest that she didn't need to fuss over me, but my stomach chose that moment to gurgle with anticipation. Plus, when she returned with a big, fleece blanket, I began to appreciate the luxury of having someone else caretake me for a while. 'Thanks,' I said.

She pursed her lips as though to remind me that she really didn't want to be harboring a fugitive from justice. 'Try to get some rest. You look terrible.'

I gave her a smile.

She pressed a remote into my hand and went off to the kitchen. I watched her through the pass-through as she gathered up various ingredients and equipment. I knew from previous experience that I was in for a treat. When Izzy made soup, it wasn't from a can. She had vegetable stock already in her refrigerator. Noodles dried on a rack.

The TV dominated the wall directly opposite my chair. Bookcases overflowing with DVDs and old videotapes surrounded either side. Some of the cases were clearly store-bought, but the majority was identified only by Izzy's precise drafting-style print. She had movies, TV series, and even video games. Several types of game consoles littered the area around the monitor.

Besides the chair I occupied, there was a slightly sagging purple suede couch under the window. Paperbacks covered the bookshelves that filled the available wall space.

Despite the amassed clutter, Izzy's house was clean. Wood floors gleamed. The warmly painted walls reflected morning sun. There was no trace of cobwebs on the chandelier that hung in the center of the living room.

The smell of sautéing onions drifted in from the kitchen. I put the remote down on the glass coffee table beside the chair and picked up the nearest paperback. It was some kind of space adventure – not my usual fare, but it was pleasantly distracting. I found my eyelids drooping after a paragraph or so.

I woke up with a naggingly full bladder and that startling sense of being somewhere unfamiliar. Stiffly, I managed to extricate myself from the chair and make my way to the toilet. Izzy's bathroom was one of those typically cramped spaces you find in older houses, but she'd livened it up by painting the walls a shocking yellow and decorating liberally with cartoon fish.

The whole thing was a little too cheery for my taste, so I didn't linger. I caught sight of a stark, smudged-makeup face in the mirror. Izzy was right. I looked like hell.

I ran some water and leaned over to splash my face. My body protested, but I gritted my teeth. I needed to feel a bit cleaner.

When I looked at my face again, I saw less mess and more fear. I *was* so completely out of my league. I didn't do cops and robbers. In fact, I was kind of surprised I'd evaded arrest this long.

I wandered back to the living room. The house was quiet. 'Izzy?'

After poking my head into the bedroom and a closet, I discovered a note on the whiteboard on the fridge. Apparently, Izzy had an afternoon shift, but I was supposed to help myself to the soup simmering in the crockpot. A sticky note stuck to the pot declared in a very Alice-in-Wonderland way: 'Eat me!'

I rummaged around for a ladle and managed, despite my wounded shoulder, to fill a coffee mug full of vegetable noodle soup. Hobbling back to the living room, I carefully lowered myself back into the easy chair. I flipped through a hundred and sixty-seven channels only to discover that daytime television programming still sucked. At least the soup was good. I slurped down several cupfuls, while skimming through the rest of the space-adventure novel.

I put the book down. I couldn't quite get into the story because I kept thinking the FBI should be kicking in the door at any minute. I mean, really, how hard could I be to find? Surely the guys in the van had recognized me and instantly ran Izzy's plates for her address. What were they waiting for? I really wished Izzy had a police procedural among all these novels. I couldn't remember if the FBI needed a warrant to arrest me or if they could just burst in and take me 'downtown' for questioning. Did Dominguez have enough evidence to make his case after I/Lilith attacked him?

Switching the TV back on, I tried to distract myself with something mindless, except everything that kept catching my interest involved hundred-year-old murder cases that brilliant forensic scientists solved in a half hour using only a microscopic fabric fiber and a single cat hair.

Crap.

I should just turn myself in.

Right now, some lab rat in Minnesota was connecting the dots from some bit of dandruff I'd shed at the crime scene. There was no way on earth I was going to get away with this. Wasn't it smarter to confess? Wouldn't the law go easier on me if I cooperated?

I fished my wallet out of my pocket and unearthed Dominguez's card. I found Izzy's phone and, with shaking fingers, I dialed the number.

'Dominguez.'

I was kind of surprised to hear his voice, especially sounding so healthy. I thought maybe he'd be in the hospital or something. Plus, now that I had him on the phone I wasn't sure what to say. 'Uh, hi.'

'Hi,' he said back. His tone was neutral. I supposed if you hand your business card out to a lot of people who are either involved in crimes or have witnessed them, you don't expect a lot witty repartee.

'It's Garnet,' I said. 'I think we need to talk.'

'Sounds good,' he said. 'Do you want to talk on the phone or should we meet somewhere?'

Meeting somewhere sounded like a profoundly bad idea, given that an entire SWAT team could descend on me. Of course, if he was tracing this call, the same could be true the longer I chatted on the phone. Strike that, he already knew where I was. He had caller ID. He would, he's FBI.

'I don't care,' I said. I started to get up off the chair, but my shoulder twinged. 'Are you okay? I mean, you're alive. Lilith didn't hurt you, did She?'

'She snapped my wrist like a twig. I've got a lovely fuchsia cast.' I noticed the correct use of pronoun. Either he was playing along with the crazy-murderer girl or maybe he did sense another presence. 'How about you?'

'You shot me.'

'Don't you mean I shot "Lilith"?'

Of course that's what I meant, but now anything I said to that effect would sound completely insane. So, instead, I pointed out, 'I always have to deal with the aftermath of Her destruction.'

There was silence on the phone for a minute as Dominguez considered my words. 'You know, I think I'd rather talk in person.' His voice dropped to a conspiratorial tone, 'I can get a better . . . uh, sense of things face-to-face.'

He wanted to be close enough to read me, psychically speaking. I don't know why, but this confession filled me with an unreasonable amount of hope. I figured that if he wanted to use his abilities to see into my mind, then maybe there was still some question in his about my guilt.

'I don't want to get arrested,' I said.

'Clearly,' he said dryly. 'I think I'll leave my cuffs at home this time. Why don't we meet somewhere you feel safe?'

Yeah, but where was that?

'Your place?' he said.

'You mean the one with the big blue van full of FBI agents parked out front?'

'Okay. Somewhere public?'

Where do I feel safe? Where's somewhere public that I feel safe? Where would the FBI be loath to burst in with guns blazing? Where? Where? 'The library!' I blurted out. 'Public library! Children's section.'

'O-kay.' He sounded like he thought I was a total nut job. 'Which one?'

Well, I'd have to be able to walk to it, since I didn't have my bike or access to a car, so I gave him the name of the nearest branch. 'I'll meet you at the Monroe Street library in forty-five minutes.'

I took a sponge bath, careful not to mess up Sebastian's precise bandaging. I struggled a bit with one-armed hair washing. Then I raided Izzy's medicine cabinet for makeup, only to find the foundation and powder several shades darker than my usual. I settled for a little eyeliner and mascara. My hair could really use some pomade, but Izzy's products were foreign to me. Besides, I felt guilty enough using her other stuff, especially considering my plan to borrow a few clothes from her closet.

Except the most exciting thing Izzy had was some kind of crazy taffeta bridesmaid dress jammed in the back that I'd have to ask her about some time – the rest was boring button downs, sweaters, sweatshirts, and T-shirts.

I borrowed a plain navy cotton oxford and shimmied back into my own black jeans. I looked at the flat-haired, conservatively dressed woman in the mirror and felt positively undercover.

As I struggled into my coat, I called Izzy and left a message on her voice mail to let her know that I borrowed some of her stuff and would probably still be out when she came back. Then I called William to check on the store and to let him know that I was okay.

'Hey,' I said, when he picked up.

'Okay, listen,' William said without preamble. 'I've got this friend whose mom works in the law department at UW, and she knows a great criminal lawyer. I think we can probably talk him into doing the thing pro bono. I figure it's going to be very high profile with the whole Witch possessed by a killer Goddess thing. Halloween murder.'

'Please tell me you have not told anyone else about Lilith.'

'Of course I did. How do you think I was going to get anyone interested in helping you?'

'William,' I said as patiently as I could. 'Non-magical people don't understand things like Vatican Witch hunters and Goddess possessions. Your lawyer friend probably thinks I'm insane.'

There was a short pause on the other end. 'I guess he did mention something about the insanity plea.'

'And being crazy doesn't get you off, it just keeps you out of jail,' I pointed out. 'I'd be locked in some mental institution instead.'

'Oh,' William said, sounding defeated. 'I still think you need a lawyer.'

'You're probably right about that,' I agreed. 'How's the store? Everything going okay? Did my orders come in?'

'Jeez, Garnet, wouldn't you rather get all the lawyer information? How long do they give you on your one phone call anyway?'

'You think I'm calling from jail? No, I haven't been arrested yet,' I said. 'Of course, I might be any minute now.'

'Where have you been? You want to hear something ironic? I've had to call in Marlena to cover for you.'

I actually chuckled a little. 'There's always Slow Bob too, you know?'

'Yeah, but then I'd have to work with Slow Bob. All he does is go off and read in the corners. He's really way more work than help.'

I knew that, but Slow Bob did really know the stock. He could recommend any book to anyone based only on his encyclopedic memory. 'I should be back soon,' I said, but then paused. I was about to go confess. I might be headed for jail. 'You should call Eugene' – Mercury Crossing's absentee owner who was currently in California communing with the Dalai

145

Lama. 'We might need to hire new staff. Have you ever thought about being store manager?'

I tried to make it a joke, but William didn't laugh. 'I thought you said you hadn't been arrested.'

'I'm off to the Monroe Street public library to confess my sins.'

'You're going to turn yourself in? At a library?'

'Yeah,' I said, feeling kind of foolish about it. 'It just seemed safe, you know?'

'Sure,' he said, sounding distracted. 'Nice and quiet.'

'I should get off the phone. I've got to get going.'

With that, we said our good-byes and I hung up. When I opened the side door to a gust of cold air, I almost reconsidered the whole thing. Then I remembered that intrepid forensic scientist who was probably right this instant parsing out my genetic signature, and decided my fate was already sealed. Time to get it over with.

I trudged down the sidewalk, my teeth clamped against the chill. The sun had come out, and so, when the wind didn't blow, I could catch a hint of warmth. A crow glided overhead and disappeared into a tall evergreen.

One of the houses on Izzy's block had gone all-out for Halloween. Orange plastic leaf bags with grinning jack-o'-lantern faces surrounded the foundation. Cardboard tombstones with names like 'Frank N. Stein' staggered strategically across the lawn. Cotton-ball cobwebs and orange Christmas lights dripped with faux menace from the trees. I suspected that come the big night, this would be the house with the stereo speakers blasting haunted house noises, and somewhere on the premises would be a cauldron full of steaming dry ice.

Halloween used to be my favorite holiday. Not only was it always the thinnest disguised pagan holiday, but also who didn't enjoy playing dress up and getting free chocolate?

Now, of course, it was a time for mourning. I couldn't see carved pumpkins without remembering the last get-together at the covenstead where we had such fun making silly and scary faces from Junko's bumper crop. She'd been so pleased that her patch had produced precisely a dozen pumpkins that year – one for each of us, she'd said, it was like the Goddess had planned it, blessed us.

Turns out it was a parting gift, some kind of booby, consolation prize. Personally, I'd have chosen the lifetime supply of Rice-A-Roni.

I took in a deep breath and tried to think about something else. It was impossible. Signs of Halloween were everywhere. Even when I averted my eyes to all the haystacks and other decorations, the air smelled of rotting oak leaves and wood smoke.

The Monroe Street branch was a little concrete box at the end of a street full of quirky little storefronts. Virginia creeper, its broad leaves now bronzed by autumn, twined in the seams. A couple of shrimpy, unhealthy-looking shrubs poked out from white quartz mulch. A sign set at an angle at the corner of the lot declared it to be a public library.

I scanned the streets for signs that Dominguez had arrived first, but he hadn't been so obvious as to park his car anywhere I could easily spot it. Since there didn't appear to be a sniper on the nearby roofs either, I squared my aching shoulders and walked up the narrow sidewalk to the doors.

A semicircle of children in costume sat in front of a library lady reading *Boo, Peek-a-Boo* – which appeared to be a story about mice having a masquerade party. Dominguez was perched at a nearby window ledge, flipping unconvincingly through *One Fish, Two Fish, Red Fish, Blue Fish*. He gave me a wave that was more of a get-over-here than a greeting.

Despite the fact that I'd convinced myself that this meeting was a good idea, I allowed myself to take my time stepping around the various pirates, clowns, Power Rangers, and hobos.

It didn't help matters that the undersized furnishings made Dominguez look like some kind of well-dressed bruiser, especially given the cast and the scratch across his cheek. In his dark tie and darker expression, his lawman power suit definitely did not fit in with the benign casual wear of the various stay-at-home parents sitting cross-legged on the floor.

I wedged myself up into the opposite corner of the window. My back pressed against the cool glass.

The story-time lady started up a new book about a friendly Witch. I tried very hard not to cringe.

Leaning in close enough to whisper, Dominguez asked, 'Who's Lilith, exactly?'

'A very powerful dark Goddess,' I said. 'Some people would say the Queen of Demons, the Mother of Evil.'

'Oh, yeah. Adam's first wife, who got exiled from Eden for wanting equality?' Before I could answer, he continued. 'You mean all that shit is real? She really exists? Christ on a crutch, I've got to start going back to church.'

One of the parents glanced back disapprovingly at Dominguez's language.

Relief flooded through me. 'So, you believe me?'

Dominguez gave me a sidelong squint. 'I don't know what to think.'

I leaned my head back against the window. A draft cooled the skin of my neck. 'You felt Her, though, didn't you? You knew it wasn't me.'

'Yes,' he said. He hadn't shaved and he had a dark speckling of five o'clock shadow, which made him look even less reputable somehow. 'But, I'm in a very serious bind here, Ms Lacey—'

'Garnet,' I insisted.

'—Previously, I'd eliminated you from the list of suspects because our profiler and our lab people agreed that there was no way you had the physical strength to murder six highly trained paramilitaries. Then, snap.' He held up his broken wrist as emphasis.

I couldn't believe what I was hearing. I hadn't been a suspect until I tried to convince Dominguez I wasn't one by revealing Lilith. Could I have screwed this up any more? Still, I was heartened to hear him call the Vatican assassins 'highly trained paramilitaries'. That meant the FBI did know something substantial about the Order of Eustace. Maybe he'd also understand that my magic had been in self-defense.

'However,' Dominguez continued. 'It's shaping up that you had motive, opportunity, and capability – except now there's a third party, isn't there? How the fuck am I supposed to factor in a Goddess?'

Two more parents gave Dominguez the evil eye. He mouthed an apology in their general direction.

I didn't know what to say. I was too busy hiding my elation that Dominguez seemed to be admitting that he didn't have a solid case against me. I could have gotten up and done the Snoopy dance of joy, except for one thing. 'Third party?' I asked, counting out Lilith and myself on my fingers. Then, it hit me. Parrish. All this time Dominguez had thought Parrish was the killer and I was the accomplice, not the other way around.

Dominguez watched my expressions carefully. Even if I didn't know he was a psychic, I would have assumed he was trying to read my thoughts.

Story time ended and the children were released in a noisy explosion. Some dashed over to the various book bins to start hunting up favorites; others struggled into coats and hats. Moms and dads chatted with each other, while giving the two of us a lot of unfriendly, yet curious glances.

A boy no more than three stared up at Dominguez and announced, 'I'm wearing Batman underwear.'

'Uh, great,' Dominguez said.

'Batman is one of my favorites too,' I said with what I hoped was a maternal smile.

'I can poop in the potty,' the boy said happily. In a second, the boy was corralled by an apologetic parent and herded off toward the exit.

'That reminds me,' Dominguez said. Taking out his wallet, he handed me a cleaner version of the bill I'd given him when we first met. 'Your counterfeit isn't. What you have is pre-Depression money.'

I wanted to hear more about that, but first I had to ask,

'What about pooping reminded you about the counterfeit bill?'

Dominguez ducked his head and rubbed the tip of his nose in embarrassment. 'Actually, it was Batman. "World's Finest Detective"?'

I gave him a sorry-you-lost-me raise of my eyebrows.

'On the banner of the comic books? Batman, World's Finest . . .' His blush deepened. 'Forget it. The point is, the dollar is real, it's just old.'

It was endearing to see Dominguez so flustered over a super-hero. I suspected some very important key to his character was wrapped up in this whole Batman thing.

'What?' he barked at my grin.

I decided to save my curiosity for a more appropriate time. 'So, is the old money some kind of collector's item? It is worth something?'

Dominguez nodded. 'A little. I'd guess it's double the face value.'

Thinking out loud, I said, 'So the sorcerer is a grave robber of another sort too?'

'What about counterfeit money made *you* think about voodoo?'

'A zombie gave me the money.'

He raised his eyebrows as if waiting for me to say some-thing more, only I didn't know what he was looking for exactly. So I stared back with a little yes-and? smile.

Dominguez sighed. 'You were serious about zombies?'

I nodded.

Shaking his head slowly, he said, 'I have to tell you that I'm having a little trouble buying the whole Goddess thing despite

151

the empirical evidence.' He indicated his cast again with a little lift. 'Do me a favor and skip zombies. I'm not up for it.'

'Aren't you curious about who's passing around old money?'

'It's not a crime to exchange a valuable antique for goods or services; it's just stupid. Stupid I can't prosecute.'

I should be so lucky.

Most of the kids had been packed off to their next activity, and the library lady busily reordered the tables and chairs that had been moved out of the way for story time. She glanced at us from time to time. I was sure we seemed more than a little out of place – Dominguez with his scratches and cast and the Dr Seuss book propped casually against his thigh, and me having the kind of bad hair day that permeates your entire body.

'Grave robbing might be,' Dominguez said, apparently still considering our conversation. 'I'd have to look it up. It's the kind of law that gets put on the books and forgotten about. Even if it were illegal, it wouldn't be a federal crime. That's state. Maybe even city.'

'What about slavery?'

'Owning slaves is definitely against the law. The Emancipation Proclamation came direct from President Lincoln so that would qualify as federal issue. Except they're dead, right? Corpses are classified as property, not people.' Dominguez stopped for a moment. He chewed on his lip, and then shot me an annoyed glance. 'You've got me talking about zombies again, haven't you?'

I smiled and nodded.

'Well, quit,' he said. 'It makes my head hurt.'

'I have that effect on people.' I smiled.

He chuckled. That little boy smile flashed across his face for a moment. 'Aw,' he said, and he ruffled my hair. I don't know if it was residue from the love spell or the awkwardness of having gotten so deeply intimate because of the enchantment, but we both started at the contact. I jumped. He snatched his hand back. We stared at each other guiltily.

'You're not hexing me again, are you?' His eyes were narrowed and suspicious.

I did my best Bullwinkle impression. 'Nothing up my sleeves.'

Dominguez smiled a little, but seemed unconvinced.

'It didn't work very well last time,' I pointed out.

'I'd disagree with that,' he said, his eyes sliding from mine. He tapped the flat of the book against his thigh.

Behind me, I heard a sharp rap on the window. I turned, expecting to see someone. Instead I was eye to beady black eye with a crow. I frowned at it, and it flapped away.

Weird.

I looked at Dominguez, wishing I'd had better luck trying to enlist his help with the whole zombie thing. He was so damned single-minded. Plus, I really wanted to ask him more about what he planned to do about me, but the line 'anything you say can and will be held against you in a court of law' kept echoing through my mind.

'I'm going to level with you, Ms Lacey—'

'Garnet,' I insisted again.

'—Interpol is breathing down my neck to close this case. Apparently, the Vatican is pressuring them, and they've been threatening to step in if I can't get the murderer found in a reasonable amount of time. Those kinds of jurisdiction fights make my boss cranky.'

Dominguez flipped the book onto a nearby table where it landed with a startlingly loud thud. I jumped. The man sitting behind the book checkout glared us at.

'You're my only link to Daniel Parrish. He's proven to be a surprisingly slick customer. I caught a break when you surfaced here in Madison.'

'You think Parrish did it? Why?'

He gave me a long, measuring glance. 'We recovered his van. We have a witness that saw him and his van entering Lakewood Cemetery, where the bodies were discovered, and at the scene of what had at first appeared to be an unrelated arson.'

I'd read about the fire much later in the *Star Tribune*. The covenstead had burned to the ground. The place was so thoroughly destroyed the authorities had trouble positively identifying the bodies of my coven, who, it had been presumed, died in the fire – though Parrish and I knew the truth. The Vatican assassins killed them. Parrish admitted to me that he'd burned the place. He said it would help muddy the trail back to me. Apparently, he'd forgotten about himself.

'A car rented by Sergio Vitale, one of the missing priests, connected the two crimes. It was parked outside of the house Mr Parrish very likely torched.'

I held my breath.

'When I looked into the arson, I found . . .' He glanced away momentarily, and I watched his jaw work as he decided what to tell me. 'A pattern our office has seen before. Seems that there are a number of unsolved murder cases that, let's just say, appear to revolve around the pagan community and a group of foreign nationals hailing from Vatican City.'

I nodded. 'The Order of Eustace.' I'd already told him all about this. At least I hadn't placed myself on the scene. I'd only said that I knew the order had taken out my coven, I didn't say I'd seen it. Unless, of course, Dominguez read it out of my mind.

'I started to follow up with whatever Wiccan organizations I could find. Of course, nobody talked. If they did, they weren't terribly helpful since nobody seems to know anybody's real name. I could never even piece together all the dead coven members, until I switched gears and asked about Mr Parrish. Turns out nobody much likes him, and they were happy to drop him in it.'

And me, by extension.

'Mr Parrish had a whole bunch of girlfriends who remembered you as the jealous one.' He flashed me an I'm-not-sure-I-approve-of-your-hippie-free-lovin'-ways sideways glance. 'Some even figured you for a Witch. Suddenly, I thought maybe Parrish might have stepped in to protect you against the . . . whatever.'

'Order,' I supplied again. 'And now?'

'Now my theory has some wrinkles.'

I wished like hell at this moment I could look deeply into Dominguez's eyes and say, 'I swear I didn't do it.' When the moment passed, I heard his soft sigh and got the distinct impression he wished I could have too.

'Why don't you tell me what happened? You said you were ready to talk.'

Yeah, that's when I thought I was deep in it, when I figured I had nothing to lose.

Studying the beige carpeting with great interest, he said, 'Listen, Ms Lacey, I already know. You broadcast your guilt every time you see me.'

But if I say it out loud, it's a confession. It's evidence.

Dominguez watched me closely for a long moment, and then his face fell in disappointment. He took in a deep breath. He glanced at me, then away again. 'I can't exactly blame you for operating in your own self-interest. Of course, there's always Mr Parrish's version of this story to consider. When my guys catch up with him, is he going to roll over on you?'

I chewed on my lip, considering. Tough call. As much as Parrish would like to consider himself an honorable gentleman, the truth of the matter was, he wasn't. More to the point, his own sense of self-preservation was highly, highly honed. He wouldn't have survived two hundred years as a vampire if it weren't. I shrugged.

'Interpol is going to chew my ass.'

I opened my mouth to tell Dominguez how sorry I was that his boss was giving him a rough time, but instead I said, 'Can I tell you something that's been pissing me off? I can't believe so much energy is being wasted avenging these . . . well, killers. I mean, they're the bad guys. They're the ones who busted in and killed innocents. And this wasn't the first time. Shouldn't the FBI be after them? And, you, of all people, being assigned this gig, it's ironic. If the Vatican Witch hunters knew you were in possession of psychic ability they'd either try to kill you or recruit you.'

156

He shrugged. 'It's my job, Ms Lacey.'

'Well, it sucks.'

And that's when I noticed William. He came barreling up to us with such fierce determination that I knew he'd come on a mission to rescue me.

Great. Now I was really screwed.

7

Libra

Key Words:
Diplomatic and Fickle

William stormed right up to Dominguez. He raised his hand, and, at first, I thought William planned to punch him. 'William, no!' I shouted.

But instead, William opened his fist and tossed a handful of amber powder into Dominguez's face.

Dominguez reacted as if he'd been hit with mace. He let out a bark of rapid-fire expletives and rubbed furiously at his eyes. Tears ran in copper-red streaks down his face.

'Water,' I shouted at William. 'Get some water to wash out his eyes.'

I looked around for signs indicating the bathrooms. One of the librarians was approaching to see what the commotion was about, and I waved her down. 'Water and paper towels,' I shouted. 'And someone call 911.'

'I don't need an ambulance, I need to kill the punk who did this,' Dominguez growled, still blindly dabbing at his eyes.

William took a step back and tugged my sleeve. 'This is a

good time to leave,' he whispered. 'This is the distraction part before the running. Let's run now, please.'

'I can't leave until I know Dominguez is okay,' I said. 'What the hell were you thinking?'

'I was thinking we'd be making our getaway about now,' William murmured.

The librarian came back with bottled water and a wad of industrial-strength paper towels from the restroom. 'Sit down on this chair and tilt your head back,' I told Dominguez. 'I'm going to try and flush out your eyes.' The librarian helped Dominguez perch in the child-size chair while I twisted off the top of the water. As soon as his head was tilted back, I liberally splashed water directly on his face. He held the paper towels by his ears to try to catch some of the excess water.

'Is that better? Does it sting?'

Dominguez squinted in my general direction with tears flowing as hard as before. 'More water,' he insisted, through clenched teeth. To William, 'If you've blinded me, kid, you're going down.'

'I'm leaving,' William said quietly, even though he didn't budge.

'Has anyone called an ambulance?' I asked, pouring more water into Dominguez's eyes.

When no one answered, William held out his cell phone. That's when I noticed his hair. William must have changed religion again because now instead of a neat ponytail, he had unruly clumps of hair that looked like a white guy's dread-lock starter kit. His John Lennon glasses perched on his nose made him look so wide-eyed, I had a flash of pity for him. I could visualize him as a kid running around his backyard with a towel pinned to his shirt, pretending to be the brave hero to the rescue. Dominguez really could, if he wanted to, arrest William for assault. I needed to get William out of here before that happened.

I took William's cell and glanced at it. 'No reception in here,' I lied. 'We'll just step outside.' I handed the nearly empty bottle to one of the gathered librarians. 'Fill this up and keep flushing his eyes until the paramedics arrive, okay?'

She nodded her agreement, and I took William outside.

'Are we leaving now?' he wanted to know when we stepped into the parking lot.

'After I make the call,' I told him. I dialed 911 and explained to dispatch that Special Agent Gabriel Dominguez had been hit in the face with unidentified powder—

'Myrrh, actually,' William interjected. 'We had it in overstock.'

—and was in need of assistance. She asked me what, if any, first aid we'd administered, and then she wanted me to identify myself. I hesitated at that last question. Part of me wanted there to be a record that I'd called the ambulance, especially if somehow Dominguez was permanently injured and all of this played into the case against me. The other part was just plain afraid. Fear won. 'Just get to the library as soon as possible,' I told her and repeated the street address.

I clapped the phone shut and handed it to William. 'You should get out of here,' I told him. 'Dominguez is pretty mad.'

'What are you going to do?'

'Stay with him until the ambulance comes.'

William kicked at the white stones around the shrubs. 'Then I'll stay too.'

'No, that's an incredibly bad idea, William. He could have you arrested.' Sirens wailed in the distance. It was probably too soon to be the ones coming here, but they made me nervous. 'Will you go, if I go?'

William nodded.

'Okay,' I said. The paramedics would take care of Dominguez. I told myself I wasn't fleeing another crime scene. I hadn't done anything wrong. 'Let's get you out of here.'

William showed me to a sleek, black VW Beetle convertible. Fishing out the keys from his pocket, he beeped the doors open.

'Is this yours?' I asked incredulously. I couldn't get over how classy this car was. In some ways it suited him. It was trendy, but kind of five minutes ago.

'Sort of,' he said, as he opened the door for me.

I lowered myself into the seat and buckled up with a minimum amount of grunting. William watched my progress curiously.

'Are you okay?' he asked once he'd snapped his safety belt and deliberately arranged the shoulder strap in a comfortable position. Watching his slow, steady progress through the motions, I decided if I ever needed someone to get me out of Dodge quickly, I would *not* call William.

'I was shot.'

In a textbook driver's manual maneuver, William adjusted his rear view before putting the key into the ignition. He turned the key, and the engine sprang to life with a well-oiled purr. He glanced over his shoulder and then signaled his entry into traffic as he pulled out from the curb. 'Like with a gun?'

Why did everyone ask that? 'Yes,' I said.

William scratched his scalp, making all his dreads bob. 'Who shot you?'

'Dominguez.'

William snuck a glance at me as he slowed for a stop sign. 'And you didn't need a rescue?'

'Well, not just now,' I said. 'Turns out he didn't even think I was the prime suspect until recently.'

We paused for precisely six seconds as William checked both ways for traffic before proceeding through the intersection. 'Who does he think did it?'

'Parrish.' The sirens were definitely approaching. I could hear them through the closed windows. 'I need to get home to warn him.'

'I'll take you there.'

Sitting back in the seat, I watched a glow-in-the-dark skeleton toy that hung from the rearview mirror sway. I changed the subject to save me from further embarrassment. 'How can this be "kind of" your car? Oh, William!' I said excitedly. 'Are you dating again?'

'Kind of,' he said to the passing scenery.

Well. This was good news. William had been having a rocky patch ever since he discovered his last girlfriend was a ghoul who preferred vampire suckage to him. I was thrilled he'd found someone new. Only, he didn't seem all that excited about it. He chewed on his lower lip.

So I asked the obvious question. 'How can you "kind of" date someone?'

'She's polyamorous.'

A lot of people in the pagan community were polyamorous.

163

There were even books out on the subject of being poly and Wiccan. Polyamorous meant just what the Latin seemed to imply – many loves. A polyamorous 'couple' might actually be a triple or a quadruple . . . or more. All of the members might be in love with each other, or with one of the people in the group who had other lovers.

The whole thing had always seemed terribly complicated to me, especially since a major component of the poly lifestyle was that these relationships had to happen with the full knowledge and consent of everyone involved.

I'd much rather stay in the dark about certain things, hence my preferred method of dealing with Sebastian's ghouls. If I didn't have to know, I didn't want to. I'd never even considered polyamory because I knew I was too damn jealous. I'd never been good at sharing, not even in kindergarten.

'So,' I said, reaching into the fuzzy corners of my memory to pull out all the various terms used to describe the types of poly arrangements. 'Are you in a Y or a triangle or what?' A Y would mean that two people shared one, who acted as a kind of focus point. A triangle meant all three people were into each other.

William nodded his approval at my attempt. 'It's a Y right now. I'm into Maureen mostly. I mean, I like Ethan and everything, but I'm just not sure he's my type.'

'You have a boy type?'

William shrugged. 'I might. I don't really know, you know?'

'Sure,' I said, though I wasn't entirely. William had always struck me as someone who could go either way, but I tended to chalk that up to his Pisces sun, which made him generally

164

indecisive. 'Wait,' I said, twigging to something he said earlier. 'You've met her other lover?'

'Oh yeah, sometimes we all have dinner.'

'How weird is that?' I managed to say before I could censor myself.

William laughed, as he turned down a street with a slow, precise hand-over-hand on the steering wheel. 'Yeah, it was a little at first, but then after a while it was no big deal. It's really important to be nonpossessive.'

'That's the part I could never hack,' I admitted. 'I like being the center of attention.'

William gave me a sidelong glance and a half smile. 'You're still thinking in the monogamous mindset. Nobody gets cheated in poly. It's different when everyone in the relationship agrees to the terms from the beginning. I knew there'd be an Ethan before I signed up.'

Yeah, and I should have factored in ghouls when I decided to take on a new vampire lover. Knowing they were part of the equation didn't make it any easier for me to accept, however. I was impressed how nonchalant William was about the whole thing; maybe it really was working for him.

'I'm really glad you found someone ... or someones,' I corrected with a big smile. 'Maureen and Ethan are really lucky.' Wow, that felt weird to say. Oh well, the grin on William's face was worth it. 'So, tell me more about them.'

'It's nice you're trying to get this, but my relationship is really just with Maureen,' he said. 'You'd like her, I think. She's magical too. I've been learning a lot from her.'

Speaking of nonpossessiveness, here was a weird bit of

jealousy. I found myself bristling at the thought of someone else acting as William's magical role model. It wasn't like I'd ever really offered to teach him Wicca, but we always shared bits of astrological trivia and he always came to me with questions he had. 'Oh, really?'

Apparently I'd kept the ice out of my tone, which was good, because I'd meant to. He went on. 'She's seriously powerful, Garnet. I've seen some things I would never have believed possible.'

Okay, now I really had to wrestle the green-eyed monster. Before he met me, William had never known vampires existed, and even after he had met two of them, he still had trouble committing to the idea their magic was real. This woman convinced him of the impossible?

So I had to know. 'What kind of magic does she practice?'

He started to say, but stopped. 'Oh,' William said, his eyes firmly on the road. 'This and that.'

I gave him a hard stare. It was very unlike him not to want to talk about magic. 'You don't approve?' I asked, though my mind was elsewhere. We were getting closer to my house, and I realized I was going to have to sneak into my apartment somehow and warn Parrish that the FBI *were* after him.

William chewed on a fingernail. Then, noticing his nervous tick, he quickly got his hands back into the proper position. 'It's kind of dark. What she's into.'

My eyes strayed to the skeleton. I thought about how William had tossed that powder into Dominguez's face. It was very *The Serpent and the Rainbow*. I shook my head. 'Please tell me it's not voodoo.'

'Uh, well.'

Before I could even react, a crow flew so low that it almost smacked into the window. William slammed on the brakes. I had to brace myself with my arms. The effort cost me in a pulsing pain. Tears came to my eyes and I let out a frustrated growl. 'What the hell is it with those crows?'

'I shouldn't have said anything about Mo's magic,' William whispered, looking genuinely freaked out. 'Please forget I said anything.'

Voodoo, like any magical/religious system, had practitioners who used their powers for good and those with darker bents. I had no reason to assume that William's new girlfriend was the same voodoo priestess who was raising legions of the undead, except for his reticence to talk about her magic and the sudden appearance of this suicidal crow.

'Are you saying these crows are Maureen's spies or something?'

He shook his head. I couldn't tell if he was denying my allegation or telling me to hush.

William turned onto my street. The big van was still there, so I told him to drop me off a couple of blocks away. His spirits seemed to perk up a bit at being asked to play spy. 'Maybe I could distract them again?' he asked. 'Do a naked Uhura dance or something?'

I smiled at the image. 'Go for it.'

Honestly, I could use any help he was willing to offer. Though I still felt somewhat incognito in Izzy's clothes and bare-minimum makeup, I didn't have any illusions about my abilities to sneak past trained FBI agents.

'Seriously?' Now there was that goofy grin I loved so much.

'Yeah, why not? Anything you could do to distract them would help. I mean, maybe even just stopping to ask them for directions or something.'

'Oh, that's clever.' A twinkle brightened his hazel eyes. 'I like that. What should I be looking for?'

'The student union?'

'Yeah, although they're probably not from around here. Maybe I better pretend I know the cross streets and see if they have a map.'

And so it was decided. I got out of William's car a couple of blocks away and he made a Y turn. I headed down the block, and as I started toward my place I caught sight of William slowing down to peer meaningfully at the street signs. I smiled; he was playing the part to the hilt.

Like a lot of Madison streets, mine didn't have an alley. Behind my apartment was a bike path, which had been converted from train tracks. As soon as I got close, I ducked onto the path. I knew there were probably agents watching all approaches to my place, but the thick undergrowth would make spotting someone more difficult.

I hoped, anyway.

Broad, bright maroon leaves of sumac shielded me from the road. At least, until it came to the next block, then I'd somehow have to pass unnoticed across the railroad bridge. I peeked through the branches of an oak sapling, its browned leaves clinging stubbornly to what seemed little more than a twig. I could see William's black Beetle sidled up to the FBI van. William leaned far out his window and pointed in the direction of the lake. I couldn't tell what was going on inside the van, but I decided to take a chance. I strolled across the bridge as slowly and purposefully as I could. Of course, my feet itched to run, but I knew hurrying would very likely catch their attention. I also tried to only spare them the most casual of glances. That was the hardest part. I desperately wanted to see how William was doing, but I didn't think staring was such a good idea. Somehow, I got across to the other side.

Once safely behind the cover of trees, I let myself jog a few steps. Then my shoulder reminded me that walking was a better option, since screaming in pain with every bounce would most certainly draw the attention of the Feds.

As I got closer to the back of my house, I didn't see anyone in a black trench coat with a walkie-talkie, so I decided to risk it. The slope was covered in long grass and milkweed stalks, and my feet slipped as I made my descent. I bit the inside of my cheek to keep from yelping as my shoulder twisted this way and that in order to keep my balance. When I was at the back fence of my place, I remembered to breathe.

I lifted the latch on the gate of the cedar fence that completely surrounded the backyard. The neighbors had left a couple of fast-food wrappers on the narrow sidewalk that led to the garage. I compulsively picked them up and tossed them in the big, brown plastic bins.

Since I was the responsible tenant, the landlord let me garden. All the flowerbeds, which neatly paralleled the lines of the fence, were covered for the coming winter. Sebastian had spent last weekend with me cleaning up the dead plants and leaves. We purposely left a cluster of spent purple cone-flower heads for the birds to perch on, as well as some dried husks of milkweed for no good reason other than the fact that I like the look of the seedpods. Sebastian had agreed that they would make an excellent winter garden 'feature'.

The cold snuck under the weave of my heavy sweater. The smell of wood smoke was strong in the air. I needed to work things out with Sebastian. This missing him thing, frankly, sucked.

I had a brief flare of panic when my keys weren't in their usual pocket, but a frantic pat down revealed that I'd merely stuck them in the wrong place. I let out another relieved breath because my spare set was hidden inside the front door behind a loose bit of baseboard. It would have been a slight bit trickier to evade notice if I had to creep through the hedges to try to sneak past where the FBI was parked.

The warmth inside felt good, though it set my shoulder aching. I trudged down to the basement to wait for Parrish to awaken.

Grabbing a metal folding chair from where they were stashed next to the dryer, I opened the door to Parrish's storage room and sat myself in front of his coffin. What I really wanted was to go upstairs to take a long, hot bath. But, as the only way into my apartment was up the front staircase, I decided not to risk the exposure. This was the best place. Besides, I couldn't afford to miss him.

I stared at his coffin. The soft pine had been scuffed and dented in places. At the 'foot', the faded remains of some certificate of passage or other lingered. I couldn't tell, but there might even have been a customs inspector's stamp.

While those details made it seem a bit more like a well-traveled packing crate, I couldn't help but visualize Parrish's corpse inside. The dank smell of the basement started giving me the feeling of being inside someone's crypt, albeit one with steamer trunks and a dresser.

To distract myself, I thumbed through the manga. It took me three minutes to figure out I was reading the Japanese comic backward, but even then starting over didn't help much. Still, the pretty pictures helped me pass the time. I started wishing I could sneak upstairs long enough to grab some of my laundry or to fetch that new astrology book on Neptune I'd begun reading or . . . anything.

Just when I was ready to risk it, I heard a rustle inside the coffin.

Despite knowing it was Parrish, my stomach still dropped the way it does during horror films when things that aren't supposed to happen do. I jumped up out of my seat and stood in the doorway. The lid tipped up, and I let out a little squeak. All the time Parrish had been sleeping in my basement, I never once watched him come out of his coffin.

No more than a plain pine box, Parrish's coffin lacked fancy hinges. The top fit neatly into grooves. To get out, he lifted the cover straight up and then tossed it to one side. The top slid to the floor with a bang. The interior revealed Parrish in all his glory; he was completely naked.

8

Scorpio

Key Words:
Sex and Death

I don't know why I expected Parrish to sleep in clothes. I suppose putting on pj's before crawling into your coffin would feel silly, but, then you'd think it would feel equally strange to undress. Yet, there he was.

It had been a while since I'd seen Parrish nude. Even lying in a cramped, stiff position inside the coffin, he was a sight to behold. He'd died before the era of bodybuilding and personal trainers, so his body was defined by the work he did. Robbing stagecoaches apparently took powerful arms and athletic legs. His stomach was taut from hunger and ambition.

Parrish rubbed his eyes and scratched himself – going through guy-waking-up rituals. He hadn't noticed me yet. I cleared my throat.

Other guys might have acted modest, not Parrish. He looked me in the eye and stretched languidly, like a cat, daring me not to notice the ripple of muscle along his lean form. When

I found my eyes sliding from his to do just that, I blushed a little. He laughed.

'Good evening,' he said, in his best Dracula impersonation. With a grunt he levered himself up out of his coffin and padded on bare feet over to the dresser near where I sat.

'Hey, um,' I said, trying not to stare at the part of him that was now at eye level. 'I wanted to warn you, the FBI thinks you killed the agents. And they have the house staked out.'

He stopped rummaging through his clothes. 'Blood.'

His change in subject seemed a little abrupt, but I tried to follow, anyway. 'Uh, yeah, about that. You might have to skip going out tonight . . .'

'You,' he interrupted me. 'You've been injured.'

My hand moved to protectively cover the gunshot wound. 'Oh, yeah.'

In a blink, using that superhuman speed of his, Parrish suddenly knelt before me. I nearly startled out of the folding chair when I found him there between my slightly parted legs. He lightly grasped the sides of my face and searched my eyes. 'What happened? Are you all right?'

I felt very self-conscious with a naked man kneeling between my thighs. I was hyperaware of every place we touched – my knees grazing his hips, my hands trying to find somewhere to be that wasn't, well, right there.

'I guess I found out Lilith can't stop bullets after all,' I said with a weak smile.

'Are you in pain?'

'Uh,' I said. It was difficult to answer when I could smell the scent of his body, a captivating combination of frankincense and leather. I really wanted to get up and move away from the temptation to touch him because not only was the timing wildly inappropriate but I *did* still have a boyfriend even if we were 'on a break'. Sebastian had all but given me permission to explore my feelings for Parrish. Even so, I doubted that running my hands all over Parrish's chest was the kind of exploration he had in mind. 'No, uh, I'm okay.'

My shoulder *had* settled into a kind of constant, yet forgettable ache. It was like my pain receptors had had enough, they weren't up to working very hard anymore, and were just phoning it in every so often.

Letting go of my face, Parrish frowned at me. 'I could help.'

'Help? How?' Sebastian had done an expert job field dressing the wound. I couldn't fathom what Parrish might have to offer, unless – 'No illegal substances, thank you. Not with the FBI on our butts.'

He snorted a laugh. 'Nothing like that. You do realize that my blood is fairly regenerative.'

'You want me to drink your blood? Parrish, I'm a vegetarian.'

With an amused shake of his head, Parrish stood up.

I swear he lingered there, right in front of my face, showing off his manly attributes, just a few seconds longer than necessary before returning to the task of retrieving his clothes from one of his steamer trunks. 'Well, as long as you have your priorities straight,' he said.

The trunk was about two feet high and not terribly sturdy-looking. It was constructed mostly of pine, which had been painted black. There were strips of oak and tin ornamental corner protectors burnished to look like brass. Two wide, well-worn leather belts held the box together.

When Parrish lifted the top, I expected to smell cedar, but didn't. Yet it was clearly an antique, just not an especially well built one. Probably it had been cheap when it was young. Not unlike Parrish himself, honestly, I thought with a wry, fond smile.

I watched in complete fascination as he pulled on the sleaziest pair of silky leopard-print underwear I'd ever seen.

'You're not seriously going to wear those, are you?'

He looked down at himself, considering. I had to admit that despite the tacky pattern, the material did flatter him. It clung like a second skin, barely concealing him. Then he noticed me noticing, and he said, 'Yes, I think I shall.'

'I don't know why you're bothering getting dressed.' Then I stopped myself, realizing how much like an invitation that sounded, especially given the lascivious smile that slowly spread across Parrish's face. 'That is, you might want to consider hiding out for a while. You know, lay low.'

Parrish's mouth twitched into a kind of a sad smile. 'That's not really my style is it, darling?'

'But, I was serious when I said that the FBI have the place staked out. They're right outside.'

He stomped into a pair of black jeans.

'Didn't you hear me? Dominguez thinks *you* did it.'

Pulling on a black T-shirt, which, incredibly, appeared to be manufactured by Armani, he shook out his auburn hair. 'Yes, and sooner or later he'll get his man.'

'What do you mean by that?'

176

'It means, my love, I'm going to lead them away from you. If they have me to chase, they'll leave you alone.'

'Why would you do that?' I stood up from my folding chair when Parrish brushed past me on his way around to the other side of his coffin. I tried to catch his sleeve, but he shrugged off the contact. I stood there waiting for an answer as he busied himself with setting the long, narrow cover back into place.

'Hey, you know, it's not that I don't appreciate the gesture, but you don't have to do this for me,' I continued, when it was clear he wouldn't give me an answer.

He sat down on the lid of the coffin and pulled on socks and motorcycle boots. 'What you continually fail to appreciate, Garnet, is that I *want* to.'

Oh.

'You don't have to prove anything to me by being all noble,' I said without adding, *you already reminded me that you love me better than I love you.*

He'd finished putting on his boots. With his elbows resting on his knees, he stared at the floor momentarily before looking up at me. 'I'd ask you to run away with me if I had any hope at all that the answer would be yes.'

I didn't have a response for that.

Parrish stood up and studied the wall with a deep frown. Then, he reached out and slapped the concrete. 'Gross,' he said, when he pulled his hand away. 'I need to wash. And, given that I'm about to throw myself on my sword for you, any chance I could borrow a final use of your bath?'

'I . . . uh.' I stopped. I wanted to press the issue, but Parrish

177

was right. This was hardly the best place for this kind of intense conversation. 'Yeah, come on.'

If we were careful, the guys in the van might not spot us. Keeping our heads low, we snuck upstairs. The main hallway always had a light on, so, although crawling killed my shoulder, it was easy going.

When we reached my apartment door, I had to crouch in a funny position to get the key in and turn it. I fumbled a couple of times because of the pain, but eventually I got it open. Parrish went down on all fours and crawled across the living room like a seasoned Marine. Me, I waited at the door for a moment while my eyes adjusted to the darkness.

In deference to my injury, I stooped my way to my bedroom. At least in that room, I always kept my curtains closed since that day I spotted the neighbor kid watching me from his back patio. I could probably light a candle without alerting the guys outside.

Parrish had crept into the bathroom before I could gesture for him to follow me. He shut the door.

I pulled myself up onto my bed and listened to the sound of the shower in the darkness. Barney hopped up and bonked her head against my arm until I relented and petted her. I scratched her ears and stroked her fur until she hummed with pleasure. It was nice to be loved, but I suspected she really wanted to remind me that I hadn't fed her in days.

When she nipped slightly at my hand, I knew it for a fact. I gave Barney a one-armed shove off my bed and slunk into the kitchen to fetch fresh water and kibbles. Once I'd managed to fill both bowls, the volume of her purr increased tenfold and came interspersed between wet, snarfing munches.

I sat on the kitchen floor listening to my cat inhale her food.

If Parrish left, I might not see him again. I had a lot of faith in Parrish's ability to evade capture, but these guys were the FBI. What if they caught him? He was supernaturally fast and a helluva lot stronger than your average guy, but he wasn't Superman. More important, he couldn't turn into mist or transform into a bat. If he got locked into a jail cell and the sun came up, poof!

That'd be all she wrote.

If they didn't capture him, it wasn't like he could come back here. He'd have to stay gone for a long, long time. Eventually, he'd stop being Dominguez's priority, but it would still be foolish to risk it. One of the reasons Parrish was successful in his life of crime was because he was ruthless about cutting ties. When he walked away, it was for good.

Mostly. After all, he had a weak spot for me.

Barney's purring stopped abruptly, and she sat back on her haunches and began to lick her paw.

The apartment smelled of rosemary, which had bloomed in the sunroom despite my neglect. From where I sat underneath the cabinets, I could see the faint lavender star-shaped flowers in the silvery moonlight. Not everything else had fared so well in my absence. The sandbur had shriveled to a dried husk, littering its spiny seeds all over the floor around the pot.

Seeing the burs reminded me of all the effort I'd put into the love spell. How ironic, then, that it was Parrish who was so ready to sacrifice for love.

Barney padded across the floor to lay down beside me with

a heavy thump. She offered her belly for scratches with a purring grunt. I obliged, wishing people were as easy to satisfy as cats.

Well, I thought, there was one thing I *could* give Parrish. It wasn't precisely what he wanted, but it might pass for close enough. I crawled toward the bathroom, and as soon as I was out of sight of the windows I tried to squiggle out of my pants. They didn't come off in the quick, smooth gesture I'd hoped for, and instead hitched against my knees. I fell flat on my face. Worse, I tried to cushion my fall and strained my shoulder.

I lay on the floor with my pants around my knees and howled with pain.

'Garnet?'

Parrish stood over me, dripping water onto my hardwood floor and my head. He'd grabbed my favorite fuzzy blue towel and wrapped it around his waist. I couldn't quite catch my breath. Luckily, I'd stopped making noise, or I was sure the FBI would be knocking down the door any second.

'What happened to your pants?' he asked, helping me into an upright position.

How could I explain to him that some part of my addled brain had thought offering a pity fuck was a good idea but the Goddess struck me down, thus saving me from my own stupidity. Not only would Parrish have seen my attempt to seduce him for what it was, but also I would have undeniably betrayed Sebastian. Both monumentally inane ideas.

I'd been having a lot of those lately.

'Wardrobe malfunction?' I gasped.

'What the bloody hell does that mean?' He propped me up

180

against the hallway wall, while I tried to scootch up my jeans. Every move made my shoulder spasm. I bit my lip to keep from screaming. 'This is ridiculous. Look how much pain you're in. You have to let me do something.'

Considering what I'd been imagining we'd be doing right now, I had to laugh. I wouldn't have lasted two minutes doing any kind of, shall we say, strenuous exercise. What had I been thinking? Oh, right. I hadn't. Good thing some higher power had been doing the thinking for both of us. Sometimes the Goddess interceded in great, big monumental ways, and other times She tripped you in the hallway and exposed your pink frilly underwear to the world.

Parrish, meanwhile, wasn't in on the joke. He frowned at me. 'After all this time, you don't trust me.'

I'd gotten my pants around my hips and, even though my underwear was wedged up my butt and the zipper was still wide open, I just couldn't spare the energy for any more modesty than that. 'Would your bite really heal me? Without making me undead?'

Parrish sat down beside me, pressing his back against the wall. He stretched out his legs, which went on significantly longer than mine, and appeared to be admiring his toenails in the dark. 'Yeo.'

Barney wandered in and sat near his toes. She blinked her yellow eyes innocently and then sneezed hard enough to spray a fine mist of snot in our general direction.

'Ugh,' I said, nudging her with a toe. 'You can make your point a lot less disgustingly, you know. I know vampire bites are magical.'

181

Barney rubbed delicately at her nose and then padded off to the bedroom.

Parrish shook his head. 'You have the strangest relationship with your cat.'

I nodded, but my mind was focused on the ramifications of accepting Parrish's bite. 'So, if we did this, what would happen? I mean, I'm not going to turn into a bite junkie, am I?'

'You might,' Parrish admitted. 'But you're not really the sort, Garnet. Worst-case scenario, you'll occasionally crave rare steak.'

'Be serious!' I snapped. I was nervous. I didn't mind dating them, but I didn't want to *be* a vampire.

Parrish put a wet hand on my knee. 'You wouldn't need to taste that much. We could keep things this side of a blood bond. If we play things right, you won't even have to call me "master".'

I smiled despite the way my guts roiled. 'You'd have liked that, wouldn't you?'

'You know me well,' he said, touching a finger to my nose briefly. 'You know, I *have* done this before.'

Though I was extremely glad to hear I wasn't a guinea pig in his blood-transfusion experiment, I was strangely hurt to hear I wasn't the first. 'Oh?'

'He lived a normal life, and I stood by his grave for days. He never rose.'

My mind flashed to being entombed alive, but I shook my head. 'You're certain.'

'One hundred percent.'

I felt relief and no small amount of curiosity. 'Who was he?'

'Someone special. Like you.'

Like me? 'A lover?'

Parrish's expression revealed nothing. 'Someone worth saving.'

'Sounds serious.'

'It was.'

I waited, hoping to get the whole story, but he offered nothing. 'I'm – you were joking about the steak, weren't you?'

'Not really. You'll probably discover you burn easier in the sun too.'

'No.'

'Yes. But, as a bonus, the regenerative powers will stay in your system for a couple of months. With flu season coming up, that's always a plus.'

Even though Parrish's last comment seemed more ominous than comforting, I decided to go for it. 'I trust you,' I said finally. 'In fact, it looks like I'm ready to trust you with my life.'

'About damn time.'

We decided to 'do it' in my bedroom. Making sure my curtains were securely closed, I lit a few candles for mood, and, frankly, so I could see. Parrish helped me onto the bed and then, in a strange reversal of what I'd expected would be happening right about now, disappeared into the bathroom to put his clothes *on*. I managed to get my jeans all the way back on, but the effort left me collapsed in a sprawl on top of my green-and-white moose-print down comforter. Barney continued to register her disapproval of my decision by lurking under a fold of the blanket and occasionally leaping out to poke my leg with her needle-sharp claws. Not that it even registered given the throbbing pain in my shoulder.

I was just wondering if I should find some reserve strength and strip the bed to put down plastic to catch any stray blood – I mean, I didn't want to ruin the comforter – when Parrish sat down beside me. Neither Barney nor I had heard him come in, and we both started. She bolted for the windowsill; I made an annoyingly feminine peep. Then, as if that wasn't embarrassing enough, a giggle slipped out. I couldn't believe how much like a blushing schoolgirl I felt.

Despite having dated two vampires, I hardly ever let them really bite me. Thing is, contrary to what Parrish thought about me, I knew I liked it. A lot. Part of my jealousy of Sebastian's ghouls came from the fact that I could all too easily see myself as one of them.

'Shhh,' Parrish said. Propping himself up on his elbow, he lay down beside me. He stroked my cheek with his finger.

The intimacy of the gesture and the intense look in his eyes made me reconsider. 'I don't know if this is such a good idea after all, Parrish.'

'Daniel,' he said. Then with a quirk of a smile I could only barely see in the candlelight, he added, 'I mean, if you're not going to call me master, you should at least use my Christian name.'

'I thought you didn't like it.'

'I don't,' he said with a little laugh. 'It just seems more appropriate, don't you think?'

'I do,' I said. 'Daniel.'

He did have such a beautiful smile, even with his fangs extended. Auburn curls glittered red-gold in the muted light. With my good hand, I ran my fingers through the silken strands. Parrish lowered his head and kissed me, softly, on the top of my head. Despite the gentleness of the gesture, I flinched slightly with anticipation. Pain stabbed my shoulder.

Parrish had pulled back and now watched my reactions with a furrowed brow. 'So much for foreplay,' he sighed.

'It's okay,' I hissed through clenched teeth. 'I can handle it, really, I like it, in fact—'

I didn't get to finish my thought. His fangs sunk into my neck. My neck! I'd always heard that neck bites were fatal. I could feel my blood pounding in rhythm with my heart. Panic washed over me. Parrish's hair covered my face, making me feel suddenly smothered. His body draped over mine, effectively pinning me down. I felt trapped. I started to struggle, only it didn't take much effort on Parrish's part to still me. Between the searing pain and the hand he put firmly on my wounded shoulder, I couldn't move.

Parrish's thumb rubbed slow, steady circles on my shoulder. Either he had the strangest tick when he sucked someone lifeless, or this was a signal to me to calm down and trust him. Even though I swore I felt my blood gushing into his mouth, I told myself he knew what he was doing. If Parrish was an expert at anything, this was it.

I steadied my breath, but, even so, trust didn't come easily. I decided, in fact, that the best way for me to cope with my mounting fear was to just give in to it. I wrapped my good hand around Parrish's waist, and dug my nails in deep. Maybe if I could hold on tight enough, I'd feel safe.

Releasing my neck with a wet sound, Parrish lifted his head. I expected him to be smeared with my blood, proof positive that the comforter was stained beyond repair, but he wasn't. Only the slightest hint of red colored his lower lip, like he'd smeared a bit of lipstick onto himself during a kiss. Then, he slashed his own lip with a sharp fang.

Parrish covered my mouth in a sudden, desperate kiss. The coppery taste of blood filled my mouth. I should have been repulsed, but his passion distracted me. I forgot to close my eyes, so I stared, unfocused at the nearness of him. I watched his eyelashes flutter as his tongue slipped into my mouth. It was a beautiful kiss, except for the salty blood. I started to pull away, but his hands held me firmly. Besides, his tongue started probing my mouth in a way I found irresistible, and I couldn't help but follow the familiar, erotic dance.

My hand trailed along the contours of the muscles of his back, reveling in their firmness, evident despite the fabric between us. Our lips parted, and met again. My fingers twisted through his hair, outlined the ridges of his earlobes. He kissed my nose, and then returned passionately to my mouth. I let my palms map out the dimensions of shoulders, waist, and back again.

We must have kissed and stroked each other for twenty minutes or more. There was passion in each touch, but no urgency. We were exploring each other like virgins, savoring every sensation.

All this without a single article of clothing removed. I

completely forgot I'd been bitten; I only remembered being kissed.

We reached the point when things either needed to go a lot further, or we needed to stop. Just before I was going to say something, Parrish pulled away from me and rolled onto his back.

'That should last you a couple of months, I'd think,' he said as if he'd just repaired a leaky window for me.

I stretched my injured arm experimentally. I pre-winced, but there was no pain other than the faint stretchy feeling of pushing against the tape and bandage of Sebastian's field dressing.

'Thanks,' I said, feeling sort of awkward now that everything was over.

The votive candles on my dresser top had nearly burned down, so I pulled myself upright to fetch more from the box of them I kept in my sock drawer. Parrish lay on the bed with his eyes closed and his arms behind his head. His expression was blank, but I thought I sensed a bit of wistfulness around the corners of his mouth.

'Where are you going to go?' I asked.

'I don't know, exactly. Depends on how deeply I need to bury myself. I might sleep for a while, or I might go home.'

I sat down on the edge of the bed. 'Sleep? You're talking about something other than a nap, right?'

He opened his eyes a crack. 'I'm talking about death sleep.' My confused expression must have made him explain, 'It's a kind of extended torpor. Older vampires use it to sleep out a

187

generation or two, so you don't have your neighbors wondering why you haven't grown old. You wake up and reinvent yourself. I hear it works like a charm.'

'You've never done it?'

He stretched is arms and yawned. 'Never longer than a year, and that was somewhat unintentional. I'd planned to death sleep only a couple of months, but the temptation to stay in torpor is surprisingly strong.'

Yikes. 'So,' I said, 'what's your plan, exactly?'

He sat up and leaned his back against my headboard. 'I have one?'

'I hope you do.'

'I thought I'd let the FBI or whoever make the first move, actually. I plan to leave as normal, and if they approach me, well, run.'

'Run? That's your plan?'

He smiled at me, as if to say, 'Clever, isn't it?'

'Parrish,' I felt the need to add, 'they have guns.'

'I'm actually rather hoping they'll shoot.'

'What? Why?'

'So I can die.'

It took a few seconds for Parrish's words to register as anything other than completely suicidal.

'I've found death avoids all those expensive legal fees,' he said. 'Not to mention life imprisonment, which would be rather short come sunrise.'

Incredulous, I stared at him in the flickering candlelight. 'Okay, your plan? It blows,' I said, standing up.

Parrish looked crestfallen. 'Why?'

'Do you think they're going to just walk away from your dead body?'

'No, they'll take me to the morgue. From which you will collect me.'

My voice squeaked. 'Me?'

'Yes. You can't let them cremate me or, worse, embalm. Then I'm truly fucked.'

'Why?' I asked. 'I mean, I get cremation; fire bad. But what happens if you're embalmed?'

'I'd die. Think about it, Garnet. A complete blood drain and then formaldehyde pumped in my veins? That'd kill just about anyone. Haven't you ever wondered why you don't see many post–Civil War vampires?'

I hadn't known there weren't any, but I was game. 'No why?'

'Embalming became standard practice for shipping the dead long distances during that time. Of course, now the majority of people are cremated. Plus with increased numbers of autopsies, and all the concrete vaults, there's really no way for a vampire to survive all the post-death violation.'

'Isn't embalming the law?'

'Not in Wisconsin. Why do you think there are so many vampires here?'

Were there a lot? Should Wisconsin change its motto from 'America's Dairyland' to 'America's Vampire Haven'?

Parrish continued lightly, as though thrilled to be conveying all of his intimate knowledge of postmortem laws. 'There are other states that don't require embalming, but thanks to the Amish, Wisconsin is surprisingly liberal regarding burial requirements.'

'Okay.' This conversation had gotten decidedly weird. 'This so isn't going to work. Wouldn't it be smarter for you to run and just keep on running?'

'I can't avoid this rap without dying, Garnet. At least here, with you, I can control what happens to my body afterward.'

'Why would they give your body to me? What if they do an autopsy?'

'If they shoot me dead, they know the cause of death. I highly doubt they'll autopsy in that case. As for releasing my body, you're the closest thing I have to next of kin. You'll just have to work your damnedest to convince Agent Dominguez that you're my fiancée.'

'This is crazy,' I said, starting to pace. The candles made my shadow do a jerky dance along the wall. 'I don't even have a ring.'

'I do.' Parrish's voice was low. 'Two, in fact. Matching. In my steamer trunk.'

Would the surprises never cease? 'You do?'

'Yes.' I waited for more information, but instead, he continued, 'With any luck, it'll fit. If not, we could wear them on chains around our necks. Might be smarter, since Dominguez never spotted a ring on your finger before.'

'This is crazy,' I repeated. 'Insane.'

'It is, and very dangerous.' Parrish ran his fingers through his hair. He looked surprisingly casual for someone talking about getting killed.

'Your sacrifice might not solve anything. Dominguez knows I was there that night.'

Parrish sat up straighter. 'What does he know exactly?'

'Everything.'

Parrish's fists clenched, and for a second I thought he might jump up and shake me. Instead, he snarled, 'Are you mad, woman? I told you not to confess to anything.'

'I didn't! Not out loud, anyway. He's psychic.'

That caused Parrish to pause. His anger morphed into confusion. 'Sorry? Did you say psychic?' When I nodded, he said, 'He read your mind?'

'He said I broadcast my guilt whenever I look at him.'

Parrish's lip twisted into an I-can-see-that grimace. 'But he has nothing else?'

'Well, he's seen Lilith.' I hid my embarrassment by pulling out a pair of jeans from my closet. They were my scary-Goth-girl pair – ripped and patched together in places with rows of safety pins. If I was going to have to try to pull off vampire fiancée later tonight, I thought I might try to look the part. I tossed them onto the bed to change into later. 'That's how I got shot.'

Lying back down, Parrish chewed on his lip. Meanwhile, I tossed a tight-fitting knit black top onto the pile. I added pentacle earrings and had started work on my makeup when he said, 'It'll never hold up.'

'What?' I asked, looking at my outfit.

'Lilith, in court, I mean. I doubt anyone would even believe an eyewitness account. He'd lose all credibility trying to explain Her. I think my plan could work. If he's built a case around me, let him have me.'

Even though I'd planned to dress for it, I didn't like the idea. 'Parrish, so much could go wrong. What if they don't shoot you?'

191

'I plan to provoke them. Trust me, I'm very good at making people want to see me dead.'

I was sure that was true.

Parrish stretched, as if waking, and pulled himself upright. 'We should go or they might be tempted to come in looking for me. Usually, I'm on the street well before now. I don't want them to find us together, because then they'll know you tipped me off.'

'Okay,' I said, because I didn't know what else I could say. Reminding him that his plan was stupid didn't seem to dissuade him, no matter how many times I repeated it.

'Let's get the rings, and I'll go.'

'I just want to change,' I insisted. He stepped out of the room, and I quickly got re-dressed. I took a few moments to remove all the sticky tape and gauze from my shoulder. It was strange to see only a small pink pucker on the flesh just below my collarbone.

After pulling on my shirt and stomping into a pair of combat boots, I grabbed a silver chain from my jewelry box and looped it around my neck. Blowing out the candles, I joined him just outside the door. We snuck down the way we'd come up. It was a lot easier for me to crawl without the pain in my shoulder.

'Someday,' I whispered to him as we crept down the stairs, 'you're going to tell me about that special friend of yours.'

Parrish shook his head. 'I don't kiss and tell.'

'So he was a lover!'

Parrish put a finger to his lips. 'If you must know, yes.' We reached the shared hallway. The floorboards creaked, so we moved quickly. Parrish glanced over his shoulder at me. 'Don't look at me like that. I've tried just about every flavor, you know. You tend to lose your inhibitions after a couple of centuries.'

I supposed you would. Of course, it was one thing to think about such things in theory, another to imagine them on a personal level. Had Sebastian been with a man? He'd been around for a thousand years, which made it seem much more likely. How did I feel about it? I couldn't decide. So, I distracted myself with the other question I'd been burning to ask, 'So, you have rings? Were you married?'

At the basement stairs, we straightened up, but Parrish didn't switch on any lights. I grasped for his hand and tried not to think about all the bugs that could be crawling around at my feet.

'Yes,' he said.

'When?'

Parrish didn't respond, but I could feel the sadness in his silence. I didn't press him further. When we reached his storage area, he let go of my hand. I got the sense he wanted to retrieve the rings privately, so I waited outside the door. Light from the street filtered in from the small window above the washing machine and softly illuminated the dusty strands of cobwebs between the pipes on the ceiling. As difficult as it was for me to imagine Parrish sleeping with a guy, I had much more trouble seeing him going down the aisle.

When he finally stepped out of the room, he had two white-gold rings in his hand.

I couldn't help but go all girly when he offered me one. 'Oh, Parrish, it's gorgeous!'

He seemed proud. 'Black Hills gold.'

Taking my hand in his, Parrish slipped the band on my ring finger. My heart did a strange flip-flop watching the intense solemnity with which he performed the traditional ritual. The ring was a size or so too big, but it glittered enchantingly against my skin. I splayed my fingers to admire it.

He started to put the other band on his own finger, but I closed my hand over his. 'Let me do it,' I said. At first I didn't think Parrish would let go, so I added. 'Please. I want to.'

Releasing the ring, he gave it to me. We faced each other, and I took his hand in mine. With trembling fingers I slipped the ring smoothly over his knuckle.

Parrish said nothing. I wasn't even sure he was breathing.

'Do you think, after all this is over . . . ? I mean, would it be okay if I kept this?' I asked. 'I know it's not mine, it's just that it would always remind me of you and if you have to be gone for a long time, I'd really like . . .' Before I could finish my thought, I felt his hand cup my chin and I was pulled into a soft but heartfelt kiss.

'I have to go, or I never will.'

I nodded. There were a thousand things I wanted to say, but the only thing that came out was, 'You should wear a coat. It's cold out.'

He gave me a fierce, final kiss.

When he released me it was sudden, almost like a push.

In absence of his arms, I held myself. He grabbed his jacket from a hook just inside the door. I watched him shrug into that worn, familiar leather and thought about all the times I had snuggled against it. 'When . . . ? I mean, you're not going to let them shoot you in my front yard, are you?'

'Actually, I'm going out the back,' he said with a crooked smile. When I didn't return it, he added, 'No, Garnet, my love, there won't be a shoot-out here. I suspect they'll follow me around downtown for a while and then decide to approach me. That's when I plan to get belligerent and run. I'll give chase for a while, draw them away, and make them convinced of my guilt and desperation.'

He looked at the stairs, but didn't make a move to leave.

'So, this is it, then,' I said.

'So it is.'

Pretending it needed adjusting, I reached out to fiddle with the zipper of his coat. 'I really wish that I . . . I'm going to miss you.'

Parrish said nothing, just shrugged out of my grip and walked away. Tears filled my eyes as I followed his progress up the steps. The screen door squeaked on rusty hinges, and then snapped shut. Cold October air brushed my cheek.

When a spider dropped into my hair, I brushed at the ticklish, silken strands of its web until I was certain it was elsewhere. I blinked in the darkness. I realized I'd been standing in the basement, staring at the door, for over twenty minutes. Wiping at my eyes with my knuckle, I headed back upstairs. I doubted I could sleep. I wanted to go somewhere, do something, but what?

I crept to the front hallway and peeked out the main door. I had to stand on my tiptoes to see out through the narrow leaded glass. I couldn't spot the van anywhere, but I wasn't convinced that didn't mean my apartment wasn't still being watched.

'They're totally gone, man.'

I jumped at the sound of the gravely, groggy voice.

Sticking out from the doorway to the first-floor apartment was a mop of stringy, sun-bleached blond hair. A thin, angular face erupted in odd bits of hair – dark sideburns and a scraggly soul patch. I could barely see his eyes, though given the strong herbal scent wafting from the door, I suspected his pupils would be wildly dilated.

'Dude,' he said slowly, as if I were the addled one. 'I'm telling you the feebs have vacated, vamoosed. It's all clear. Back to business as usual.' For some reason, this declaration made him laugh a scratchy sort of evil chuckle.

'Uh. Okay, thanks, neighbor,' I said.

He nodded sagely, flashed me the peace sign, and disappeared back into his hole.

Wow. I'd never actually spoken to my neighbor before. Weirdly, our brief, cryptic exchange actually made me more warmly disposed toward the guy. I shook my head and snuck back upstairs.

I thought about turning on the light when I got in, but I couldn't quite bring myself to trust stoner boy. As I headed to the bedroom to get a few more candles, I noticed my answering machine was an insistent red flash in the darkness.

The first call was from my mother – who complained about having to track down this number through a series of my old friends – wanting to let me know that they might have to sell the farm. I rolled my eyes at that, she went through this panic every other year, it seemed. Also, she added, a very nice-looking FBI fellow came to chat a couple of weeks ago, and I shouldn't worry because she and dad had 'kept things cool'.

Typical of my mother to consider the FBI visit as an after-thought. She wasn't being coy, she'd probably forgotten all about it ten seconds after the door closed on Dominguez. The truth? Let's just say more than the eggs were organic on my parents' farm.

My folks were also stoners.

Most of the time they were pretty high functioning. They successfully ran an egg ranch, after all. Having fried a lot of synapses over the years, interpersonal relationships, however, were not their forte. When everything went down last Halloween, I'd called to let my folks know I was alive but needed to keep it a secret. For my efforts I got a dazed 'cool,' and a suggestion that if I wanted to keep in touch I should use the P.O. box they'd set up in one of their more paranoid moments.

I didn't really write, except on birthdays. I loved them, but considered myself benignly estranged. Still, if Mom made the effort to call, I should return the favor just to let her know that I was okay – well, I thought, maybe I should wait a bit to make sure that was true.

The next several calls were from Sebastian, at least I assumed they were. It sounded like his angry growl.

I grabbed the phone and hit speed dial. When he picked up, I blurted, 'Don't be mad. Parrish is gone. For good.'

Sebastian said nothing.

The sound of my own breathing was loud in the receiver, and it made me wonder who could be listening in. 'Look, maybe you could come over later?'

'I could come now.'

'No,' I said. 'I know you're going to think I'm shutting you out again, but . . . I need, oh, Great Goddess,' I said, hating myself for having to resort to therapy speak, 'I need time to process, okay?'

'Sure,' he said, and I wished I could see his expression as he said it because his voice was either resolved or flat. 'I respect that.'

'Listen, I want to tell you about this,' I said sincerely. 'But, not on the phone, you know?'

He laughed softly. 'I lived through the sixties. I know.'

I wasn't entirely sure what that meant, but I liked the smile I could hear in his voice. 'How about you come over in a couple of hours?'

'I'll be there.'

'Great,' I said, and we hung up.

I kicked around the apartment for a few aimless minutes, then decided what I really needed was a walk. Grabbing my long leather coat, I headed down the stairs and out the door. After checking down the block for cars or vans that looked government-issue, I decided I'd try to find some place to eat. It was after ten, so my options were becoming limited. I could always head back toward State Street and do bar food. As a vegetarian, that sometimes meant I got the onion rings and pretended I didn't know they'd been fried in animal fat. Completely ignoring my politics, my stomach growled.

198

The residential streets were quiet. As I passed two-story Victorians, bright interior lights showed me glimpses of other people's lives – IKEA furniture and abstract prints; flickering bluish light of a television set; warm yellow walls, folksy pottery and handcrafted bookshelves.

I kicked at the leaves that had gathered at the edge of the sidewalk, making them rustle. The wind was crisp, the kind of temperature that snapped your eyes wide open and brought a blush to your cheeks. Dogs barked through cedar fences. A stray cat slunk low under a parked car.

Somewhere in the distance I heard the roar of a motorcycle, and I thought about Parrish. Beneath my shirt, the gold ring felt cold and smooth against my skin. I hoped his crazy plan worked. What if the FBI never thought to call me? I mean, unless he managed to croak out, 'For Goddess's sake, call my fiancée, Garnet,' why would they think of me? As soon as I got somewhere with a phone, I'd call Dominguez and tell him Parrish had run off and I was worried he'd do something stupid (which he had), and then maybe, just maybe, he'd get word to me if – when Parrish pretended to take a swan dive.

Taped to the porch window of one of the houses I passed was a Dollar Store cardboard version of a vampire, complete with widow's peak and blood dripping from his fangs. He stared at me with dark-rimmed eyes.

I should have laughed at the ridiculousness of the thing, but instead I just felt sad. 'Don't get yourself *really* killed,' I told it.

'Ha. Ha.'

The figure of a crow perching atop the streetlamp was just barely discernible in the evening gloom.

I stopped walking to stare at it accusingly. 'You've been watching me.'

It glided down into the soft pool of light and hopped onto a pile of leaves left on the boulevard. Cocking its head, it gave me that inscrutable, impenetrable, beady-eyed stare crows have perfected.

'You creep me out. Deeply,' I told it, intending to continue on my way to the bar.

It fluttered ahead of me to the next streetlamp. It waited for me to catch up, then took off to a street I hadn't intended to go down. Sitting where I could see it, it cawed noisily.

Clearly, I was supposed to follow it.

I hesitated. I had no idea whose 'side' this crow was on. That it was a tool of the voodoo priest seemed pretty likely, but it hadn't done anything specifically to harm me, yet. I was curious enough that I wanted to know where it would lead me, but sensible enough to think maybe dinner and beer was the better idea.

The crow noticed my indecision and hopped impatiently. I shook my head at it and pointed in the direction of my dinner. Taking a broad jump into the air, it swooped just past my head, making me duck. If I didn't comply, the damned thing was going to herd me like some demented, winged sheepdog.

'All right! All right!' I told it. 'I'll go.'

We played the streetlight game for several blocks. Then, I thought I lost sight of it when we came to Regent. A gas station's floodlights cast a surreal brightness over the entire corner of the block. I scanned for black feathers between the brightly colored pumps and advertisements for cigarettes and beer. I squinted at the sloped roof, but all I saw was dark sky.

Not knowing what else to do, I kept walking. Just past the driveway and outside of the range of the service station's artificial daylight, the crow cawed, startling me. It perched on a bus-stop sign. I paused, waiting for it to show me where to go next. As I looked up at it, it started to preen its pinfeathers.

I glanced at the bench and then at the bird. 'You want me to take the bus?'

The crow bobbed its whole body in an affirmative.

Well, I thought as I sat down, I guess I should be relieved the voodoo sorcerer wasn't my neighbor. The chill of the plastic bench slats penetrated through a rip in the thigh of my jeans. I wondered how long I would give this silly adventure before I took my chances against the crow's beak and talons.

With the squeak and hiss of well-worn brakes, the bus announced its arrival. I fished the appropriate change out of my purse and got on. The bus driver eyed me as though he thought my kind was trouble. Even so, he managed a pleasant enough greeting, which I returned, as I found a seat near the front. The doors sighed shut. Through the window, I watched the crow take wing.

When the bus lurched back into the flow of traffic, I wondered how I was supposed to know where to get off. We sped past darkened strip malls, murky bars, and flickering neon signs on tattoo parlors. I pressed my nose to the window. I thought I spotted the flat expanse of wings soaring through the parking lot of a chain grocery store, but I couldn't be sure.

What was I doing here, anyway? Parrish was off doing Goddess knew what to try to get himself killed. I wanted to be *there*, not riding around on a dingy bus headed south of the Beltline. What I'd really rather be doing was helping Parrish somehow. I felt so useless, yet so responsible for all his trouble. Though I wasn't much for prayer, I decided to say a quick one to Athena. I'd felt Her presence touch me in the past when I was desperately in need of protection, and Her association with justice seemed appropriate somehow.

'Shield him,' I pleaded. 'Take him under your aegis.'

I let out a breath, hoping to calm myself. Instead, my feet tapped, restless to be doing something, going somewhere. Oh, fuck it, I thought, sitting back against the metal headrest. I'm getting off at the next restaurant I see – even if it's a McDonald's.

There was only one other person on the bus. A woman wearing a gray, hooded sweater sat a few seats in front of me on the opposite side. Her head nodded in rhythm to each bump and jostle, as if she were asleep. On impulse, I squinted at her. In the weird too-bright/not-quite-light-enough glow of the bus, it was difficult to read her aura. One thing was for damn certain, there wasn't enough of it. She was dead. Or nearly so.

Zombie.

Well. That was certainly convenient.

I glanced at the window, searching for the crow again. All I saw was my own reflection against the darkened glass.

Sitting forward in my seat, I rested my forearms against the seats in front of me. I buried my nose in leather sleeves, worrying. I'd originally assumed the crow was a spy. I'd known plenty of Witches, particularly those who practiced shamanism, who could, in a sense, become completely merged with an animal for short periods. Watching and Seeing, however, were two different things. To be able to sense the pattern of the universe, to predict that the zombie would be on this bus and arrange for me to also be there . . . well, that was the sort of thing I usually chalked up to the Goddess Herself.

You know, coincidence. Destiny. Fate.

I suddenly got that gut rattling sense that I was *supposed* to be here and that if the crow worked for anyone, it was for Her.

The zombie dinged the stop-request strip. She stood up very deliberately as the bus jerked to a halt. We were in a neighborhood I didn't recognize. The doors opened in front of a concrete-block, industrial apartment complex. As the zombie shuffled out the front, I had plenty of time to slip out the back door.

The bus took off with a warm waft of diesel fumes. I loitered beside a scraggly ginkgo. The tree's trunk was only as big around as a soda can, and it wobbled precariously when I leaned against it. I tried to look inconspicuous, but I needn't have bothered. The zombie never even glanced in my direction; she just plodded forward one laborious step at a time. I followed, and quickly realized that by walking my normal speed I'd outpace her in a matter of seconds. When I tried to match her gait, it was patently clear I was trailing her.

I thought about trying to act drunk, but when I tried it, I

just felt silly, and then I just looked like some kind of wino detective.

I wasn't even sure it mattered. So far, the zombie paid no attention to me. For all I knew, I could just walk up to her and strike up a conversation as she led me back to the voodoo priest's lair. If that was even where she was going.

Bits of broken glass crunched underfoot as we walked. The sidewalks were concrete and asphalt all the way to the curb. A few holes had been cut for mountain ash saplings that, despite the wrought-iron grate surrounding their trunks, were heavy with clusters of berries. The streetlights had become the kind you find on the highway, with halogen bulbs that gave everything a kind of greenish tint and threw elongated shadows at my feet.

She turned, cutting across an elementary school playground. I hung back by the monkey bars as she continued across the crabgrass-and-sandbur-speckled baseball field. Beyond the chain-link fence, the streetlamps became scarce. I dashed across the hard-packed ground before the darkness swallowed her.

The houses were all postwar Cape Cods packed together in tight rows. Lawn maintenance, however, appeared to be optional. Dandelion was the neighborhood flower of choice, and trash trees like mulberry and buckthorn grew in abundance, crowding walkways and foundations.

Even so, occasionally one of the residences would be decked out for Halloween and be otherwise clearly well loved, featuring neat little gardens and painted concrete gnomes. It was into one of these that the zombie turned. Two pink flamingos guarded a raised flowerbed, and bright plastic orange garbage bags with jack-o'-lantern faces ringed the house.

I took note of the address and kept walking.

Circling the block I tried to decide what the hell to do.

I considered the bold approach. You know, the insane one, where I just walked up to the door and knocked and the voodoo sorcerer answered. What I imagined happening next tended to involve hurled accusations and me on the receiving end of some extremely bad-ass spell.

After all, I always considered voodoo to be in a league of its own, and, at the very least, not something I personally ever wanted to mess with, and this from a woman who'd made a bond with Lilith, Queen of Demons.

Yeah, I thought, as the gnarled shadows of a buckthorn hedge passed over me, going home and ordering a pizza is sounding better and better. Even so, I kept my eyes trained on the house as I passed it. Which is probably why I bumped smack into William.

9

Sagittarius

Key Words:
Philosophical and Pushy

'What the hell are you doing here?' we asked simultaneously.

I stepped back a pace and crossed my arms, giving William my best 'boss' stare, hoping he'd cave under its no-doubt withering effect and start talking. The truth of the matter was that I didn't really want to start off our conversation with 'I followed a crow here, you?'

'I live here,' he said, slipping his hands into the pockets of his low-riding jeans. The waist was so far down, only the tips of his fingers fit.

I looked at the house we were standing in front of. Pink flamingos. 'You live *here*?'

William shrugged. 'Mostly.'

Like the car was 'kind of' his. 'Your girlfriend,' I said, suddenly remembering the voodoo priestess. 'Does Izzy know?'

He chewed on a cuticle. 'She should. She introduced us.' At my blank stare, he added, 'Maureen is Izzy's cousin.'

'Izzy's cousin is the voodoo priestess who's been making all the zombies?'

William laughed. 'Zombies? I have no idea what you're talking about. Sure, she practices voodoo, but it's benign.'

'Ha,' said the crow as it landed in the silver maple on the boulevard; I tended to agree. Though I loved him dearly, William was hardly the best judge of character, especially when it came to girlfriends.

'Oh,' I said, trying to cover my skepticism with a light tone. 'Cool.'

William's shoulders seemed to relax, and I caught the glint of a smile in the moonlight. 'Yeah, I've been learning a lot from her.'

I didn't even want to touch that.

'So, uh, you never did tell me what you were doing here,' William asked. 'You're kind of a long way from home.'

A half a dozen vaguely plausible lies flitted through my head, but this was William. Looking into that earnest face, I had to tell him the truth. 'A bird led me here.'

'Aw,' said the crow, as if it had hoped for a better answer, or maybe it objected at being identified as merely a bird.

The vehemence of William's response surprised me. 'Those fucking crows.'

'Argh,' the crow replied and took off in a loud flapping of wings.

'Yeah, and don't come back,' William muttered. To me, 'You see how it is? They persecute us!'

Crows, it's true, generally have a bad reputation. They often get associated with destructive and/or battlefield Gods and

Goddesses because they eat dead things, carrion. It doesn't help that they're smart, crafty, and have a fondness for other people's pretty, shiny things. *But* – crows are smart, some of the most intelligent birds. They also have a number of surprising traits, including expressions of grief. They (and their cousins, ravens) are trickster Gods in certain Native American myths. The Goddess Hecate, Queen of Witches, is sometimes associated with a crow. So it unnerved me to hear William curse with such anger at the crow.

And it made me more and more convinced that whatever this Maureen woman was teaching William, it wasn't good.

I wanted to punch her for corrupting William.

Trying very hard to keep all that out of my voice, I asked, 'You're having trouble with crows?'

'Let's just say you're not the first person that damn bird brought here.'

I was glad for the darkness because I had no idea what William would read in my expression otherwise. I wondered what happened to the others. Were they all Witches, like me? They'd have to, at the very least, be the sort to willingly follow a crow across town, which made them either crazy or some kind of sensitive.

'I can hardly go outside without being dive-bombed,' William said. 'And you saw it, if I even mention my girl-friend—' William twitched, looking up at the sky.

'Doesn't all this seem like a bad sign?' I couldn't stop myself from pointing out what seemed to me to be obvious.

William's shoulders straightened. 'Clearly, the magic we're practicing here bothers somebody.'

Yeah, I thought, Somebody with a capital 'S'. 'It's possible that maybe your girlfriend is . . .' I didn't get a chance to finish my sentence. The porch light flicked on and the screen door opened with the squeak of rusty hinges.

'Billy, honey? Is that you?' Despite the warmth in her tone, her voice made both of us jump in surprise. 'Who are you talking to?'

William stepped a little closer to the porch. 'Sorry I'm late, Mo,' he said. 'My friend Garnet's here.'

'The one you went to rescue? Cool. Come on in,' she said to me. 'We're just sitting down to a late supper. Care to join us?'

I couldn't really see Maureen, silhouetted as she was by the light from her front room, but her voice was pure Southern charm. I could see why William/Billy-honey had fallen for it, since I surprised myself by saying, 'Sounds delightful. If you're sure you don't mind?'

'The more the merrier, I always say,' she said, and for some reason this made her laugh in a throaty, sexual way.

As I followed William up the sidewalk, my skin tightened along the back of my neck. The fly entered the spider's den.

Maureen, or Mo, as she insisted several times that I call her, was, in point of fact, gorgeous. It was irritating, actually, how much she looked like a model. She had the same mocha-colored, flawless complexion that always made Izzy look so much like Nefertiti, but her hair was a fascinating concoction of tight, blond corkscrews that fell just past her shoulders. Even at this hour and in the comfort of her own home, she wore a form-fitting tube dress in a glittery gold as equally artificial as her dye job, but just as striking. Really, Mo should have looked trashy prancing around in that dress and heels among the shag carpeting and linoleum, but somehow she pulled it off. Maybe it was her height or her slender build, but she almost seemed regal as she motioned for us to take our places around the oak dining-room table. I noted with no small amount of surprise that a place had already been set for me.

The whole house smelled of curry. A man – another lover? – came out of the kitchen bearing a big kettle, which he held with thick potholders in each hand. I looked at what I'd assumed to be an extra plate. Ah, I realized, this is his.

He smiled at me, and, once the pot was safely deposited in the center of the table, offered a hand.

'I'm Ethan,' he said, as I shook. 'Secondary.'

'Garnet,' I said, resisting the urge to say, 'Primary,' since I had no idea what he meant by his comment.

'I'll get another plate.' Ethan was what my mother would classify as a 'nice young man'. In his early twenties, he was thin and reedy. His hair and eyes were the color of sandstone, and he had a shy, reserved nature about him that made me picture him instantly as an accountant or an Episcopal minister.

Could I see myself replicating this scene with Sebastian and his ghouls? Would I ever be able to politely ask for the butter from someone I knew was doing my boyfriend? How awkward would it be when sexual innuendos started bantering around the table?

I shook my head. I had to give William some credit; he dealt so maturely with all of this.

211

William inspected the contents of the ladle before helping himself to a large portion. From what I could tell, we were having some kind of curry fish stew. Ethan excused himself to fetch freshly baked bread from the oven.

When Ethan placed a slice of crusty French bread on my plate, Mo leaned close to me to whisper conspiratorially, 'You see why Ethan's a keeper.'

I smiled politely, but I couldn't shake the feeling that eating anything in the house of the voodoo priestess was an extraordinarily bad idea. Too bad my rumbling stomach couldn't keep its opinion to itself.

Mo laughed. 'You sound ravenous, darling.'

I didn't like the use of the familiar pet name, especially since it was a favorite of Parrish's, nor did I like the lingering way her hand touched my forearm. 'I kind of skipped dinner,' I explained, so as not to seem rude.

'Well, how fortunate you ended up here.'

William snorted, and then completely busted me. 'Crow brought her.'

I kicked his shins hard under the table.

Mo frowned at me. 'I see,' she said coolly. She arched her frosted eyebrow to give me an once-over that set my teeth on edge and my Spidey sense tingling.

Somehow I knew she'd checked my aura. 'Yeah, well,' I said, 'see anything you like?'

The lurid smile returned. 'Oh, darling, you have no idea.'

Lilith tightened across my stomach. I could almost hear Her growl.

Ethan sucked in a breath. A cat, which had been lounging

on a nearby radiator, jumped up and hissed. Mo crossed herself.

And William obliviously poked at the fish and potatoes. 'You know it totally annoys me when you flirt with new people when Ethan and I are sitting right here,' he said, his eyes focused on his plate.

Mo laughed as though William's complaint delighted her. 'You're so cute when you're jealous.'

I looked at William. He gritted his teeth, and a blush bloomed in angry spots across his cheekbones. 'I hardly get that much time with you as it is.'

Oops. Then again, maybe William's maturity was a façade.

'I'm not exactly taking away from our time together by flirting,' Mo countered.

'Actually,' William said, meeting her gaze hotly, 'you are. Whenever there's fresh meat, I might as well be invisible.'

Well, William certainly had all our attention right now. I kept feeling like maybe I should excuse myself from this domestic squabble, but I was wedged between the dining-room table and a buffet. The physical act of getting out would cause a stir. Then again, maybe that's just what this party needed.

I pushed myself up from the table. 'I just forgot. There's somewhere I need to be.'

'Let me show you to the door,' Ethan said, standing up nearly as fast as I had.

Before either William or Mo could open their mouths to protest, we were halfway across the living room to the door.

'Just another day in paradise,' Ethan said under his breath. 'It was nice to meet you.'

I nodded, distracted by a sudden thought: where was the zombie I saw go in here? 'The meal was delicious,' I said, though I'd barely had more than a taste. 'Did you cook it yourself?'

He shook his head. 'I'm just the bread baker.'

'Mo made it?'

'Look, I can get you the recipe if you'd like.' He sounded a little irritated by my questions.

'No, that's okay. Just curious.'

'Yeah, well, I have to go mediate World War III in there,' he said, jerking his head in the direction of the dining room.

I gave him a sympathetic smile. 'Why do you put up with it?'

'Are you kidding? I live for it. It's better drama than anything on TV.'

I wished him luck and said good-bye. I walked out toward the street and kept going until I heard the screen door slam. I walked another few steps before turning around and edging my way toward the back of the house.

I snuck around a neighbor's hedge and peered into the kitchen window of Mo's house. All I saw was an empty kitchen filled with Holstein kitsch. Where had the zombie gone?

The other window revealed a fairly ordinary bedroom. A lamp had been left on near the bed, so I could see most of the room clearly. Mo, it seemed, had a penchant for gold and purple, as the bed was decked out in blankets and pillows of those colors. One wall held a shelf of creepy/cute stuffed animals, like the nearly realistic dog plushies with oversized heads, but still no sign of the zombie.

Where was she?

Tall boards fenced in the backyard. I scouted along the perimeter, looking for a knothole or some other way to see in. It was too dark for me to make out anything much, other than a concrete slab patio, a picnic table, and a gas grill.

The garage was detached, modern, and could easily fit two cars. It was almost as large as the house and completely windowless. Feeling a little guilty, I stepped over a calf-high chicken-wire fence and through some mums into the neighboring yard. I crept back to the alley along Mo's fence.

The bulb in the alley streetlight had been smashed, so the only light came from the moon. Brown tubs and tin cans of garbage lined the alleyway in clusters. The scent of something rotten lingered in the air. Then I heard it – the rustle of feet, and a low, sad moan.

Mo kept her zombies in the garage?

I tried the lift handle on the roll-up door. No surprise, it was locked.

I felt a sharp poke in the gut. Lilith reminded me there hasn't been a lock made yet that could stop a Goddess.

With my hand on the latch, I took a deep, slow breath, centering myself. I felt a tremor move up my torso to my shoulder and arm. Heat poured along my veins. The power felt like the rush of a drug hitting my system. Ah, it had been far too long since the last time I called on Lilith. I let the heady sensation carry me away. I fell into a black, welcoming oblivion.

When my eyes refocused, the handle was in the upright, open position. Tendrils of steam drifted from the back of my hand. Experimentally, I tugged on the door. It rolled upward easily. Lifting it over my head, I gave it a push and it continued to the ceiling.

Inside, zombies surrounded the black VW bug.

There must have been a dozen of them. They sat on folding chairs with their hands in their laps. They stared straight ahead, unblinking. I recognized the hockey jock, the deli waitress, and the hooded bus rider. None of them spoke or even registered my presence. Piled in the corner next to a tool bench was a collection of spades, pick axes, and shovels, all crusted with mud. There seemed to be a pile of something on the table. I took a step closer, my eyes trained on the zombies. None of them moved, though I noticed a number of eyes tracking me.

It was darker inside the garage, and much smellier. I held my breath and tried to determine what exactly was on the table, but my eyes failed. I reached out a hand and found myself holding rings and paper with the texture of and feel of currency.

A zombie moaned. I dropped what was in my hand. I wasn't sure I wanted to be touching it anyway. Given what Dominguez had told me about the money the zombie passed to me, it was probably antique, which, given its proximity to the muddy shovels, might mean it was plundered from someone's grave. To that, all I could say was, 'Ewww.'

I was getting William out of that house. Now.

Backing out slowly, I reached around by the edge of the door until I found the pull. I shut the door on the zombies. The latch hung at an angle that clearly suggested it had been broken, and I tried to straighten it a couple of times before I had to give up. No one was going to steal anything out of this garage. Not with all those zombies sitting there.

After pulling out an earring and tucking it into my pocket, I made a mad dash for the front door. I banged with my fist until I noticed a bell. Mo answered. 'You're back? Is something wrong?'

'I think I lost my earring,' I said. 'I got to the bus stop and realized it was missing. It's probably not here, but – do you mind if I just check?' I touched the remaining skull bead with my fingertip. 'These are favorites. Sentimental, really.'

Mo didn't even look at me twice; she totally bought it. 'Sure thing, honey,' she said. 'I know what it's like.'

When I got inside, she gave me an appraising glance that made me feel almost naked, and a smile that said you-dropped-it-on-purpose-to-come-back-here,-didn't-you?

'Uh,' I said, feeling a blush creep up my ears. 'I'll just check around on the floor.'

'You do that,' she said, eyeing my backside.

William came out of the kitchen with a dishtowel slung over his shoulder. When he noticed me, he had the decency to look chagrined. 'Oh, hey, Garnet.'

'She lost her earring,' Mo supplied.

'Uh, let me help,' he said. He flashed Mo a wide-eyed look that seemed to imply he wanted some alone time with me.

Surprisingly, she obliged. 'I'll be in the kitchen,' she said, with a disappointed last look at me.

The swinging door hadn't even shut before William said, 'I'm sorry, Garnet. I completely gave into my baser instincts.

It's hard to shake the lizard brain, you know? It's disgustingly instinctual – this whole desire to protect a mate from all other competitors.'

Hello, yikes? 'Uh, yeah, sure,' I said.

'Seriously, Garnet. I acted like a Neanderthal . . . okay, actually Homo sapiens, which I technically am, since Neanderthals were a completely different species, but the point is, I'm sorry.'

I spotted the salt and pepper shakers on the buffet. I could never remember which one was supposed to be the salt, the one with two holes or many. So, I grabbed them both.

'Are you stealing the silver?' William asked incredulously.

'No. Borrowing.' I tucked the shakers into my pocket.

'Is that a euphemism? Because if you need cash or something I could help you out.'

'I don't need money, William.' I leaned in conspiratorially. 'You need to come with me to the back alley. Tell Mo I enlisted you to help find the earring outside. Bring a flashlight.'

'What's this about?' he whispered back. Though his tone was suspicious, his eyes glittered with excitement. 'Is this some kind of vampire thing? Oh, or maybe the FBI?'

'Better,' I assured him.

He smiled. He was in.

As I waited by the door, Ethan hunted up a flashlight for William. 'Are you sure you don't want us to help?' he asked. 'Four of us could cover more ground.'

'That's sweet of you, but I don't want to, uh, interrupt anything.' I gave Mo a little wink to let her know what I thought she planned to be up to.

Mo, however, misinterpreted. 'Four is always better,' she

grinned. Then wrapping an arm around William and Ethan, 'Think of how grateful she'd be if we found it for her, boys.'

I tried again. 'This earring really is important to me,' I said. 'If I don't find it here, I'm going to keep looking.' Not stop to have sex with you, I added silently. 'I'll have to phone the bus company and retrace my steps.'

'I'm pretty sure it's somewhere nearby,' Ethan said, completely unhelpfully. 'I remembered you having them both at dinner.'

'Oh, okay,' I said, because what else could I say? They were so damned insistent. 'Look, why don't William and I get started outside since we've got the flashlight, and you two check in here and meet us when you're done?'

Finally, it was agreed.

We weren't going to have much time to free the zombies. I grabbed William's hand, as Ethan and Mo discussed the best way to make quick work of checking the floor. 'Come on,' I said to William.

'Hey,' William said as I tugged him through the brambles. 'Your arm seems a lot better.'

'I . . . I got a little blood transfusion from a vampire.'

I heard the vacuum cleaner start up as we passed the dining-room window.

'A blood transfusion? Doesn't that usually involve a lot of IVs and other specialized equipment?'

'Honestly, you'd be surprised how easy it is to accidentally swallow some blood.'

'Not really,' William agreed. 'Just the other day I got spattered with some chicken blood and . . .'

'I don't really need to know details.'

'Right,' William said with a nod. 'Anyway, I understand how it happens.'

Not unless that chicken lost its life during some really nice kissing on the bed, I didn't think so. Then, what he implied caught up with me. 'You killed a chicken? Like, for a ritual?'

William peered at me in the darkness, the round circles of his glasses glinting in the flash of a passing car's headlights. 'I thought you didn't want to know.'

We stood in front of the garage. 'I don't. I'm just surprised you'd kill a chicken. I mean, that seems kind of cruel.'

William leaned against the siding. He crossed his arms in front of his chest. 'I've been doing a lot of thinking about magic since that day that you showed me that vampires are real.' William's eyes focused on the wooden light pole on the opposite side of the asphalt, but I could tell that his mind was elsewhere. 'Creation and destruction are linked, Garnet. Nothing lives without killing something. Look around,' he said, pointing to the browning tendrils of ivy clinging to the neighbor's fence, the flies buzzing around the garbage cans. 'It's totally obvious. Flowers might look pretty, but they're leeching nutrients from the soil to live. We have to consume. Death is the only real magic.'

I pursed my lips. Of course, that was only half the equation. If life came from death, then it followed that from death came life. I doubted I could convince William to expand his philosophy in the amount of time we had before Mo and Ethan came out to find us. 'Look, you can be a nihilist all you want,' I said. 'Just tell me you weren't involved in this.' I jerked up the garage door with a dramatic shove. The zombies didn't even blink.

Neither did William.

10

Capricorn

Key Words:
Serious and Fatalistic

'Look, William, zombies!' I said, gesturing wildly at the dozen or so glassy-eyed living dead sitting around Mo's black VW Beetle.

He continued to be unimpressed.

'Look,' I said again, though this time with a growing sense of dread. 'Zombies, William,' I thought maybe if I repeated myself one more time, William would suddenly realize that these moaning, shifting animated corpses were all the proof he needed that his girlfriend was bad, bad news. Then, he'd thank me for opening his eyes and join me in the quest to destroy her and her evil ways.

Only it wasn't happening that way at all.

And now I heard the sounds of people coming through the backyard, and Mo saying, 'I thought I saw them heading out back.'

William turned and gave me a look. It wasn't a nice one, and suddenly it dawned on me that he was completely under the sorceress's spell. It wasn't like William to be a nihilist, kill chickens, curse crows, or even toss myrrh in the face of FBI agents. She'd possessed him somehow.

'Oh, William,' I said sadly.

'Get in the garage,' he said, as Mo and Ethan came through the gate to stand behind me.

Mo gave me a little shove in that direction. I stumbled, but didn't quite step past the threshold. I glanced at the pick ax and shovel, thinking to use them as a weapon, only Ethan – who had seemed so nice – grabbed both. 'You heard the man.'

They were closing in around me, but I tried to make a break for it anyway. William grabbed me. I was startled by his wiry strength. And his utter betrayal.

'William,' I said to him. 'This isn't you.'

In the movies, he might have crumbled in his resolve just a little to show me that the true William was still in there some-where, but he didn't. He just gave me a ruthless push that sent me sprawling against the hood of the Beetle and shut the door with a slam.

In the dark, the smell of rotting meat filled my nostrils, threat-ening to gag me. I held my breath, comforting myself with the knowledge I'd earlier broken the lock. That was, until I heard the scrape of the shovel – or maybe the pick ax – being hooked over the handle and then propped snugly against the door.

Great.

Outside, I heard words being exchanged. Something about whether or not I had a cell, and who was going to clean up in the morning.

Clean up?

When a folding chair clattered to the floor, I squeaked. A moan followed by shuffling, then more sounds of chairs being pushed aside.

The zombies were going to eat me? Did they really do that?

When I felt a hand touch my elbow and smelled fetid breath far too close to my face, I decided I didn't want to wait around to find out. I started screaming, but realized pretty quickly there wasn't much point to it. My noises didn't deter the zombies, made my throat scratchy, and probably couldn't be heard very well beyond the immediate vicinity of the garage. Plus, it was the middle of the night. Who, besides me, would be out wandering this late?

I grabbed the shakers from my pocket and waved them around menacingly. The sharp scent of pepper hit my nose, and I sneezed. The zombies followed suit. Well, I thought, this wasn't my intended effect, but maybe the sneezes would keep them off balance. I held my breath and continued to dash salt and pepper in the air.

The one who had ahold of me let go, although he didn't seem terribly deterred by my random condiment waving. In fact, it seemed zombies could see pretty well in the dark, because one of them managed to grab the shaker right out of my hand.

Okay, Plan B.

I tossed the remaining shaker at the nearest zombie. Then, with all the speed I possessed, I clambered on top of the Bug. The rounded hood and sloped windshield made my feet slip, but the combat boots had good traction. I soon found myself crouching on top of the car, my head scraping the rafters. Feeling around the dusty, rough wood for a grip, I hooked my arms and tried to haul myself all the way up. Upper arm strength had never been my forte, having flunked chin-ups in gym class and, despite Parrish's transfusion, my shoulder was not up to full strength. So, I flailed around, secretly kind of glad no one could see how stupid I looked in the dark. As a bonus side effect, my lame efforts apparently ended up landing a few good face kicks to the zombies who were in hot pursuit. Eventually, I was able to blindly use someone's head to give myself an extra boost to swing my legs up and over.

Now that I was perched on the rafters, I discovered the boards were actually quite narrow and of dubious structural integrity. In other words, they shook under my weight. Of course, now that I was up I wondered what to do next.

From the sliding, thudding noises coming from below, I suspected that the zombies were none too agile and were finding the slick, curved vehicle somewhat difficult to climb up. That, at least, bought me some time.

I tried looking around and all I saw was dark, dark, and even more dark. Except there, just ahead, was a patch of slightly less blackness. I blinked. Some kind of mirage caused by desperation? I strained to make sense of what I saw. Further inspection revealed a square section that appeared downright gray. A painted-over window? Could I be so lucky?

Maybe. Only now I had to pray that it was big enough for me to squeeze through, and not, say, facing the house full of bad guys from whom I was attempting to escape. Not too much to ask, was it?

Except getting there involved moving across the rafters in the dark. I put my hand out, attempting to get a feel of the beams. The rough wood and exposed nails scratched my palms, and I found myself trying to remember when my last tetanus shot had been. The moans below were becoming more like howls of desperate animals, which reminded me I had bigger things to worry about than lockjaw.

I leaned forward, testing my weight on the beams. I did *not* like the way everything seemed to sway when I shifted up onto all fours. I kept my eyes trained on the gray patch and the possibility of freedom. I could do this. It was all just a matter of one trembling, inching movement after another.

The narrow width of the rafters cut into my knees sharply. But I had the phantom sensation of hands reaching up to try to grab me, followed by the real sensation of someone putting weight on the boards I was trying to balance on. There was a deep creak, a kind of bending, straining noise that sounded a lot like a board before it split, that made me scurry the rest of the way.

I pressed a hand against the surface of the gray and felt the cool smoothness of glass. I pushed harder, hoping against hope that the window would just pop out. When it didn't, I felt for a latch. Finding one, I grappled with it, only to discover it had been painted shut.

The zombies had gone quiet.

I didn't like that at all. I got the creepy-crawly feeling of eyes on me, like the steel-hard gaze of a predator who has finally cornered its prey.

No time to screw around, I decided. I shifted so that I could put my combat boots up against the pane, then I reached for Lilith. I felt her heat rise, molten and sweet. Power flowed through my veins like an avalanche of lava.

The window popped off like a cork. It flew across the alley and crashed against the neighbor's garage, filling the night with the explosive sound of shattering glass.

Oops. I guess Mo was going to know I'd made an escape. I wedged myself out the window, feet first. I could feel the cool air of freedom through the rips in my jeans.

I was ready to thumb my nose at the approaching zombie, except my butt stuck. My hips, it appeared, were just a few inches too wide for the window.

And I could feel the rafters shaking. The enterprising zombie who'd managed to scale the car was closing the gap. Soon, it'd be close enough to bite me.

I tried wiggling, and that only seemed to make things tighter. If I didn't die tonight, I was going on a diet starting tomorrow. No more chocolate ice cream when I'm feeling depressed.

I smelled zombie breath.

That was, if I lived.

I gave the zombie a smack with my hand. Okay, it was meant to be a manly punch, but my awkward position and complete lack of hand-to-hand combat skills meant it was really more of a biff across the cheeks. It snarled, grabbed my head, and slammed my face down into the rafters.

Ouch.

Lilith rumbled across my stomach as if to say, 'Lemme at 'em.' I was seriously considering unleashing Her completely, despite the fact that I was more than a bit squeamish about killing zombies. Even though I suspected they were already dead. Then I felt a tug on my ankles.

Thinking it was probably Mo or one of her henchpersons, I gave whomever it was a swift kick.

'Damn it, Garnet, it's me,' came Sebastian's irritated voice. Never had someone so pissed off sound so wonderful.

I stopped kicking and let him take hold of my legs. I tried to think skinny thoughts, and he gave a mighty pull. I felt rotted wood give, my hips and shoulders bruise, and then suddenly I was falling onto the hood of Sebastian's black 1934 Cord Phaeton sedan.

Just as I was starting to enjoy the feeling of being tangled up with Sebastian, the zombie tumbled out on top of us. Then, like some kind of undead lemming, another one started to follow.

The zombie grabbed ahold of my waist and started to squeeze. As I pushed and clawed against him, I found myself noticing that he looked like he had probably been good-looking once. This guy struck me more as a swimmer. He had the body type, I thought, as a curtain started to descend in front of my vision. I heard the crack of breaking bones and assumed they were my ribs.

Then, quite amazingly, I could breathe again. Swimmer-zombie lay limply against the garage door, his arms dangling uselessly at odd, unnatural angles. Sebastian caught the next zombie before it even hit the roof of his car and gave it a push that sent it flying. Then, Sebastian noticed another one coming and flashed me a look. I didn't need any instruction. I slid off the roof and got into the passenger seat of his car as fast as my wobbly and bruised legs would carry me.

When I got in, I proceeded to concentrate on breathing. At some point, Sebastian joined me inside the car.

When he gunned the engine, I realized he'd left the car running like a good getaway driver. The tires squealed as he backed up. Zombies continued to rain from the garage window, and those on the ground slowly picked themselves up. Sebastian's car was a pre–Depression era boat, so he had to do a lot of steering wheel cranking to get into position. Meanwhile, I clutched the edge of my seat, wishing the car had seat belts, and stared out into the blank eyes of the zombies. The whole scene made me feel a little like an extra in some insane remake of *Night of the Living Dead.*

We raced down the alley, bouncing on well-oiled shocks. Sebastian wasted no time getting out of Mo's neighborhood. After about a mile or so, he slowed to his usual five miles above the posted speed limit.

So, far neither of us had said a word.

After a few more seconds of silence, I said, 'Thanks.'

'You're welcome,' he answered somewhat perfunctorily.

I stole a glance at Sebastian. He'd dressed up to come see me. My favorite silver-gray button-down clung to his broad shoulders the way only silk could. Tight black jeans and cowboy boots accented long, sleek legs. A black velvet ribbon, tied in a very eighteenth century style bow, held his long, black hair back from his face. He looked elegant and sexy – and very anachronistic sitting behind the wheel of a Mafia car.

'Sorry I ditched you,' I said. 'I didn't mean to. I was just going out for a walk.'

He grunted an acknowledgment that seemed very much a yeah-I'm-sorry-too.

'About Parrish,' I said, deciding we might as well start this

230

fight if we were going to have it. 'You don't have to worry about him. I'm never going to see him again.'

Sebastian's next grunt sounded more like a laugh. 'Oh, you will.'

'No, he's gone off to—'

Sebastian cut me off. 'I know what he's gone off to do, Garnet. The entire tristate region knows what he's gone off to do.'

'What are you talking about?'

Instead of answering, Sebastian flipped on the radio. Josh Turner crooned that I had no idea how turned on he was just to be my man. Sebastian tapped another button and a car salesman yelled about low, low prices. On the next station, ironic on so many levels, Rob Zombie thundered out 'Dracula'.

Sebastian caught my smile, returned it, and gave up trying to find whatever it was he hoped to demonstrate. We sang along and bobbed our heads to the slamming beat. When the song ended, Sebastian turned down the volume on Black Sabbath's 'War Pigs'.

'Why doesn't that ever work like it does in the movies? No one ever gives you the news when you really want it. Anyway,' Sebastian said. 'Parrish's high-speed chase was all over the news ten minutes ago.'

'Jeez.'

'Yeah, and your boy keeps veering back toward town. I get the sense maybe he doesn't want to get too far away from a certain county morgue. Honestly, if it were me, I'd have gone for the standoff and gotten myself shot long before now. He's such a drama queen.'

I chuckled despite myself.

231

'I still think you should have gone to the south of France.'

I gave Sebastian a hopeful look. 'Maybe we still could.'

'If I take you to the Côte d'Azur, you going to ditch me again?'

'Maybe,' I smiled.

'Hmph,' he grunted again, but his eyes glittered fondly.

'Thanks again for the rescue,' I said.

He tapped his belly in the spot where I usually imagined Lilith residing in me. 'If I can't occasionally be a knight in shining armor, what's the point,' he said, as we waited at a stoplight.

I finally thought to ask, 'Where are we going?'

'Parrish was last sighted on I-90 headed east. I thought we'd try to intercept.'

'What? Why?'

'So you can say good-bye.'

At first I thought Sebastian was being cruel, but he gave me a long, sad look, like, somehow, he'd been in my shoes, or maybe Parrish's, and he *understood*.

'Plus,' Sebastian said with a smile that showed just the hint of sharp canines. 'I want to see the bastard die.'

Of course, catching up to Parrish proved difficult. Like every good farmboy, Sebastian had an illegal scanner bolted to the underside of the dash. To me, the entire police frequency sounded like babbling, but occasionally I could pick out county road numbers or other directional phrases. Sebastian seemed to know where we were headed and would suddenly veer right or left accordingly.

The moon shone over empty fields. The farther out we drove

from city lights, the more stars became visible. I could make out Orion's belt low on the horizon, and the big W of Cassiopeia. The Milky Way was a thin swath, like wisps of clouds, over-head.

'Are you ever going to explain the whole zombie army thing to me?' he asked after we'd driven for a while down a gravel road I was quite certain wasn't on any map. 'Or is this one of those things I'm not privy to as your boyfriend?'

I sensed a little bitterness in that last line, but for the sake of the cease-fire we'd so recently negotiated I let it lie. 'William's new girlfriend, Izzy's cousin, is an evil voodoo priestess,' I explained. 'Izzy and I think she's been killing frat boys and wage slaves and making them into zombies.'

'Oh, is that all?' he asked dryly.

'No,' I said. 'William's been brainwashed by her.' Sitting up straighter, I suddenly added, 'Oh, Sebastian, I have to break her spell over him. It's just awful to see him like that.'

Sebastian shot me a skeptical glance. He'd switched the station back to country and western, and SheDaisy harmonized softly in the background. 'Are you absolutely sure it's not just love?'

Sebastian slowed the car suddenly, and I watched a family of whitetail deer bound out from the ditch into a nearby alfalfa field. The bright tail tufts bobbed until they disappeared into darkness.

'He's not himself,' I insisted.

'Love can do crazy things to a person,' he said.

'Yeah, but William seemed heartless. He talked about getting sprayed by chicken blood as if it were nothing.'

Sebastian seemed to contemplate that as he searched the ditches for signs of more deer. Satisfied there were none, he started back up to full speed. 'Yeah, you're right. That doesn't sound like our William, does it?'

The car curved around gentle hills. Barren branches of oak and maple stood out in sharp relief in the headlights. A white steeple, illuminated by halogen beams mounted on the ground, cast an eerie glow among the tangle of leafless trees.

'Ever fought a voodoo priestess before?' I thought it was worth a shot, after all, Sebastian was a thousand years old.

'No, but I was briefly possessed by a loa once.'

'Really?'

'It was voluntary, well, mostly. I guess the spirits that attended the ritual looked at the vampire in the audience and thought what a funny joke it would be to have Baron Samedi possess the dead guy.'

'Wow.' I mean, what else could I say?

'Yes, well, I damn near needed an exorcist. Apparently, he didn't want to leave. Luckily, even the mambo agreed that it would be an extremely poor idea to have the spirit of the grave walking around all the time in the body of some white guy.'

Having been bodily possessed by Lilith, I had some sense of how frightening that must have been, even though Sebastian did a pretty good job keeping any emotion out of his voice.

'Do you think you can help me with William?' I asked.

'Do you want me to?'

I started to say 'of course,' when the light of Parrish's motorcycle coming straight at us suddenly blinded me.

Sebastian slammed on the brakes. There wasn't much of a

shoulder to aim for, only a thin patch of loose gravel before the ground sloped into sharp incline of drainage ditch. I braced my hands on the dash. We skidded to a stop. In the headlights, I saw a brief flash of Parrish's hair streaming behind him as he shot past.

Police cars followed at quite a distance. We heard their sirens first, and then caught the flashes of red and white. Quite suddenly, they were passing us; the howl of the horns became deafening and the lights a brilliant strobe.

'Well, we found them,' Sebastian said. We had slid precariously close to the ditch, and Sebastian took his time extricating the car from the shoulder. He'd made a U-turn just as a big, white media van came careening down the highway. We let it pass and then joined the parade of taillights.

Sebastian pressed a button on his watch to make it glow a faint green, then he shook his head. 'His timing is off,' he muttered. 'He's not going to be able to keep this chase going long enough before he runs out of gas.'

'Long enough for what?'

'The shift change at the morgue. You really want to time it so your body is being brought in just as one set of workers is leaving for the day and the next is coming in.' Sebastian chewed on his lip. He surprised me by seeming genuinely concerned for Parrish. 'Next one is awfully close to dawn for him. Six a.m.'

I watched as the stream of lights made a hard right turn at the next intersection. 'Why's that important?'

'He is planning on getting up and walking out, isn't he?'

'No. He wants to be declared dead, so the FBI will close the case.'

'Why not just switch toe tags with someone? Do you know how easy it is to lose a body?'

'In Madison?'

Sebastian thought about that for a moment. 'Right. Still. The whole thing seems awfully dodgy. What about the autopsy?'

'He said they wouldn't do that if the cause of death was obvious.'

'Maybe. But he's a suspect in a federal case; they're going to be thorough, Garnet,' Sebastian said. 'If for some reason they don't autopsy, they'll take blood to test for drugs and alcohol. Did he feed before this chase started?'

I was starting to get nervous. What did Parrish's blood test like? Was it even human? Would they be able to tell he was different? 'I don't think he had time.' Other than me, of course, but this didn't seem the right time to confess that to Sebastian.

'Bummer,' Sebastian said, gunning the engine through a hairpin turn that made me slide across the bench seat and bump against the door.

I nodded. The lights turned again, and as I watched them scream through the darkness it appeared the police were closing the distance.

'He's slowing,' I said.

Parrish made a quick turn into someone's driveway and then proceeded to attempt to go off-road through a cornfield. From the wild bumping of his headlight, I guessed that the cornstalks had recently been plowed under and the ground was both uneven and soft. One of the cop cars had pulled off to the side of the road and trained its floodlight on the field. I could see Parrish struggling with his Harley. Dirt sprayed everywhere, and the bike bucked and skidded wildly. The cops, meanwhile, stopped in a semicircle at the edge of the field. They cut their sirens. The silence unnerved me.

We were a quarter-mile away, at the top of a hill. Sebastian turned off his own headlights and glided us to a stop. Not far from us, the media van did the same. As soon as the engine was off, I had the car door open and was running down the road.

'Stay back, Garnet!' Sebastian shouted, but I couldn't.

Parrish's engine roared as he fought to gain purchase. One wheel caught something and the bike spun out from Parrish's grasp. The wind and distance garbled the command projected by police megaphone. Whatever was said caused Parrish to pull himself upright, flip the cops the bird, and pull his Colt revolver.

There would be no question about the cause of death.

Surreally, the sound reminded me of Fourth of July fireworks. Parrish jerked spastically under the barrage of bullets. Then, he fell. No slow motion, time lapse, or graceful swan song, just splat, onto his back in the mud and broken cornstalks.

Everything was silent, except for the sputtering of the Harley's engine, the chatter of police radios, and my screaming.

I don't know when I started yelling, but, like the running, I couldn't stop. It was like I was on automatic pilot as I scrambled down into the ditch and started across the field toward Parrish's motionless body. Even when a powerful grip caught me and held me back, my feet kept pumping and my arms continued reaching.

Dominguez set me down in the backseat of a squad car. The

interior was warm and smelled faintly of disinfectant soap, reminding me of a hospital.

'I'm sorry you had to see that,' he said, handing me a paper cup of coffee. 'What were you doing out here, anyway?' He propped the elbow of his cast on the ridge of the open car door.

'A friend picked up the chase on his scanner.' I sniffed the coffee, and was surprised by its pleasant, dark aroma. Where had this come from?

'Leonard brought some in,' Dominguez answered, jerking his chin in the direction of one of the squads. 'It's going to be a long night for some of us.'

I nodded. Even though I knew Parrish wasn't really dead, I couldn't shake the image of the bullets ripping into him, the jerky, unnatural way he fell. Details revealed themselves in the replays of my memory – a fine mist of blood spraying from each puncture, the twist of pain in his expression. That fall, so sudden and final. I shook my head to clear it.

Dominguez laid a hand on my shoulder. I could feel the sympathy in the brief squeeze. Then, 'Don't go anywhere. I may need to take a statement.'

I watched him walk away and merge with the flurry of activity. An ambulance arrived, as did the medical examiner. The county sheriff, the crew from the media van, and curious onlookers from nearby farms all milled about aimlessly. I sat with my head against the seat, snuggled into a blanket someone had offered me.

From my vantage point, I could see several people standing over Parrish's body, talking and occasionally gesturing at his prone, motionless body. The ambulance guys were making their way across the field with unhurried steps. A uniformed cop had taken the keys out of Parrish's motorcycle and pushed it back up the slight hill to where a tow truck waited to haul it off to . . . I didn't know where. The impound lot? Police auction?

The aftermath of violence was very regulated. Everyone seemed to know their part. Except me.

The blanket around my shoulders was coarse and scratchy, but I hugged it tighter, anyway. I couldn't help but wonder if this strange ordered chaos is what things might have been like if I'd called the police instead of Parrish after Lilith killed the Vatican agents. Except, instead of sitting with my feet hanging out an open door, I'd be handcuffed behind a locked one.

A passing uniform gave me a curious glance. I returned the midwestern nod of friendly acknowledgment. That seemed to satisfy him, and he went on with whatever he was doing, though he spared me a final suspicious glance. Who knows? Maybe I'd still leave here under arrest. Even though Parrish had made his ultimate sacrifice it didn't mean I wasn't still an accomplice. Dominguez could still have me locked away.

Out in the field, which was still bathed in an unearthly white light, the EMTs hoisted Parrish onto the gurney with a rolling move, which gave my heart a little pause. Something about that movement, the practiced, respectable ease in which it was executed made Parrish's death seem just a little too real.

What would it have been like to see the members of my coven transported with this professional calm? I remembered in my hysteria of that night, the one thing I couldn't abide was the thought that, in death, the dead Vatican agents and my friends would be treated the same way. Emergency medical types didn't distinguish between the good guys and the bad. To them, it was about doing the job right. That was part of why I'd called Parrish and told him we had to separate the Vatican agents from the others. He'd wanted to burn them all together in the house, but I'd said no.

It was the hysteria of grief, and of ... well, in retrospect, I knew the other thing that drove my insane insistence of removing the Vatican agent's bodies was guilt. I didn't want to put the two crimes on the same level because, if I did, then what I'd done was no better than what they had.

So lost in my memories, I didn't even hear Sebastian approach. He crouched down beside me and gave me a big grin. 'He couldn't have planned a more dramatic exit,' Sebastian said. 'Very Last Stand at the O.K. Corral."

'Remind me that he's okay,' I said desperately.

'He's a vampire. Being shot hurts – at least, it hurts me. I don't know very many traditional vampires, maybe he doesn't feel a thing, but, regardless, he's fine. Nothing a little sleep won't cure.'

'You're sure?'

Sebastian's smile waned a touch, but he held on to it as he tugged a bit of my hair. 'Try not to worry. Parrish never would have let this happen if there was any real danger of him dying. He's a fighter.'

Sebastian was right. I remembered Parrish's story of how he was made. He apparently picked the wrong stagecoach to rob one night. Instead of relieving a lady of her jewels, she nearly relieved him of his life. But rather than go down without a fight, he decided to bite back. She was so impressed with his chutzpah, she turned him.

'You've certainly come around about Parrish,' I said.

'It's not him I've come around about; it's you.'

I pulled Sebastian into a hug. Nuzzling against his shoulder, I took in his scent – a manly musk with the hint of something exotic, yet familiar, like cinnamon. I could have stayed like that forever, wrapped in his comforting strength, except someone cleared her throat.

'Ms. Lacey?' An Asian woman in her fifties with a shock of snow-white hair cut in a bob stood a respectful distance from Sebastian and me. She wore a yellow windbreaker, dark nylon slacks, and sturdy, practical ankle-high boots. 'I'm the medical examiner. I'll be issuing the death certificate for Mr Parrish, and I was wondering if you might know how I might get in touch with his immediate family.'

'He doesn't have any family. But I'm his fiancée.' Sebastian's eyebrows shot up, as I fished the ring from under my shirt.

The ME tucked a strand of hair behind her ear, clearly considering. 'Are you certain there's no other living family member? No estranged sibling, uncle, anyone?'

'His parents have been dead for some time,' Sebastian supplied without even a trace of amusement in his voice, as he turned to address her.

She nodded. Her face was impassive, but she didn't seem very pleased with the information. 'Will you be handling the funeral arrangements?'

'I own a family plot,' Sebastian said. 'We wish to care for him ourselves.'

It was my turn to stare in shock at Sebastian. What was he suggesting, exactly?

The ME tried to hide a scowl of disapproval. 'That's somewhat unusual outside of the Amish community,' she said. 'Without a blood relative, you might have some trouble getting all the approval you'll need.'

'I'm well aware of the state requirements,' Sebastian said. Sebastian and the ME got into a stare down. Out of the corner of my eye, I saw the stretcher being loaded into the ambulance.

'Uh, so are you going to do an autopsy?' I asked.

'In cases of violent death it's usually required by law,' she said. 'However, when there is a known and undisputed cause of death, it can be omitted at my discretion.'

I'm sure I looked visibly relieved.

She gave me a hard stare. Her eyes flicked over the safety pins on my jeans, the skull earring, and then over to Sebastian's equally monochromatic clothes. 'You're part of some cult, aren't you?'

I'm sure my mouth dropped open. When I dressed as a Goth, people made a lot of assumptions about me, but this was the first time anyone had accused me of being in a cult. 'I'm Wiccan, thank you very much.'

'As pagans,' Sebastian cut in; no doubt sensing a rant was imminent, 'we're against all the artificiality surrounding death.'

Of course, the funny part was that Sebastian was Catholic. Still, I was grateful he stepped in. What I would have said wouldn't have been nearly so articulate or diplomatic.

'I've heard about you people,' she said with a nod. 'You've got a pagan cemetery on that crazy commune of yours.'

'Circle Sanctuary is not a commune,' Sebastian supplied. 'And, we are not "you people".'

'Whatever,' the ME said. The scowl she had been suppressing twitched across her thin lips. 'Well, if you can assemble all the appropriate forms and you follow the law, I don't care what you do with him. Be sure everything's in order before you try to collect the body from the morgue.'

'Yes, ma'am,' Sebastian said as deferentially as he possibly could.

She walked away. Which was good because I really, really wanted to smack her.

With the ambulance gone, the crowd thinned considerably. A few squads remained to collect evidence and secure the scene or whatever they were doing. I didn't really care. I felt emotionally exhausted.

'I wonder if we can go,' Sebastian asked no one in particular.

'You can,' Dominguez said coming up out of the ditch. 'But, I'd like to talk to Ms Lacey for a moment.'

'Garnet?' Sebastian didn't even really acknowledge Dominguez's authority in the matter. He looked at me expectantly.

'It's okay,' I told Sebastian. 'Why don't you bring the car up?'

Sebastian nodded, but before he left, he took a moment to give Dominguez an appraising look that suggested you-hurt-her-and-I'll-kick-your-ass.

Dominguez waited for Sebastian to move off before speaking. He watched Sebastian with a curious expression on his face, like he was examining a bug under a magnifying glass. Finally, Dominguez announced, 'He's different.'

In the Midwest, calling someone 'different' was a major insult; it was the Norwegian equivalent of 'Wow, he's completely fucked-up.' The only thing worse you could say might be 'unique' – that implied someone was a true psycho.

'What makes you say that?' I bristled. 'You hardly know him.'

Dominguez shrugged. 'I read people as part of my job. There's something about your friend that's out of step with the ordinary. I can smell it on him.'

Not to mention the fact that he probably 'read' differently being a vampire. 'So, you just came over here to insult my friends?'

'No, I came over here to tell you that I know.'

Fear stabbed through me. To hide my concern, I folded up the silvery blanket and set it on the seat beside me. 'Know what?'

'Parrish isn't dead.'

I tried to act incredulous. 'How can you even say something like that?'

He tapped his temple with a finger. 'I felt it. His consciousness is still in there.'

Well, that was good to know.

'Tell me he's not one of those zombies you were talking about,' Dominguez said wearily.

'He's not a zombie.'

'Thank God,' Dominguez said. 'Don't tell me anything else. I don't want to know.'

That surprised me. 'You don't?'

'No,' he said. 'As far as I'm concerned, case closed.'

'Really?'

'Don't push it,' he said, with a raise of a finger at my hopeful tone. 'It's easier this way. Parrish is a straightforward suspect with a history of violent crime, and for all intents and purposes he's dead. Anything else, I don't want to know.'

I wanted to say 'thank you,' but that seemed inappropriate. 'Okay.'

He shoved his hands into the pockets of his jeans. 'Okay.'

When he looked at me the way he was now, I couldn't help but remember the hot and heavy in his car. I could feel a blush heat my cheeks. 'Uh, well, I guess I'll see you around, then.'

He snorted a little laugh. 'Isn't that supposed to be the guy's line?'

'Look, I'm really sorry about the love spell. It was way more powerful than I expected.'

'Forget it,' he said.

How could I, now that I thought about it again? The moon was high in the sky. Bats darted overhead, chasing the season's remaining mosquitoes. 'Any chance you'd help me take down a voodoo priestess who's killing frat boys?'

Dominguez smiled and shook his head. 'Sounds like a local problem.'

'Ah,' I said, disappointed, but what could I do about it? Sebastian and I would have to think of something.

'Seeing as I'm currently between assignments,' Dominguez said. 'Maybe I could, you know, act as a liaison or something.'

'You would?'

'Nobody else is going to believe this whole zombie thing, you realize.'

'Don't I know it,' I said with a wry smile.

Sebastian honked. I asked Dominguez if it was okay for me to head out, and he waved me away.

'I'll call you,' I said.

'Sure,' Dominguez said, sounding like a girl who doesn't expect to hear from a lover ever again.

Lost in our own thoughts, neither of us spoke much on the way back to Sebastian's farm. Once there, Sebastian guided me to the big, comfy couch in his living room, put a cup of tea in my hand, and tossed a couple of logs in the fireplace.

I always loved Sebastian's living room. It was full of books and curios he'd collected in his long and interesting life. Every time I scanned the shelves I'd notice something new, something that would reveal a new facet of Sebastian.

Meanwhile, everything Parrish had owned fit in a steamer trunk and a couple of saddlebags.

I sipped my tea, tasting honey and chamomile. 'Do you think he's going to be okay?'

Sebastian sat down beside me, and put his stocking feet up on the coffee table. He shrugged, his eyes on the fire. 'If the ME keeps her promise and doesn't perform an autopsy, he should be fine. We can take possession as soon as the death certificate is issued and we file the Report for Final Disposition with the Office of the Registrar. All that might take a couple of days. But, we've made it clear we want to care for him and bury him ourselves, so they won't embalm. Wisconsin doesn't require it, at any rate.'

'Do I want to know why you're up on all this?'

'Teréza,' he said, casually mentioning the dead/not dead

mother of his son. Teréza was, or is, a failed attempt by Sebastian to pass on his vampirism. She is locked in stasis between the dead and the living, a corpse with a soul. Because Sebastian became a vampire through alchemy instead of the traditional Blood Sire, he can't create others of his kind. However, he could produce children – real, live children. Anyway, Sebastian and Mátyás, his son, disagreed about what to do about Teréza. Sebastian felt it was wisest to bury her to let her rest, Mátyás kept disinterring her. Their family dysfunction was especially odd.

'When you have a corpse lying around your house, it helps to know the local regulations.'

'Ah,' I said, so not wanting to talk about how creepy I found that.

We lapsed into silence. I allowed myself to be mesmerized by the dance of flame across log. The wood creaked and popped as moisture evaporated. The room began to smell faintly of birch.

Sebastian set down his empty teacup. 'Are you planning a wake or a funeral? Do you want to write an obituary?'

I hadn't thought about all of that. 'I suppose we should. They'll be expecting it, won't they?'

'It's what people do.'

Except, I hadn't.

When my coven died I'd fled Minneapolis, leaving other people to perform the duties surrounding death. Some of my friends, like Jasmine, hadn't been 'out of the broom closet'. I wondered if she'd been buried as a Lutheran, with some pastor who didn't know her life at all merely filling in the blanks.

I never saw an obituary for any of them – not that I would have necessarily recognized their mundane names since our identities were so highly guarded. Still. Did anyone eulogize them? Or recount favorite stories around a quiet glass of beer?

Someone must have, but I didn't.

Sebastian got up and retrieved a leather-bound scrapbook. Returning to his seat beside me, he held it in his lap. 'I've had to write a few obits,' he said. He ran a finger along the edge of the binding and then set the book on the coffee table unopened.

'Anything in there you don't want me to see?' I asked, feeling Parrish's ring resting against my chest.

'Probably,' he said. 'I've been alive a long time.'

That reminded me, but how to ask? 'So, any, uh, guys in there?'

'Guys?' Sebastian asked.

'Yeah, you know, survived by their loving partner, Sebastian.'

His reaction couldn't have been faked. 'Garnet! I'm Catholic.'

I gave him a quirk of an eyebrow as if to say like-that-would-really-stop-some-people.

He scratched the tip of his nose. 'Look, I'm sure it's sort of expected that a vampire be bisexual, but I'm straight. Guys just have never, ever done it for me. It's tragic, really. Doomed for all eternity to only be able to get off with one sex.'

'Did you try?'

'What does that mean, did I try? Sure, there were some very lovely men in my acquaintance over the years who made certain intentions known, but, look, it never worked out.' He crossed his arms in front of his chest, and his lip pulled into a tiny pout. 'I don't want to talk about it.'

I laughed. I had a pretty good idea what it meant when he said things hadn't worked out. I patted his thigh. 'Oh, honey.'

'Shut up,' he said teasingly. 'I take it Parrish has broken the hearts of every gender?'

'According to him,' I said and we both laughed a little at that. Then we were silent, both of our gazes settled on his scrapbook.

I leaned into Sebastian, and he wrapped an arm around me. He nuzzled his nose against my ear, took in a long, sighing breath, and then jumped back as if I'd hit him. 'Your shoulder is better,' he started. 'Oh, Garnet, you drank his blood, didn't you?'

Aw, and we'd been getting along so nicely too.

'I hate him,' Sebastian snarled. 'I hate that Parrish's blood can heal you, when my own is poison.'

'I said no when he first suggested it. But the pain was intense, Sebastian. I mean, I'd be going along fine for a while and then all I'd have to do is move wrong and . . .' I stopped making up excuses. 'In the end, it was an easy solution. I didn't really think about how you'd feel about it. I should have. I'm sorry.'

The muscles of Sebastian's jaw flexed. 'Can I tell you how glad I am that man is playing dead for the next few months?'

And yet Sebastian offered to bury him right next door. At first I'd thought that was an act of somewhat uncharacteristic kindness, now I wasn't so sure. 'You're not planning on staking Parrish once he's buried next door, are you?'

'I hadn't been, but, of course, that was before I knew you two had swapped bloody kisses. No, transfixing him would be too kind.' Sebastian frowned into his cup of tea as if wishing it were filled with something more potent. 'Unfortunately, if I dragged his body into the sunlight and watched him shrivel like a raisin while dancing, quite literally, on his grave, you'd hate me. Despite how much instant gratification killing him would give me, the price is too high. He's not worth losing you.'

'You mean it?'

Sebastian sighed wearily. 'My life would be so much simpler if I didn't.'

I gave him a kiss. It was meant to be just a thank-you sort of peck on the lips, but kissing him once made me want to do it again. After a long, extended reunion of our lips and tongues, I pulled away and said, 'I love you, Sebastian Von Traum.'

'I love you, Garnet Lacey,' he said. 'Come on, let's go to bed.'

It wasn't that I wasn't in the mood, because I was looking forward to what else we could reunite, but with everything that had happened with Parrish I felt sort of like I needed tonight to be about him.

Sebastian noticed my hesitation and understood. 'Take your time,' he said. 'If I'm asleep when you come up, don't take it personally.'

I smiled. 'I won't. Oh, and thanks.'

He shrugged. 'You owe me a relationship coupon.'

'What's that?'

'You'll know when I call it in.' He gave me a toothy grin. Then he stifled a yawn. 'See you in the morning.'

'Yeah,' I said, my eyes straying to the book of obituaries on the table in front of me. 'I'm sorry about this, I know he's not dead, but I'm still sad.'

Sebastian paused and leaned over the polished maple railing. 'He's gone, isn't he?'

I nodded, not trusting myself to speak over the lump in my throat.

'Then you need to grieve him.'

I made myself a peanut butter and jelly sandwich in Sebastian's kitchen. I switched the radio on for company. NPR broadcast the BBC live. I drank a glass of milk and let the British accents fill my head with memories of Parrish.

Sometime later, I found myself sitting on the couch leafing through Sebastian's book of obituaries. There were hundreds of them. Some were undoubtedly lovers, but there were also notices of friends – war buddies, neighbors, and the like. All people Sebastian had known and cared about in some fashion. It didn't go back very far, only until the early seventies. When I scanned the shelves, there appeared to be other volumes.

I shut the book and set it down. Looking at all of the lives of these people made me realize what I needed to do. Parrish needed a funeral – more than that, he needed a wake. One big, final party with lots and lots of whiskey. I would even invite all his ghoulfriends; they'd know he wasn't dead, but they'd appreciate the opportunity to toast him, anyway.

Then, I dug out a pen and a sheet of paper from Sebastian's junk drawer. I started writing Parrish's obit.

When I finished his, I wrote 'a remembrance' notice for each of the friends I'd lost last Halloween. I started by thinking I'd just place a short notice listing everyone's craft name. Pretty soon I was recounting bits of physical detail – Martingale's twinkling green eyes, Junko's salt-and-pepper hair – which led to other things I wanted to remember, like Jasmine's home-baked zucchini bread and Cloverleaf's amazing hand-sewn belly-dancing dress. What I ended up with were stream-of-consciousness, almost poetic snippets, and a sense I should have done this long ago.

I was frying breakfast eggs when Sebastian shuffled into the kitchen in a bathrobe. His eyes brightened when he saw the coffee brewing. Sun shone in through the windows, and he squinted miserably as he did the fast switch with the coffeemaker. With minimal spill, Sebastian slipped his cup under the steady brown stream. I flipped the eggs, smiling.

'You look remarkably cheerful for someone who didn't sleep,' he grumbled. Sliding the pot back into its holder, Sebastian leaned his hip against the countertop. He gave me a suspicious glare while taking a long draught from his mug.

'You look remarkably . . .' I stopped. What I wanted to say was that he looked surprisingly *human* with his hair a tangle and stubble on his cheeks, but it seemed a bit rude. 'Tired,' I said instead. 'For someone who went to bed early.'

'If I don't get my sleep, I don't regenerate as easily,' he said with a shrug. 'Even my kind of vampire needs a few hours of torpor to maintain my youthful figure.'

When he ran a hand along his hips like a movie starlet, I giggled. The eggs were done, so I pulled a couple of plates from the cabinets and pressed the switch on the toaster where I'd preloaded a couple of slices of multi-grain bread.

'I took the liberty of finding out the hours of the registrar's office,' Sebastian said. Moving over to the kitchen table he set his cup down and moved aside a tincture of anise, clove, and nutmeg. Automatically, he shook it once before finding a place for it among the crowd of oils and ointments on top of the refrigerator. 'And I left a message at the hospital that we need a copy of Parrish's death certificate ASAP.'

I set a plate of over-easy up eggs in front of him. Fetching a couple of forks from the drawer, I refilled my own cup with coffee. 'All this before a shower?'

'I know you're anxious to get closure about Parrish,' he said. After getting the butter bowl from the fridge, he paused to crumble a handful of dried basil and something I didn't immediately recognize into it. He popped the dish in the microwave for a few seconds, grabbed the toast, and settled back into his chair.

The scent from the herbed butter made my mouth water. 'I guess I can fax the obituary to the paper,' I said. 'I set the date for the wake for Wednesday.'

He spread a large dollop of butter onto a piece of toast and handed it to me. 'That's Halloween,' Sebastian said, a little surprised.

I took a bite of toast. The mystery ingredient in the butter turned out to be oregano. 'I know,' I said. 'I thought, maybe, if I had Parrish's wake on Halloween, I could put a lot of ghosts to rest, as it were.'

Sebastian nodded. 'The veil between the worlds is thinnest,' he said, recounting the pagan belief that on Samhain the barriers between the living and the dead were easiest to cross. It was a night for communicating and communing with souls who had

253

passed on into the Summerland. The idea of dressing up as ghosts and other frightening things came from a pagan super-stition that the malicious spirits, which walked that night, wouldn't recognize you in costume. The scary faces of the jack-o'-lanterns kept your house safe, as well.

'Well,' I said, when my coffee was drained and my breakfast eaten. 'Let's go collect Parrish's body, shall we?'

Sebastian and I spent most of the day in and out of various government offices. I must have filled out a million and a half forms. We had to do a little fast-talking to convince the regis-trar to accept me as Parrish's 'spouse', given that I had no marriage certificate. But since Parrish had no one else and the registrar, like any other government office, was overworked and understaffed, they found a few more forms for me to make it all legal, or at least waive them of any responsibility if I turned out to be a grave robber or some kind of sick necrophiliac.

I dressed the part of the grieving fiancée, going ultra conser-vative (for me) in a tea-length black skirt and one of Sebastian's white, silk button-downs. I wore the shirt open just enough to show off Parrish's ring. Before hitting all the various govern-ment offices, we'd made a pit stop at a Walgreens to buy a pair of hose and back at my place to pick up my only pair of black flats. If anyone noticed the silver bat buckle, they didn't comment.

I wouldn't be able to pick Parrish up until tomorrow, but I was assured everything was in order so there shouldn't be a problem.

I worried about him stuck in the morgue, but I thought it

would be mighty suspicious to drop by just to see him. Most people didn't go visiting the dead.

Wanting just to be busy for a while, I convinced Sebastian to drop me off at work. I was a bit dismayed when I walked in to discover no one staffing the register. I checked through the store and discovered William hiding in the astrology section. He sat on an unopened box of books and held his head in his hands.

'Are you okay?' I asked him.

His eyes were rimmed with red, and his face looked mottled. When he saw me, he squealed with joy. 'Oh my god, Garnet. I thought you were dead.'

My eyes narrowed. 'You mean: you thought you'd killed me.'

William didn't deny it, but he looked sort of muddled and yet offended, like the stereotypical kicked puppy. 'Mo is very persuasive,' William said. 'When I'm around her. When I'm not . . . Garnet, I've been having these terrible nightmares where I sacrifice chickens and raise the dead. Then, last night, I dreamt I shoved you into a garage full of flesh-eating zombies.'

'You know that wasn't a dream, William.'

He shut his eyes and hung his head. Limp strands of brown and dyed-green hair hung in front of his face. 'I was afraid you'd say that,' he mumbled to the floor.

I put a hand on his shoulder in sympathy. The tips of my fingers buzzed, like I'd touched an electrical current. I jerked back, cradling my hand.

When he glanced up at me his eyes had changed. The look in them was unlike anything I'd ever seen William express – he seemed focused, certain . . . and deadly.

255

11

Aquarius

Key Words:
Inventive and Unpredictable

He stood with slow menace, the letter opener he'd been using to unwrap the boxes gripped tightly in his hand. Even his stance was different, his posture more erect and purposeful. I knew instantly he'd been possessed.

Lilith jittered across my abdomen as William advanced. If I let Her take over, I figured more than the loa would be destroyed. I couldn't let Her kill William, not even in self-defense. I would have to find another way.

So I ran.

I turned on my heels and dashed out the door and down the street, screaming my fool head off that I needed help. Glancing behind me, I saw William burst from the store, weapon in hand. The dinner crowd on State Street erupted in noise and confusion. I slowed when William looked flustered at all the attention he'd drawn, dropped the knife, and took off in the opposite direction.

I stopped to catch my breath. Passersby offered help, which

I brushed away politely. I didn't realize I'd started crying, however, until some kind soul offered me a Kleenex. I touched my belly where Lilith lay dormant, knowing now, for the first time, I'd had at least one other viable option that night. When I saw the Vatican agents in the covenstead, I could have run. I could have called for help.

If I had only . . .

I stopped myself, because if I had run that night there was a strong possibility one of the agents might have caught me, killed me. Running would only have meant that those six agents would be alive today, knowing what I'd looked like. If the FBI could find me, a supersecret order of assassins surely would have.

And, despite the fact that it felt good, running hadn't solved the overall problem. William might not have killed me this time, but he was still possessed by a loa. I would still have to come up with a way to destroy it, and now any element of surprise I might have had at my disposal was gone.

I made my way back to the store. At least one good thing came from running away; now I had more time to think about what I was going to do to save William.

I stayed at Mercury Crossing well past closing. William had left the place in terrible disorder with orders unplaced, invoices unpaid, and, from what it looked like in the safe, deposits unmade. Sebastian dropped by at nine o'clock with sandwiches. He helped reorganize the stock room and even volunteered to drop the money in the night deposit box at the bank for me. I felt too guilty to let him. The store was my responsibility, after all, and I'd neglected it for days.

So, instead, I set him to taking care of some Parrish details I hadn't been able to get around to. Using the store's computer, I had him rekey the obit I'd written for Parrish and the remembrances for the coven on the newspaper's website. He paid for the notices electronically as well. Then, I had him print up some posters for Parrish's wake. Since I didn't know the names and address of Parrish's ghouls, I thought I'd post details in the places Parrish haunted. It would probably mean we'd get more than our share of freeloaders, but part of me figured Parrish wouldn't mind as long as his wake was remembered as a damn good party.

Sebastian went out with a staple gun to hang the notices, while I finished up putting my store back in order. I had just laid my head down to 'rest my eyes', when Sebastian returned. I have a vague recollection of getting bundled into his car, but almost none at all of getting tucked into bed.

I dreamt of the dead.

Trick or treating, dressed as a Witch. The first doorbell I ring opens to the smiling face of Jasmine. She's wearing a new necklace and wants to show off the lapis lazuli and malachite beadwork. I admire it, thinking, something's wrong. I notice a crow, no, a vulture, circling overhead. 'Jasmine,' I ask, 'aren't you supposed to be dead?' She smiles, teeth showing all the way to the roots.

I woke up with a start. The room was dark, and Sebastian lay beside me, as motionless as a corpse. The red light of the digital clock read 2:52. I rolled over to spoon with Sebastian. Even though his body was all twisted up, I managed to tuck my arm around his slender waist and gripped him tightly. He made no sound, not even the gentle huff of measured breathing. At least his skin was warm. I folded the feather comforter around our shoulders and shut my eyes.

This was the first time I'd dreamt of a coven member. Though the dream certainly unnerved me, the majority of it gave me the sensation of catching up with an old, albeit dead, friend. Scary, but comforting. Not unlike snuggling up to a vampire lover.

The next morning I slept in. Sebastian woke me up with a cup of coffee, a bagel with cream cheese, and a nervous smile. Even though they seemed highly suspicious, I accepted his offerings. I munched on the toasted bagel and waited for Sebastian to explain why he perched on the edge of the bed so precariously.

'So,' he said finally. 'What are your plans today?'

I brushed a few crumbs from the comforter. 'I thought I'd go into work for a while and finish taking care of some of the stuff I couldn't get to yesterday. Then, I'm going to call Slow Bob and have him cover for me so we can pick up Parrish. At some point, I need to figure out how to de-possess William.' I took a sip of coffee. 'Why?'

'There are some things I need to attend to today,' he said ominously.

'Oh?'

He glanced out the window. The sky was robin's-egg blue. A flock of geese made a noisy exodus south. He cleared his throat. 'I was thinking that maybe if we adopted a policy of full disclosure things would be, you know, better.'

I took another hit of coffee hoping the caffeine would help

me make sense of Sebastian's words. When it didn't, I tried again. After four sips, I finally had to say, 'What?'

'I need to feed, Garnet. I thought you should know.'

Did I feel better knowing Sebastian was headed off to suck someone else's blood?

'Okay,' I said. It wasn't like I could demand he starve to death. 'You know, you could . . .' What was I about to offer?

Sebastian looked equally intrigued.

' . . . Just not tell me in the future,' I said. 'I think ignorance is best.'

Getting back into town was a hassle. Calling a taxi would involve spending more cash than I had on me. I tried Izzy's cell, but she was probably working since it was switched off. I couldn't call William for obvious reasons, and Sebastian was . . . well, busy.

I ended up borrowing Sebastian's rusty ten-speed, which I found covered in cobwebs propped in a corner of the barn. The tires were flat, but a bit more investigation turned up an air pump and a wrench to adjust the seat with. I left him a note about it, but given the state of the bike I doubted he would be in a hurry to get it back.

Previous experience taught me that Sebastian's farm was about an hour or so from the store by bicycle. It was a long ride, but not impossible, especially given crisp, clear weather like today's.

I started down the road toward home. Glancing at the grave-yard opposite the driveway, I hoped Parrish was still safe and sound in the morgue.

The asphalt was broken and bumpy where a season's worth of traffic had made it rough. A sparrow hawk circled above fields of dried cornhusks. My eyes watered at the scent of skunk roadkill. I pushed the bike faster uphill.

Rounding the curve, I crested the hill and was able to coast down past farmhouses and fields. As gravity carried me along, I tried to figure out what to do about William and the zombie queen. Maybe I could still convince Dominguez to arrest her. I was sure trafficking in humans was a federal crime, even if the people involved were dead. Even if it wasn't, he had said he would act as a liaison for me with the local authorities. Besides, I still owed him a natal chart. Maybe I could lure him over to my place for Parrish's wake, and then all I'd have to do was convince William and Mo to also attend.

The smell of dead skunk was eventually replaced by the much more pleasant odor of burning leaves. Tall grass growing in the ditch rasped in the wind. A sandpiper darted along the road.

The old William would definitely come to Parrish's wake. They knew each other from our previous misadventures, and for a while I suspected William could have been counted in the ranks of Parrish's ghouls. Going Goth had been another phase of William's, but like all the other spiritualities/lifestyles he'd tried, it didn't stick. He later confessed to me that he couldn't hack the late hours; William was a morning person.

A black covered wagon pulled by a pair of dark brown horses clomped alongside the ditch in the other lane. I waved a cheerful hello. I turned my head to watch them pass, marveling, as always, at how the bright orange slow-moving triangle fastened to the center of the wagon always seemed like such an anachronism.

I had to help William return to his usual, fuddled self. I was sure there was a spell to counteract the possession. Maybe Izzy could help.

By the time I pulled up to Holy Grounds, my butt ached from sitting on an unfamiliar seat and all I wanted was a cool glass of something. A notice about Parrish's wake was taped to the window. We'd picked a good picture of him, one I'd snapped with a friend's digital camera to settle a bet that a vampire's images would reproduce electronically, despite the myth they didn't on film. I'd tried to explain to Parrish that no one used silver to develop pictures anymore. And even if they did, there'd still be a photograph, because vampires aren't allergic to silver, werewolves are. Needless to say, I won that bet.

When I opened the door, a few leaves followed the gust of wind inside. The coffee shop was quiet. It was one of those between-rush times, when only a few patrons sat clacking at laptops and nursing lattes they'd ordered hours ago. Izzy had a newspaper open on the counter. She glanced up when the door opened. When she saw me, she scurried around the bar.

'Sebastian told me about your friend,' she said, embracing me in a hug. 'Are you okay?'

Izzy and Parrish had never met. She had no idea he wasn't really dead. 'I don't know,' I admitted. Parrish's 'death' had shaken me, bringing up all the unspent grief with my coven. 'I have to pick up his body today.'

Izzy stepped back and held me at arm's length. 'And *why* do you have to pick up his body, exactly? Shouldn't the funeral home take care of all that?'

'He can't be embalmed,' I said. Then, because there was no reason she shouldn't know, I added, 'He's a vampire.'

'But he's dead?'

'Officially, he's in torpor. He called it a "long sleep" or something like that.'

'He's playin' possum,' she summed up nicely with an appreciative grin.

'Yeah,' I smiled. 'Precisely.'

'But, you're going through all the motions? Wake, burial, and all that. I noticed the obit today,' she said jerking her thumb in the direction of the paper she'd left discarded on the bar.

'He's taking the fall for me,' I said. Then glancing around the room, I whispered, 'With the FBI.'

Izzy gave me that smile that sometimes seemed more like an exasperated grimace and shook her head. 'All in a day in the life, eh?'

I shrugged. Izzy went back to her position as barkeep, and I pulled up a tall stool next to the jars of biscotti and foil-wrapped imported chocolates. 'Can I trouble you for an iced coffee?'

'Sure,' she said, then automatically, 'For here?'

I laughed. 'Yeah, I need to sit awhile. And, we need to talk about William.'

She scooped ice from a bucket into a pint glass. Removing a pitcher of chilled coffee from the fridge, she added that and a bit of milk to the glass. 'What's wrong with William now?'

'He's possessed by a loa or . . . something. He tried to kill me.'

264

Izzy set the glass down in front of me. 'Honey, he doesn't
need to be possessed to want to do that.'

'He's dating your cousin,' I said, ignoring her quip. 'Mo? The
one who's making all the frat zombies?'

Izzy didn't look nearly as surprised as I wanted her to be.

'You knew about all of this?' I asked. 'Is that why the zombies
were after you?'

Slowly folding the newspaper back together, Izzy shrugged.
'I feel responsible for all of this. I helped Mo relocate after the
hurricane. It was tough when she first arrived. She'd lost so
much . . . I should never have told her about the money.'

'What money?'

Izzy leaned against the refrigerator. The surface of it was
covered in cartoons featuring coffee and/or coffee shops.
Magnets in the shape of cups and saucers held everything in
place. Crossing her arms, she said, 'I hear a lot in this job. People
like to tell stories to me, just like they would to their bartender.
This guy came in once, said he was writing a book about grave
traditions, and he'd heard about some Italians or gypsies that
buried money with the deceased. He'd done research, knew
names. I told her about it after work, you know, like you would.'

Izzy trailed off, but I could guess the end of the story.

'When I found out what she was doing, I kicked her out.
We've been feuding ever since.'

'She took your barista, Suzette,' I remembered. 'And now
she's got William.'

'Well, I didn't say I was winning.'

Izzy returned the newspaper to a pile at the edge of the bar,
and I drank my coffee, considering. When she came back, I

said, 'How mad would you be if I had your cousin arrested for human trafficking?'

'Pretty damn mad,' she said. 'I brought her up here because I wanted to help her.'

'She's killing those people, Iz.'

'Pot calling the kettle, don't you think?' she snapped.

Izzy was comparing what I did in self-defense to what her cousin did for fun and profit. My mouth hung open for a moment. The way her eyes slid away from mine, I could tell Izzy regretted what she'd said the instant she'd spoken. But, it was too late, we'd started something that apparently needed saying.

'That wasn't the same,' I insisted.

Izzy's gaze drifted to the espresso machine. Her lips compressed into a thin line, and she shrugged. 'I'm just saying that the other day you thought you'd killed that FBI agent. It's not like you don't abuse your power sometimes. Jesus, Garnet, you date people who prey on others and drink their blood. That's like romancing some kind of giant tick. You don't have a lot of moral high ground to stand on here.'

Did she just call Sebastian and Parrish wood ticks? I shook my head, not even knowing which accusation to refute first. Instead, I said, 'I think I should go.'

'Probably best,' she agreed. Pivoting in the direction of the stainless-steel sink, Izzy turned her back to me and pretended there were dishes that needed her attention.

William never came to work. The first thing I did was phone every auxiliary staff member I had to set up a schedule that would allow me to pick up Parrish this afternoon *and* keep the store open during its busiest month while assuming William as a long-term no-show . . . in case I couldn't reverse Mo's possession spell. Then, I picked out every title on voodoo we had in the store and piled them next to the register. When I wasn't ringing up sales of last-minute Halloween costume jewelry to giggling customers, I skimmed the sections regarding possession.

I didn't find anything terribly helpful, since most of what was described happened in ritual to practitioners. Plus, I felt very uncertain about using a magical system so different from my own. Finally, I decided that I'd try a general hex-breaking spell. As I sold the fifteenth black wool cloak and pointy cap to a UW student, I felt a pang of loss. I missed my coven. Someone there would have had some experience with this sort of thing, and if not, they still would have lent their magical support to the spell. I had a feeling that breaking Mo's hold on William was going to take more oomph than a single Witch could muster.

Thinking of William, I called his home number and left a message inviting him to my house for the wake. 'This is for Daniel . . . and for me,' I said. 'I want you to know you're welcome to come. Mo too. Please consider it, William.'

Then, I dialed Dominguez's number. I was surprised when he answered after the first ring. 'Don't you have work to do?'

'This *is* my work,' he said gruffly. 'What do you want?'

Here I go, lying to an FBI agent again. 'I finished your astrological chart. I thought maybe you'd like to come over for a reading some time. Maybe this evening?'

There was a long pause on the other end. For a brief moment, I thought we'd been disconnected.

'Uh, Dominguez? Are you there?'

'I'm thinking,' he said. More silence. I thought I could hear the sounds of people talking in the background. 'What time?'

The wake was at nine. We'd set it for a late hour intentionally to appeal to Parrish's ghoulfriends. 'Seven?'

Dominguez cleared his throat. 'Just to be clear, are you asking me out on a date?'

'Would you be more or less inclined to come if I said no?'

'More.'

'Then no.'

'Okay, I'll be at your place by seven. See you then.'

Despite insisting this wasn't a date, Dominguez sounded kind of excited. I wondered if my love spell had entirely broken. I'd lost the amulet when Lilith tried to kill him. Maybe it was still mostly together somewhere, still brewing up trouble.

Just what I needed.

Slow Bob came in at noon. Slow Bob was a portly, more-than-middle-aged man with a keen mind and a deep need to avoid most social interactions. He had a grandfatherly salt-and-pepper beard, and, when appropriately provoked, a bright, warm smile. Despite the fact that he would never make employee of the month, I liked Bob. He was a Virgo; he organized like a demon. The store was always more orderly after his shift; he just did things in his own time. I knew he was a Witch – I'd actually run into him at the Pagan Gathering one year when both of us were practicing the 'clothing optional' rule. He never revealed much of that wilder side of himself at work, except for the occasional surprising quip interjected into a discussion William and I were having about some esoteric topic or another.

268

'Hey, Bob,' I said.

He tipped an imaginary hat at me, flashed a shy grin, and disappeared into the back. I didn't see him again until Sebastian showed up after one. I reluctantly left Slow Bob in charge of the store with strict orders for him not to spend his time hiding in the astrology section. Bob sat behind the register with a hangdog expression that would likely chase off any potential customers. My profit margin was so doomed.

Oh well. I had bigger things to worry about. Like picking up my ex-boyfriend from the morgue.

'I see you borrowed my bike,' Sebastian said, as he showed me to the minivan he'd rented. It was bright red, not exactly a somber color for transporting the dead. As I got in, I could see that Sebastian had removed all the seats. Parrish's coffin sat in the middle of the carpet.

'Everything work out for you?' Sebastian asked, then quickly added, 'With the bike, I mean.' There was something strained in his tone, and I realized we hadn't spoken since I nearly offered to be his meal.

Even now, some part of me found the idea tempting, and I didn't want that. So instead, I blurted, 'Izzy thinks you're a parasite. Actually, she called you a tick.'

Sebastian chuckled. 'Well, I suppose that's better than a leech. Is she mad at me for some reason?'

I shook my head. 'No,' I said, 'at me. Her cousin is the person responsible for all the zombies, and I'm planning on trying to get her arrested.'

'Izzy?'

'No, the cousin Mo – Maureen.'

Before unbuckling, I double-checked to make sure I had all the proper forms and paperwork. Satisfied everything was in order, I followed Sebastian up a set of concrete stairs littered with cigarette butts. Apparently, being a hospital worker didn't require living a particularly healthy life.

It was only after the third turn down a maze of hallways did I think to wonder how it was that Sebastian knew his way around the basement of the hospital. 'Have you been to the morgue before?'

Sebastian had come from work. He had stripped off his coveralls, but he still had traces of motor oil and grease on his face and hands. Sebastian had a day job as a car mechanic. He fixed antique cars down at Jensen's. He didn't need the money; he just enjoyed the work.

He'd tucked his hair up into a ball cap, and could easily pass as any one of Wisconsin's regular joes, if it wasn't for the aristocratic cut of his features. 'I dated a nurse,' he confessed.

I wasn't sure that entirely explained it, but I let it go.

The farther into the building we got, the more the air smelled of hospital – that distinctive combination of disinfectant and disease. The overhead fluorescents stripped the dingy, brightly painted hallway of any natural warmth. I shivered, grateful that I'd started to see signs directing us to the morgue.

A stretcher was pushed up against one wall. Only when I walked right beside the bed did I realize that there was a body under the white sheet. I hurried to catch up with Sebastian and took his hand.

We walked into the front office. An attendant sat behind a nursing station desk. He wore a white tunic and looked to be about twentyish with blond curls. He flashed us the civilians-usually-don't-just-wander-in-here look, before saying, somewhat skeptically, 'Can I help you?'

'We're here for Daniel Parrish,' I said. I pulled out all my documentation and flashed it at the attendant.

The attendant nodded with only the briefest glance in the direction of all my hard-gained legal paperwork, and said, 'Where's the coffin?'

'In the van,' Sebastian said. 'I was hoping you'd loan us a stretcher or something.'

'Sure thing,' he said, disappearing behind a set of ominous looking double doors. In a moment, he was back with one of those flexible stretchers you see ambulances use. 'I'll help you,' he said. To me, 'Stay here and make sure nobody walks off.' He laughed at his own joke, and he and Sebastian headed down the hallway together.

I was sure the attendant wasn't supposed to leave his post, and I was twice as certain I didn't want to be in this place alone. There was nothing inherently creepy about the plastic potted plants covered in a thin layer of dust, the threadbare waiting room furniture, or the pervasive scent of air fresher, but just knowing that there were dozens of dead bodies just behind those doors gave me the willies. I paced the industrial-grade carpeting for the entire fifteen minutes it took for Sebastian and the attendant guy to come back with Parrish's coffin.

I wasn't quite ready for what came next. The attendant, who introduced himself as Gary, motioned us both in past the dreaded double doors. Noticing the look on my face, Gary said, 'Hey, you're going through upright. It's all good.'

I tried to smile, but found my expression froze at the sight of stainless-steel exam tables and drains. Lots of drains. For all the bodily fluids, I imagined. The acrid stench of formaldehyde stuck in the back of my throat.

All the Court TV I'd watched at Izzy's had prepared me for the rows of metal refrigerator boxes, at least. The door pulled out like a macabre lazy susan to reveal Parrish, covered modestly in a sheet. A slight film of frost covered Parrish's skin, and his lips looked bluish. Great Goddess, I hoped he was okay! I reached out a hand to touch his cheek, searching for some sign of life.

'I'll give you a minute, shall I?' Gary offered kindly.

'Yeah, but only a minute,' Sebastian said. When I glanced at his rudeness, Sebastian whispered in my ear, 'He's already been frozen too long. He's going to have a morgue hangover.' To my questioning look, he replied. 'It's like an ice cream headache, only worse.'

'How would you know?'

'Had a similar experience with a frozen lake up north. Ice fishing gone bad.'

'Let's get him out of here,' I agreed.

Sebastian waved Gary back from where he was standing at the far side of the room. Gary compared my documents to Parrish's toe tag, and then Sebastian and he did the hospital sheet trick and neatly dumped Parrish into the open coffin.

'Awesome pine coffin,' Gary said, running his fingers on the freight stickers. 'You don't see a lot of antiques of this sort. I mean, most people are still using their coffins.'

Eek. Good point. Maybe we should have bought new?

'Got it on eBay,' Sebastian lied smoothly. 'It was prebought and shipped empty, I guess.'

'And what? The guy moves without taking his coffin and the family keeps it in the garage for generations?' Sebastian and I exchanged nervous glances, but Gary answered himself. 'People are so weird.'

'Yeah, well, it was cheap,' Sebastian said. 'Better than paying the extortionist prices through the funeral home.'

'True,' Gary said with a nod. 'You can keep the sheet, by the way. No need to return it.'

'Thanks,' I said, trying to imagine the people who tried to give a used funerary sheet back.

The frost on Parrish's face had started to bead. Sebastian and I set the wooden cover in place. I didn't want to. In fact, it felt sort of wrong not to see Parrish's face, but the sunlight would kill him.

Gary walked with us back to the van.

'So, you guys are Witches, right?' Gary asked as we strolled down the hall. Everyone we encountered averted their gaze when they noticed the coffin.

'I am,' I said. 'He's an alchemist.'

'Technically, I'm an excommunicated Catholic,' Sebastian corrected with a crooked smile.

'Why, did you want to ask something?' I wondered.

I held the doors open as Sebastian steered the gurney. The sun was bright. Not a cloud in the sky, other than the plume from the smokers in scrubs huddled under the eaves. Gary directed us down a ramp. I held on to the lid tightly, as the wheels jittered over some bumps.

'Nah,' said Gary with mischievous grin. 'I just wanted to say "Merry Meet."'

Attendant dude was a Witch too. Gary had just given the secret handshake. 'Seriously?'

'Every Beltane and Samhain,' he said with a wink.

'Cool.' I smiled, and shook his hand. Sebastian followed suit. Then once we reached our cherry-red Death Mobile, Sebastian opened up the back doors. He hopped inside to lever Parrish up. I started to help, but the two of them hefted the coffin in that manly way of two guys hauling a load. I felt pretty useless, honestly.

'So,' Gary said, once Parrish was inside, 'I hope you won't mind me saying: he's too light,' he gestured with his thumb at the coffin. 'Dead guys weigh a ton. Your friend here is weightless as air in comparison. It's not right. Something's out of whack, spiritually speaking, if you know what I'm saying.'

Sebastian nodded solemnly. 'That's why we're taking care of him ourselves.'

Gary considered this. 'Good plan, my man.' He raised his hand in the peace sign like a benediction. 'Blessed be.'

'Blessed be,' I replied automatically, like responding to an amen.

Sebastian and I watched Gary amble back inside. 'Well, that was certainly interesting,' Sebastian said, as he shut the van doors with a slam that made me jump.

'What? That he was so weird, or so right?'

'Both.'

Despite Gary's claims that Parrish wasn't heavy, it was a bitch getting him up the stairs to my apartment. Thank the Mother for Sebastian's superhuman strength and the duct tape we used to secure the lid. It was still awkward and slow going. More than once I suggested we forget the whole lying in the parlor thing, and change our plans instead to involve an outdoor barbeque despite early frost warnings.

Once upstairs, we had to decide where to put him. He fit nicely on the end table, but he sat just low enough to be an inviting bench. The last thing I wanted was for some drunken ghouls to sit on him and tip him over in the middle of the festivities. The dining-room table looked wrong too. The coffin hung off the edges and, well, seemed like an overlarge serving plate. Just not very dignified. Again, I imagined a lot of plates being set on him.

'How about we take him out of the coffin and just sprawl his body on the couch?' Sebastian suggested wryly. 'It'd look very natural.'

I imagined him propped up stiffly with a beer can in his hand like something out of a grisly comedy. 'Wouldn't that wake him up?'

Sebastian shrugged. 'Probably. Any other ideas?'

I had one. Sebastian and I hauled out a couple of dressers from my bedroom. They were just the right size, and when placed a short distance apart, even fairly sturdy. They put Parrish at good 'viewing' height, but not so low as to be easily mistaken as someplace to sit.

Of course, the instant we got the coffin in place, Barney leaped up on top and began to give herself a full body wash. Sebastian scratched her shoulder ruff. 'You always did like him better.'

She answered Sebastian with a sneeze.

After a rest on the couch and a couple of energy drinks, Sebastian decided it was probably time to fetch and carry from the caterers. 'I don't even like the guy this much,' Sebastian muttered. 'Do you want to come along?'

I explained that I was expecting Dominguez early for an astrological date and that I was hoping to convince him he needed to hang around to help nab Izzy's cousin. 'Plus,' I added. 'I'm going to prepare a de-hexing spell for William.'

'I should help with that,' Sebastian said, laying a hand on the flat expanse of his stomach. 'My part of Lilith could add a bit of extra power to that spell.'

I hadn't thought of that, but Sebastian and I made a whole Goddess. 'Would you? I feel like I need all the help I can get on this one.'

'Absolutely, love,' Sebastian said, leaning in to give me a peck on the cheek. 'I'll hurry home.' Barney, who had hopped off the coffin to twine around our legs, sneezed wetly on his shoe. Reaching down to scratch behind her ear, Sebastian said, 'Love you too, puss.'

Watching his car putter away, I was pleased how quickly Sebastian and I got back into a routine. He was a good guy, really.

Smiling to myself, I turned around and came face-to-face with Parrish's coffin. Despite seeing it in my storage space in the basement all the time, it still looked ominous in the middle of my living room. I skittered around it to the kitchen. I made myself some ramen noodles for dinner and settled in at my favorite spot at the kitchen table to cast Dominguez's chart.

Most people only know about astrology from their daily news-paper and don't realize the complexity of a full natal chart. A natal chart is like a snapshot of the sky as seen from the exact location on earth on the day and exact hour you were born, showing all the planets – sun, moon, and some asteroids included – above and below the horizon. It also details all interactions those heavenly bodies have with each other, what sign of the zodiac they appear in, and into which house they fall. It's a complicated affair. Casting one by hand could take hours, which was why most people did their computations by computer these days.

I, being some kind of last holdout from another era, didn't own a computer. No TV, no computer, no cell phone. I lived in the damn dark ages.

So, I set to work. The doorbell rang just as I marked the last aspect on Dominguez's chart.

I met Dominguez at the downstairs door. He wore faded blue jeans. A pearl-gray, almost silver, light-cotton button-down shirt opened at the throat to reveal a tiny golden baptismal cross. To ward off the chill of Halloween night, and, no doubt, hide a shoulder holster, he had on a tailored black sport coat. Dominguez's hair curled at the nape of his neck and just above his ears, as though he'd just stepped from a hot shower.

The only thing that looked out of place at all on him was the clunky fuchsia cast covering his arm to his elbow.

'Come on in,' I said.

As he strolled past me, I caught the scent of soap with a hint of gun oil.

He thrust a cellophane-wrapped bundle of painted daisies at me. 'These are for you, Ms Lacey,' he said gruffly.

'Garnet,' I insisted. I took them, noticing that he'd failed to remove the SuperAmerica price sticker. Clearly, these were a kind of impulse gift, but what impulse? We'd said this wasn't a date, yet flowers were the romantic gift of choice. Or maybe his mother's voice called to him at the gas station reminding him that you don't show up at someone's house without bringing something, anything. Though I was absurdly touched, chips and salsa would have been more useful, given that I was expecting a crowd in a couple of hours. Still, the flowers might help distinguish Parrish's coffin from the other seating areas.

'Oh!' I said, suddenly having a vision of Dominguez's face when he saw Parrish's coffin in the living room. 'Wait!'

But, he'd already reached the top of the stairs, where I'd left the door open. 'What the hell?'

He sounded kind of mad and surprised, or surprised and mad, it was hard to tell exactly. His face was red, just as I'd pictured, when I came up behind him. 'About that . . . I'm having a wake later tonight.'

'For the guy I shot?' His jaw twitched and his eyes glistened; rage looked kind of hot on him.

'Uh, yeah,' I said casually. 'You know, your chart implied you'd have the inner peace to deal with this sort of thing.'

His face contorted for a second, then he said, 'That's crap.'

'Clearly inner peace is not your forte.' I laughed. 'Anyway, I made that up. Your chart says nothing like that. Come on in, I'll show you.' When he didn't budge, I waved the bouquet under his nose. 'Plus, I have to put these in some water.'

278

'Oh, right,' he said, stepping aside to let me through. I purposefully strode past Parrish's coffin into the kitchen. I resisted the urge to look behind me to see if Dominguez followed, but I could easily imagine his eyes riveted to the cloth-draped box. I kicked out the doorstop and let the kitchen door swing shut behind us. Then, I busied myself with finding a vase.

'Can I offer you anything to drink?' I asked, wondering if the cheap, rummage sale 'I Heart London' pint glass would work for the flowers. Barney appeared instantly, her eyes following the foliage with the tenacity of a heat-seeking missile. One of the reasons I didn't own any real vases was because, among her other skills, Barney was a champion flower muncher and destroyer of glassware.

'Got any beer?' he asked. Instead of sitting, he perched on the ledge of the window that faced the back door.

'Tons,' I said, snipping the ends of the flowers into the garbage with a kitchen scissors. 'Plus several kegs are arriving shortly.'

He looked confused, but only for a moment. 'For the wake.'

'Yeah, so mostly I have cases of crap beer in the back hallway. The good stuff is hidden in a cooler in my bedroom behind locked doors, along with the family heirlooms, and anything else I don't want to walk off by itself tonight.' I fluffed the arrangement in the glass. The pastel lavender, pink, and rose daisies were cheery. I set them on the kitchen table.

Dominguez chuckled. 'So, Parrish's friends are thieves?'

And worse, I figured. 'Plus, I don't know who they all are. He's been . . .' Did I bring up the fact that Parrish had been prostituting himself? Nah, best not to speak ill of the not-really-dead in case he could hear me from the other room, and besides,

Dominguez probably already suspected the truth ' . . . seeing a lot of people lately, so I put up signs around town. I'm expecting some freeloaders.'

He gestured to the bowl of mini Snickers on the table. 'And trick-or-treaters.'

Sebastian had actually been the one to think to bring them. I was just glad he picked a candy I'd eat, in case there were any leftovers. 'I have to leave my porch light on for the people coming for Parrish's wake,' I said. 'I figured I'd get a few kids by accident, and it's always better to be prepared.'

'Sounds like one helluva party,' Dominguez said, as I handed him one of the bottles from the fridge. He looked at the label and sneered, but twisted the top off anyway.

'I hope so,' I said more wistfully than I'd intended. And suddenly, there was Daniel, dead, between us – me the grieving girlfriend, and Dominguez party to his shooting.

'Is that my chart?' Dominguez said, pointing to the paper with the picture of the pie-cut circle with symbols neatly printed around the edges.

Grateful for the distraction, I pulled up a chair with a smile. I pointed the C-shaped glyph, 'My favorite interpretation for Moon in Gemini? "You may be too shrewd for your own good." Tell me that's not totally you!'

He laughed, slipping into a chair beside me to peer meaningfully at the squiggles on the paper. 'Okay, you got me.'

My finger pointed to his Sun in the fourth house. 'And, of course, you share this placement with Liberace.'

'Ugh.' He grimaced.

'Aw, come on. I think that's *fab*-u-lous.' I laughed.

'Tell me more.' He grinned, as he took a long pull on the bottle.

By the time Sebastian arrived with the food and even more beer, Dominguez had told me all about his complicated relationship with his father, his fondness for combining edibles and sex – which I'd told him perfectly complemented his Venus/sensual nature – and we had laughed ourselves sick over some of the other odd quirks his natal chart had revealed to me.

It had all remained very platonic, but we still jumped apart like guilty lovers when Sebastian entered the room.

Dominguez recovered much more quickly and smoothly than I did. 'Have you had this done?' Dominguez asked Sebastian with a comradely grin. 'This interpretation is awesome. I've become a convert.'

'Do ephemerises go that far back?' I asked before I could stop myself.

'There were star charts in existence when I was born,' Sebastian said dryly.

Dominguez laughed, thinking we were making the usual jokes about old age. 'Jeez, he doesn't look that much older than you. In fact, if I had had to guess, I'd have said you were the elder in this relationship.'

Now Sebastian chuckled. 'You really know how to score with the ladies, friend.'

It occurred to me that I never introduced them properly, so I did. 'Gabriel Dominguez,' I said, 'this is my boyfriend, Sebastian Von Traum.'

'Von Traum? German? Dutch?'

'Austrian,' Sebastian corrected politely, his eyes resting, fleetingly, on the vase of flowers. 'Are you staying for the wake?'

'Uh . . . It doesn't really seem right,' Dominguez started.

'Please?' I asked, 'I mean, you're more than welcome to. Plus, we have more beer than God. Someone has to help us drink it.'

Dominguez laughed.

'Besides,' Sebastian said, gesturing at the chart and books on the table. 'I'm sure you have more to talk about. Have you even gotten to minor aspects with asteroids or midpoints?'

With the enthusiasm of a new believer, Dominguez's eyes brightened. 'No.' He turned to me. 'What's that? Tell me about those.'

I shot Sebastian an are-you-sure-you-want-to-encourage-this look, but he ignored it to reach between us for the flowers. 'Mind if I put these on Parrish?'

'Go ahead,' I told him. Dominguez blanched slightly, but didn't protest.

With his free hand, Sebastian grabbed the bowl full of Snickers. 'And trick-or-treaters are arriving. I'll man the front door for a while.'

'Okay, uh, thanks,' I said, uncertain if Sebastian was covering hurt feelings again or not.

He caught my eyes and said, 'It's really okay, Garnet. Honestly.'

So Dominguez and I went back to reading his chart. In the middle of discussing his midpoints, Dominguez leaned close and asked, 'What does it say about love?'

At the door, someone yelled, 'Trick or treat!' I could hear

Sebastian complimenting the children on their costumes and admonishing them to only take one candy bar.

I'd already explained his Venus, so I was confused. 'What do you mean?'

Dominguez's gray eyes twinkled mischievously. 'Where in my chart does it say I'm a sucker for a pretty Goth?'

'Oh, that's not on here,' I said, waving a dismissive hand over the chart. 'That's probably the love spell talking.'

'I thought you broke that.'

'I did.' But Lilith cast it aside at some point after Dominguez shot me, so who knew where it was or what condition it was in?

His lips were close to mine. 'Then why do I still want to kiss you?'

I was saved from having to answer by the sound of someone coming up the steps. I checked the clock over the sink. 'Guests are arriving,' I announced, standing up so fast, the chair nearly tipped over.

Dominguez caught it with the tips of his fingers that poked out from the cast. He was still smiling at me, as if he knew that part of me felt the same. I mean, he was awfully sexy for a cop. And, he'd been kind to me. No, more than that – he'd let me get away with murder.

I shook my head. That didn't mean I owed him any more than my gratitude. That love spell must be clouding my judgment too.

Or maybe I liked him.

To avoid thinking about that, I grabbed a few cold beer bottles from the fridge to offer the guests. Dominguez stood up as I pushed the door shut with my elbow. 'Can I help with anything?' he asked.

I pointed to the bags of chips. 'Do you want to bring in those?'

When I swung open the door to the living room, I was pretty sure the first arrivals were Parrish's ghouls. One of them, a very pretty young man in leather and denim with long, raven-black hair and brilliant colored-contact-lens green eyes was leaning close to the coffin whispering something that sounded like, 'About that twenty bucks I owe you . . .'

He stood up and smiled a Hollywood grin – all teeth and snake-oil charm – when I offered him a beer. 'Mighty kind of you, ma'am,' he drawled.

'I'm Garnet,' I said, 'And this is Gabriel Dominguez.'

'Adrian,' he said, taking in Dominguez with a suspicious once-over. 'No one said anything about cops.'

'Dominguez is here as my friend,' I said.

Two other people, both of them women in short skirts, stood near the door eyeing Sebastian and the candy bowl. 'Oh.' The tallest one, with red hair sweeping past her shoulders, smiled warmly at Sebastian. 'So, you're not her boyfriend?'

'He is,' I said, just as Sebastian said, 'I am.'

'Pity,' she murmured, and wandered over to the coffee table where Sebastian had put out cold cuts and vegetables. She sat herself down, crossing her legs in a way that either intentionally or unconsciously showed off their shapeliness. Even though I wasn't much of a connoisseur of feminine beauty, I had to be impressed by the expensive Italian leather pumps. In her blazer, silk tank top and freshwater pearls, she looked almost too polished and elegant to be one of Parrish's friends. Except here she was.

The other woman, who had wide blue eyes and a nervous expression, sidled up to me. She brushed short blond curls from her eyes from a pale, freckled face. 'About Parrish,' she whispered. 'Is he . . . he's not really . . . all the way dead is he?'

I glanced at Dominguez to see if he'd overheard.

Dominguez, like Sebastian, seemed captivated by the red-haired woman on the couch. For her part, she munched on a carrot stick and leafed through an old issue of *In Touch* I'd left on the end table.

'Daniel is going to be back, isn't he?' nervous blonde asked. 'Later tonight maybe?'

I was stunned to hear her so casually use Parrish's first name that I couldn't even formulate the words to explain the situation.

Noticing my distress apparently, Adrian put an arm around me and turned us away from where Dominguez lounged against the dinning-room table. Adrian smelled surprisingly good, like fresh lavender and mint. Though it should have felt presumptuous, his touch was casual and light. He held his arm there with a kind of confidence that was almost, but not entirely, attractive. 'Britta isn't exactly the soul of discretion.'

'Adrian, aren't you worried?' Britta asked. 'What if? I mean, where will . . . we, you know?'

Adrian glanced at Sebastian briefly. 'There are others,' he said, and I wondered how he could tell. It wasn't like Sebastian had 'vampire' tattooed on his forehead, and, in point of fact, the sun was only just now setting. Sebastian had dressed appropriately for the wake in a black suit and tie. His hair was pulled back in a neat ponytail. Sure, he was the best-looking guy in the room, but nothing about him should have said 'bloodsucker'. Maybe Adrian could smell some kind of pheromone or something, like a wolfhound tracking prey.

Adrian leaned over to speak into Britta's ear and his dark purple silk shirt shifted. I could see a dark bruise on his collarbone. 'Remember the news? The master is obviously playing a game with the police.'

The master? Cripes, had Parrish been serious about that? I shrugged out from under Adrian's arm and moved over to where Sebastian munched on some potato chips near the door. When I got up close enough to speak softly, I asked, 'Please tell me you don't have your ghouls call you master.'

'If they did, it would be purely voluntarily.' He smiled wickedly.

The woman on the couch, who had been close enough to hear our exchange, flashed Sebastian a knowing look. She sucked the dip off the tip of the carrot stick suggestively.

I gave her my best don't-mess-with-my-man stare.

Britta flounced over to flirt with Dominguez; I heard her opening gambit of 'are you really a police officer?' with accompanying shy giggle. Adrian sauntered over to join the redhead, both of them looking far too pretty for my ratty couch.

'So, Adrian, what is it that you do?' Sebastian asked in that sort of bored/sort of interested I-guess-we-should-make-small-talk tone.

The redhead chuckled. 'What doesn't he do?'

'I'm up for just about anything,' Adrian agreed in a way that made me ponder his use of the term 'up'.

Strangely, I could sort of understand why Parrish would like this guy. After all, he was apparently sexually adventurous, overtly available, breathing, and smelled good. For Parrish that was kind of a win-win-win-win.

The ringing of the doorbell interrupted my speculation about Parrish's tastes. I went down to answer it. I nabbed the candy bowl just in case it was trick-or-treaters. I opened the door to a fairy princess and a mummy. The fairy princess was in his mid-twenties and should have probably considered shaving his legs for the pink glitter tutu, though the wings went well with the cobra tattoo on his naked chest. 'Dude,' he said, 'is this the party-wake thing?'

The mummy nodded enthusiastically. I suspected his 'wrappings' were merely toilet paper. Though I could see his jeans poking out in places, he'd done a good job covering his whole body. I suspected several dorms' restrooms had been pilfered in the making of his costume.

'Sorry,' I said. 'Wrong house.'

The fairy looked especially crestfallen. The mummy took two Snickers and mumbled an apology. Though they walked off, the fairy kept glancing back at my somber black skirt and poking his mummy-buddy in the ribs. I suspected they'd be back later to try again.

Some real trick-or-treaters came next, all skeleton masks and superhero costumes. I gave them each a candy and headed back upstairs somewhat reluctantly.

The social shuffling that had happened in my brief absence horrified me. Sebastian was speaking quite earnestly about something to Adrian next to the spider plant. Dominguez sat on the couch between Britta and the smoldering redhead.

I was just trying to decide who I wanted to break up the most when the bell rang again. This time I answered the door to a gaggle of college-age girls. They wore black, but they each had on some kind of Halloween hairpiece – cat ears, devil horns, antennae, and Playboy bunny ears. I was about to turn them away when I noticed the bruise on Playboy bunny's inside arm, which looked suspiciously like a bite mark. It might have been a coincidence, but in the absence of any other calling card, I let them in.

With the addition of the four coeds, the party started to get a bit livelier. Playboy bunny had a little hysterical fit when she saw the coffin and demanded to know if he was really in there.

'This is a traditional wake,' I explained, hoping that maybe the addition of an actual corpse might convince them this party wasn't crash-worthy. But Playboy surprised me by being moved to tears. Adrian was quick with a handkerchief and a shoulder to blubber on.

The doorbell rang again and this time I found myself admitting a trim, athletic Asian man in a fabulous paisley suit. Even if he wasn't one of Parrish's ghouls, he was just too eye-catching not to let in on sheer principle. I was rewarded when I noticed Adrian sneer in Paisley's general direction.

Sebastian answered the next ring and came back with a slightly lighter candy bowl. Dominguez seemed to be chatting up Cat-ears, while Antenna and Devil Horns stood close enough to mount a girlfriend rescue. Paisley made a beeline for the coffin and started talking to it in hushed, loving tones. I suspected a lot of people would, especially those in the know, but it was still fairly disconcerting to see.

Someone I didn't know let in a group of people including a bearded biker in a black leather kilt and his harem of Renaissance Festival girlfriends in plaids wrapped as tight as saris. Sebastian tapped the keg and Barney disappeared under the couch.

The noise of conversation and laughter grew. My apartment was wall-to-wall strangers eating my food and drinking my beer at alarming rates. I pulled some emergency blue corn chips from the top of the fridge to refill the rapidly emptying bowls. Luckily, people seemed to be bringing their own alcohol, apparently even some good stuff since a bottle of Jameson Irish whiskey appeared on top of Parrish's casket.

When I next went to answer the door for trick-or-treaters, I noticed my downstairs neighbors had opened their apartment to partygoers. A strong scent of marijuana came from their living room. Some kind of thrash metal had been turned up on the stereo.

It was getting late, so the trick-or-treaters were starting to become the preteen variety. They had barely cobbled-together costumes that I suspected came from their everyday clothes, since one of them was a football player and the other a cheerleader. Both held very large sacks of candy. I wanted to ask them which little kid they mugged to get such a big stash, but instead divided the remaining candy between them and turned off the porch light, the universal signal to trick-or-treaters that the house was off limits.

If only I could come up with a similar signal to stem the tide of people arriving for Parrish's wake. Maybe running out of beer . . . I sighed. This party was already truly out of control. Parrish should be proud.

I stood on the steps for a moment reveling in the fresh air when I smelled the distinct odor of bratwurst coming from the backyard – my backyard. Walking around the side of the house, I found several people standing around the chiminea I used in outdoor rituals. A fire blazed – made from what, I wasn't sure I wanted to know. A former U.S. president, a hobo, and a sailor waved brats near the fire, while intermittently taking swigs of cheap beer. They used my bamboo fencing for skewers, dirt and all. Nixon might have been impeached, but he was the only one smart enough to be holding the dirty end of the stick.

Elbowing my way through the thickening crowd toward them, I intended to explain the fire hazards involved with alcohol and open flames when I spotted a zombie, a real one, near the compost pile. Maybe she was trying to blend in with the other dead things, but she was doing a piss-poor job of it. She rocked from one foot to the other, while staring unblinkingly at me.

Besides, I recognized her. She was the waitress from the deli. When our eyes met, she began shuffling toward me.

Out of the corner of my eye, I noticed the book-buying jock moving in my direction also. Before they could surround me, I ran. I tried to head back inside toward the kitchen. I needed a big, fat container of Morton salt, ASAP.

Unfortunately, going anywhere fast was hampered by the press of partiers. I bumped into a bride of Frankenstein and jostled a white-haired, black-suited undertaker who may or may not have been in costume. After a dozen 'excuse mes' and 'coming throughs' my progress could be measured in negative numbers; I was farther from the back door than when I started. The zombies were within grabbing range.

When a hand touched my shoulder, I swung violently. My fist connected satisfyingly with flesh, until I noticed the person I'd hit was Sebastian. His hand cupped his chin and he gave me a long-suffering look over the tips of his fingers.

'It is a very good thing I regenerate,' he murmured. 'Life with you is a damn hazard.'

'You didn't happen to bring any salt with you, did you?'

Sebastian shook his head. 'And I bear bad news.'

My eyes stayed focused on the waitress zombie, who looked to me the most ready to strike. 'What could be worse than killer zombies?'

'Turn around. I'll watch your back,' he said.

I pivoted slowly on my heels, afraid of what I might see. Directly in front of me stood William, dressed quite dapperly in a dark suit and bow tie, and Maureen, looking somber in a black dress with only the hint of gold at her neck and wrists. William had that frighteningly purposeful look of possession in his eyes and gripped a deadly looking cane.

'I'm so sorry for your loss,' purred Maureen, her whiskey-scratched voice imbuing every syllable with menace. The fire-light danced across her brightly dyed hair.

Somehow her magic did what mine could not; the crowd parted to give us some breathing room. There was an unimaginable empty space of five feet between us. I felt a little like the Earps at the O.K. Corral, except instead of tumbleweeds we were surrounded by a crowd of a hundred and fifty drunken onlookers all dressed for Halloween.

This was the point at which it would have been cool to say, 'The jig is up,' or 'I have you now,' except Mo totally owned this scene. I wasn't the one with the zombie army at my command or my friend as a kind of possessed hostage standing by her side. So, instead, I had to go with the much less dramatic, 'What do you want?'

She gave me that half-lidded glance that always made me feel like maybe I'd forgotten to get dressed, and said, 'Lots of things, but I'll settle for you leaving me and mine alone.'

Huh?

Other than preferring William in his usual addled state, I hadn't really considered myself after anything of hers. I mean, sure I stopped attacks, but I hadn't intentionally set out to do Mo any harm. More like the other way around.

Apparently Maureen mistook my confused frown for deepening resolve, because she said, 'Lay off salting my zombies.'

'Okay,' I said. After all, I felt I could agree to that, given that Izzy had done the most salting in the last several days. Still, I wasn't going to make any concessions without first making some demands of my own. 'Let William go.'

She laughed. Actually it was much more of a tee-hee than a full-throated villainous chuckle, but it was still pretty ominous given the circumstances. 'William volunteers for his position.'

Did I want to know about William's 'positions' with Mo? And, anyway, I didn't buy it. William was scared of her. 'What, like your zombies? That's slavery, you know. And murder.'

At this point I realized that the crowd had actually grown quieter. People stood around us in rapt attention, plastic glasses of beer forgotten in their hands. Someone in a black lace nightie that seemed far too skimpy for forty-degree weather asked, 'Dude, is this some kind of live-action role-playing game?'

Great, now we had an audience.

That's when the zombies made their move.

12

Pisces

Key Words:
Indolent and Sacrificing

Two zombies leaped quite suddenly on Sebastian. He'd been watching them, but he was still unprepared for the flying kicks coming from two directions. Superhuman strength wasn't the same as super balance, or, apparently, reaction time because Sebastian went down. Hard.

This garnered applause and hoots; others booed. The crowd was choosing sides. Meanwhile, Sebastian's face was getting ground into dormant sod. I had to do something. But what? Zombies closed in on me as well.

A second-quarter moon glowed palely in a crystal-clear, star-dappled sky. The air blew crisply against my cheek, carrying the scent of burning paper and rotting leaves. Time slowed, as Lilith made Her presence available to me. I sensed a silver cord stretching between Sebastian and me, power flowing from core to core.

Mo took a step back.

Sebastian shook loose from his attackers as easily as a dog

flicks off water. He stood beside me and grasped my hand. Skin to skin, I felt Lilith take another small step to the surface. Heat poured through my veins.

In unison, the crowd said, 'Ooooh,' like they were watching Fourth of July fireworks.

Out of the midnight sky came a single crow. It dive-bombed the zombie nearest me, foiling an attack with a war cry of 'Ah-ha!'

William came at us, cane raised. The leather-kilt-wearing biker tackled him, body-slamming William to the ground like a pro wrestler. William, not even breaking from his serious expression for surprise, twisted in the biker's meaty grasp and gave the guy a knock to the head with the carved metal handle of the cane. Biker guy let go. He sat down on his butt on the edge of the concrete patio surrounding the chiminea, pawing at his forehead. 'That fucking hurt, you twerp. This is supposed to be a game!'

I gave Sebastian's hand a squeeze. It was time to call out that loa before anyone else got injured. I'd been bringing only bits of Lilith's strength to the surface since the big, bad ritual that split Her in two, and with Sebastian's hand in mine I felt I had almost surgical control.

Of course, I had no idea if that were really true. This whole thing could end in a bloodbath if we weren't careful. The last thing I wanted was another Halloween massacre on my hands.

William rose and faced us. With my magical eye, I could see the loa coiled like a yellow snake around William's body, controlling him.

Reacting instinctively, I reached out my free hand and slid

it between the constricting image and William's chest. I pulled back on it. Resistance from the loa felt elastic – flexible, yet strong. I let go of Sebastian and worked my other hand underneath another section of loa. Surprise kept William from reacting until Sebastian grasped William's wrist, his fingers digging under yellow tendrils, loosening them at the edges. He seemed to be having more success, so I switched tactics to do the same. Besides, this way, we each held one of William's hands, so he couldn't escape or try to strike us.

William's body was also like a conduit for Lilith's power between Sebastian and me. When I realized that, I tried consciously sending a current of white-hot power along the coils of the loa. William twitched violently, but that section of loa sizzled and curled into ash.

Sebastian gave me a smile and sent a bolt back to me. It hit me like a static shock, but there was something kind of pleasurable in it too. I blasted a bit more. Sebastian sent it back. William twitched like he was having a seizure.

Part of me was aware of applause and shouts of, 'Cool special effects!'

Then, like a tick under the flame of a match, the loa was forced to retreat. In a sound like a cat in heat, it flung itself off William and howled away into the night.

I nearly fell when William's knees gave way. A quick waist hug from Sebastian kept us both upright.

'Are you okay?' I asked William, despite the fact that his eyes had rolled up into his head and he was clearly unconscious.

'His heartbeat is strong,' Sebastian said, putting an ear to

William's chest. A woman dressed as an Egyptian pharaoh helped us lower William into a lawn chair that a blue furry bear pulled from my gardening shed. 'He's breathing.'

'Is he playing or should I call an ambulance?' the bear asked.

'I already called the cops.' It was Dominguez. He stopped to expertly check William's vitals and then said in an accusing tone to me, 'This party is way out of hand. It's spilled out into the street. Let's just say I wasn't the first complaint, either.'

That was just swell.

'Wait,' I said, scanning faces. 'What happened to Mo?'

Just then I heard a ruckus on the other side of the gate. A series of shrill 'yarghs' were followed by painful 'ahs!' I could see the flutter of oily wings in the moonlight. The crow had cornered Mo.

As I opened the gate, I noticed long, bright beams of white and red lights in the street. A squad car had come to a halt at the end of the block where the teeming mass of partiers ended. To my chagrin, it looked as though some yahoo had dragged one of the kegs into the middle of the street. Uniforms were headed this way, looking pissed off.

Coming from the other direction was Izzy. The determined look on her face told me nothing about whether she'd come to side with Maureen or me.

I turned to Mo, who was wedged in the space between the wall of my house and the fence. 'I should have you arrested.'

Her eyes narrowed. 'I should turn you into a zombie!'

She reached into a hidden pocket of her dress and pulled

something into her fist. Before she could bring it to her face to blow it at me, I called on Lilith to protect me. Just as Mo's lips puckered, a sudden wind lifted the powder from her palm and tossed it back at her. She flinched at the realization of what had happened. Then she spat and tried to rub out the stuff.

I looked around for something to help her wipe with, then noticed the faucet. 'Here,' I said, as I turned the water on. 'Quick.'

Izzy came up beside me. She had a plastic cup and some paper napkins she'd wrestled from one of the partiers' hands. 'Let me help,' she said quietly.

'Of course,' I said, sensing she was offering an apology on top of her assistance.

Together, Izzy and I helped Maureen duck down and put her face into the stream of cold water. We were just helping her to her feet when Dominguez came up beside us.

'What exactly is in that powder?' he asked me, watching Mo frantically scrub at her face. Even in the moonlight I could see her face slacken a bit and her eyes dilate.

'Seriously bad drugs,' I guessed.

Izzy nodded her head. 'Killer drugs.'

'Illegal drugs,' Dominguez pointed out. 'Possession is a charge I can make stick.'

Izzy's glanced at me. She wasn't angry, just sad and resolved. To Maureen, she said, 'A friend of mine knows a good lawyer,' she said. 'I'll help you as much as I can.'

Dominguez pulled out cuffs I'd hoped he would have left at home for our 'date', but then maybe those were his typical accoutrements for romantic outings. Gently, he took Mo's wrists. 'I'm arresting you for possession of illegal substances,' he said.

'You'll have to prove it,' she slurred.

'That's the function of the American justice system, ma'am.'

Before leading Mo in the direction of the uniforms, Dominguez turned back to me. He landed a quick, light kiss on my stunned lips, and said, 'You'll always have a friend in the FBI, Ms Lacey.'

'Garnet,' I insisted with a smile.

'Garnet,' he said finally.

The party broke up immediately following Mo's arrest. Dominguez rounded up the remaining zombies as material witnesses to the drug charges, and I think my downstairs neighbors got hauled in for possession, as well. Sebastian and I spent the rest of the night cleaning up, although to my amazement a few of Parrish's loyal ghouls stayed to help, including Adrian, who slipped Sebastian a business card on his way out the door.

'I'd be very jealous if you started dating him,' I said.

Sebastian eyed the card for a moment before setting it down on my bookshelf. 'He's quite attractive,' Sebastian said wistfully. 'But not my type on so many levels. For instance, he didn't really seem terribly . . . shall we say, intellectual.'

'You prefer your food smart?'

'At least enough to be discreet.'

Sebastian had a point there. I plunked myself down on my couch, which was decidedly smellier postparty. We both looked at Parrish's coffin. 'Do you suppose he's awake?'

Sebastian shook his head. 'He took several bullets. He's regenerating.'

I rubbed my eyes and found them a little moist. I didn't even know what I would say to Parrish other than, 'Helluva party, eh?' Still, I missed not being able to debrief with him, to laugh at it all.

'You want to tell him something? I could leave,' Sebastian offered.

'No,' I said. 'Stay.'

Sebastian sat on the couch beside me, and I laid my head against his shoulder. Barney slunk out from under the couch and sniffed around the floor of the dining-room table. I heard a crunch as she found something she liked.

Outside, the moon was setting. It was bloated from the atmosphere and low on the horizon.

'There was almost no moon in the sky last year,' I remarked. Then, I found myself talking and talking, telling Sebastian everything about that night.

He stroked my hair and listened.

When I'd talked myself out, I stood up. 'There's one more thing I want to do.'

Sebastian followed me upstairs. I took Jasmine's broken necklace from the altar and slipped it into my pocket. Together, we walked outside into the predawn. All Soul's Day. The Day of the Dead.

I made my way to the lakeshore. Birds chirped as the sky lightened. Dew clung to the rusty playground equipment, and the smell of dead fish permeated the air. I pulled the prayer beads from my pocket, letting my fingers caress the pearl and amethyst one last time. Then, I handed them to Sebastian. When he looked at me questioningly, I said, pointing to the pond scum and floating bits of food wrappers, 'I can't toss it far enough. It needs to go into the heart of the lake.'

Sebastian kissed the beads in my hand and then took them from me. After a brief baseball wind up, he let them fly. They soared into the air. A flash of silver in the dawn, and then they dropped with a distant splash into the dark water.

I cried all the way home, but they were the tears of letting go.

The next day, we buried Parrish.

Sebastian hired a hearse, which drove us slowly out of town. I resented fluffy, white cotton-candy clouds and brilliant blue sky. It should be raining, or at least overcast. Morning commuters on the highway were oblivious to death in their midst.

An egret stood like a white ghost in a drainage ditch, taking flight with slow, graceful strokes of its giant wings as we passed. Sebastian squeezed my hand. 'I need to tell you,' he said quietly. 'I didn't buy a marker.'

'What?'

'For Parrish's grave,' Sebastian said. 'I didn't know his dates, and, well, given the circumstances I didn't want things to be, you know, too permanent.'

The driver glanced in the rearview.

'An unmarked grave?' I wasn't sure I liked the sound of that, despite the fact that seeing Parrish's name carved in stone would have given me a similar heart attack.

Sebastian frowned in the direction of the driver's seat. 'Well, it's not like it's his final resting place,' Sebastian murmured between tightly pressed lips. 'We can get one later,' he suggested. 'If he decides to stay.'

Speaking of that, 'How long do you think he'll . . . ?' The driver looked about ready to explode with curiosity so I didn't want to be too specific.

Sebastian shrugged. 'I once lost an entire century sleeping it off in Peru. Once you're in the ground, as it were, it's easy to stay.'

Just when I stared to suspect that the driver was taking the scenic route to hear what other strange things Sebastian and I might say, we turned into the graveyard. Undertakers had dug a hole and set up the coffin elevator. The driver stopped at the entryway of the cemetery, which was not much more than a worn spot on the grass. 'Are the other pallbearers coming separately?' he asked.

'No, it's just the two of us,' Sebastian said.

The driver lost all composure. 'No way,' he said. 'How are you going to get him over there?'

'Magic,' I smiled. I was wearing one of my ritual dresses, the white one. It was nothing more than a simply cut tunic with some lace, but I also had on a large silver pentacle necklace. Sebastian wore last night's suit. I was sure we looked like complete nutjobs to this guy.

Having schlepped Parrish up and down the stairs of my apartment, Sebastian and I had a pretty good system. He took the heavier front end, and bore nearly all the weight. I took up the opposite side rear and acted as navigator. We looked a little like we were hauling furniture instead of a corpse, but, hey, it worked.

After getting Parrish onto the grave elevator thingie, Sebastian lowered him into the ground without any ceremony. The undertakers and the driver looked a little shocked when we insisted they pack up their stuff and leave us alone. As I watched them remove the equipment, Sebastian brought me a cup of coffee from his kitchen. It was my favorite Las Vegas mug.

When they finished, Sebastian slipped everyone a few extra Benjamins and they drove away stunned, but well compensated.

'Okay,' Sebastian said, giving me a pat on the shoulder. 'He's all yours.'

I handed back the mug and rubbed my hands together to drive off the chill. I had no candles, no sacred tools, other than a shovel the undertaker had left behind. No matter. I took in a deep breath and centered myself. I listened to the sound of the tall, dry grass rustle, and watched as a flock of juncos flitted across the barren cornfield, white flashing at the fork of their tails.

If Parrish were really dead, I'd have done some kind of passing-over ritual. Instead, as I walked a circle around the open grave, I concentrated on thoughts of protection and healing. I envisioned the circle as a birch grove, interwoven with grapevines, heavy with fruit. No guardians, except for one spirit to stand over him, a warrior Goddess with snakes on her shield shedding their skin.

Returning to the place I started, I picked up a handful of

dirt. Sandstone and rich farm loam sifted together in my palm. I gave it a toss, and it landed with a hollow spatter on Parrish's coffin. 'Let the earth heal and protect you,' I said. 'Rise from Her womb whole and healthy.'

Picking a few stones from the pile, I placed them at the quarters as wards. Then, I opened the circle by retracing my steps, counterclockwise. I imagined the birches and vines being absorbed into the ground, returning to seed.

After blowing Parrish a final kiss, I walked across the driveway for breakfast.

I spent the day reconnecting with Sebastian. We read our favorite sections of the paper while stretched out on either ends of the couch. Of course, Sebastian and I combined were longer than the whole sofa, so our legs entwined. It was comfortable and familiar.

'Did you get fired?' I asked him after finishing an article about a local spelling bee champion. 'You hardly even pretend to go to work anymore.'

Sebastian set aside the business section. 'I go in when they have a car I'm interested in,' he said casually, like most mechanics had such a laissez-faire attitude toward their schedules and paychecks. 'I've become the resident specialist in classic English cars.'

'Nice for some,' I teased.

Sebastian smiled. 'It is, actually. This way I have more time for the important things.' Under the cover, his toe rubbed affectionately against my side. 'Good thing too,' his voice was full of faux exasperation, as he flipped his paper open again with a snap. 'Since you're constantly in the middle of some crisis or another.'

'You make me sound like a drama queen.'

He peeked around the edge of the stock listings. 'You're not?'

I shot him the why-I-oughta squint and then grabbed his paper in mock indignation. We wrestled. I giggled. He kissed me. I tickled him. He nipped my ear. The newspaper crinkled noisily as I pressed my arms around his shoulders.

'You love me like this,' I told him, kissing him lightly.

'You know I do,' he agreed, returning my kiss with more passion.

I propped myself up on my elbows. I felt his body stretched out beneath mine. 'I've come to an important realization,' I said seriously, though I had a fond smile on my lips.

Amusement glittered in the golden starburst around his chestnut brown eyes. 'I can hardly wait to hear these pearls of wisdom.'

'Love isn't meant to be hoarded,' I said. 'It has a kind of half-life. Not like a Twinkie. You can't leave love on a shelf and expect it to be sweet forever.'

Sebastian's fingers tapped where they rested against my back. 'Let me get this straight. Your big revelation is that love isn't a plastic-wrapped artificial pastry?'

'Precisely,' I told him. 'Love is something you need to eat right away.'

His eyebrows rose suggestively. 'Now there's a philosophy I can get behind.'

After copious amounts of tickling and giggling, Sebastian chased me upstairs to the bedroom after informing me all good theories needed lots of field-testing.

The bedroom was sunny. Lace curtains glowed yellow, and bright patches shown on the purple feather comforter. Despite the cold outside, the room was comfortably warm. We undressed slowly, taking time to remember each freckle and birthmark.

I kissed Sebastian's hair. His lips brushed my cheek. With each touch, I felt my response heightened by his. With each slow stroke of fingertip across naked skin, something thrummed deep inside.

Sebastian's hands caressed my breasts and nipples. Echoes of the pleasure he felt touching me accented the sense of his palms on my body. It was hard to even concentrate. My attempts to breathe ended as moans.

Then it was my turn. I peppered Sebastian's shoulders and chest with feather-light kisses. I felt him tremble beneath my lips, but also inside my own chest. As my kisses moved lower and lower, his response swelled between us, inside me.

I didn't have to ask for what I wanted; Sebastian knew. Switching places, Sebastian's tongue stroked between my thighs. A nip here and there caught me by surprise and made me yelp with delight. Then, when I was ready, he entered me, strong and steady.

We moved in perfect harmony, each anticipating the other's satisfaction. My pleasure rose with his, and vice versa. We climaxed together in a hot, exhausting rush.

Panting and slick with sweat I smiled into Sebastian's face. 'I missed you,' I said.

He returned my broad grin. 'Go again?'

And how could I resist such a romantic request?

Sometime after midnight we fell asleep pleasantly, bone-achingly exhausted and tangled up in each other. Though I should have slept soundly after so much exercise, I had strange and restless dreams. At one point, I thought I woke up to see Parrish standing over our bed, silently watching me in the darkness. Except, I knew it must be a dream, because Benjamin the attack ghost would never let him in Sebastian's house uninvited, and, even more telling, he was wearing one of Sebastian's 'McGovern for President' T-shirts. Parrish would rather be well and truly dead than be caught in anything so square.

'Daniel,' I murmured at the apparition.

He leaned over and kissed me, tasting of cobwebs and freshly turned dirt.

'Nice shirt,' I teased, clumsily flashing him the peace sign.

The second kiss was more pleasant than the first and lulled me back into less disturbing dreams. Though I had one of those moments where you wish you had better control over your subconscious so you could spend the night replaying those kisses.

In fact, I kept feeling the cool brush of Parrish's lips as I sipped coffee in Sebastian's kitchen. When Sebastian started singing along to a Hank Williams song, I headed out the back door to 'stretch my legs'.

I got as far as the driveway before I noticed the caved-in section of the cemetery. Someone, probably one of Parrish's ghouls, had dug out a coffin-sized hole. I would have panicked, thinking someone had run off with his body, but remembering the dream, I knew.

Parrish was gone.

TATE HALLAWAY

Tall, Dark and Dead

'The line between magic and sanity is very thin. That's part of why I, Garnet Lacey, quit cold turkey. Never touch the stuff. No exceptions'

Trouble is magic is so addictive, especially when you've got inner goddesses like Lilith to contend with. And it doesn't stop there for Garnet; if you are going to run an occult bookstore then you've got to expect customers like Sebastian Von Traum, with his piercing brown eyes, sexy accent, killer body and total lack of an aura; which means he's dead . . .

Trouble can be so hard to resist, and what with Vatican witch hunters, long-lost vampire exes and a boyfriend with an ex-wife who is literally stirring in her grave, Garnet Lacey has trouble enough for everyone.

'Curl up on the couch and settle in – *Tall, Dark and Dead* is a great way to pass an evening' Lynsay Sands, *USA Today* bestselling author of *A Quick Bite*

'What's not to adore about a heroine who frets equally about the Vatican and ripped pantyhose . . . Tate Hallaway has a wonderful gift. Garnet is a gem of a heroine, and *Tall, Dark and Dead* is enthralling from the first page' MaryJanice Davidson, *USA Today* bestselling author of *Undead and Unreturnable*

978 0 7553 3655 5

headline
review

Now you can buy any of these other bestselling
books from your bookshop
or *direct from the publisher*.

The Island	Victoria Hislop	£7.99
Left Bank	Kate Muir	£6.99
Wicked	Gregory Maguire	£7.99
Cuban Heels	Emily Barr	£7.99
The Vanishing Act of Esme Lennox	Maggie O'Farrell	£7.99
Blue Water	Manette Ansay	£6.99
Sparkles	Louise Bagshawe	£6.99
A Perfect Life	Raffaella Barker	£6.99
The Lost Art of Keeping Secrets	Eva Rice	£6.99
The Godmother	Carrie Adams	£6.99